HOME

Hidden Book Three

COLLEEN VANDERLINDEN

Home: Hidden Book Three
Colleen Vanderlinden

Published in the United States
by Building Block Studios LLC

ISBN 0615965911
ISBN-13 978-0615965918

http://www.colleenvanderlinden.com/hidden
http://www.buildingblockstudios.com

DEDICATION

As always,
for Roger.
Here's to twenty more amazing years.

CONTENTS

DEDICATION   iii

CONTENTS   v

ACKNOWLEDGMENTS   i

CHAPTER ONE   1

CHAPTER TWO   11

CHAPTER THREE   24

CHAPTER FOUR   43

CHAPTER FIVE   57

CHAPTER SIX   71

CHAPTER SEVEN   79

CHAPTER EIGHT   88

CHAPTER NINE   102

CHAPTER TEN   114

CHAPTER ELEVEN   129

CHAPTER TWELVE   143

CHAPTER THIRTEEN   154

CHAPTER FOURTEEN   170

CHAPTER FIFTEEN   185

CHAPTER SIXTEEN   203

CHAPTER SEVENTEEN   219

CHAPTER EIGHTEEN   239

CHAPTER NINTEEN   250

EPILOGUE   257

SNEAK PEEK   260

ABOUT THE AUTHOR   267

ACKNOWLEDGMENTS

I am grateful, as always, to my amazing family.

Thank you to my husband, Roger, for being the one to talk me down when I get stressed, for being my rock and my best friend, and for handling the technical and design aspects of publishing *Hidden*. Thank you for listening to me talk about my characters as if they're real people and reacting as if that's totally normal. Love you, babe.

Thanks and hugs and kisses to my kids, who make me smile every single day of my life and are living proof that there is magic in this world. Thanks also to Peggy, Roger, and Will Vanderlinden for their support and enthusiasm.

Huge thanks to *Hidden's* first readers, especially Jayna Longstreet and Kellie Roach. You ladies have been with Molly and company from the beginning, and I will always be grateful for your support, encouragement, and friendship.

Thank you to the lovely Elizabeth Hunter. I am eternally grateful for the advice and encouragement you've given me.

I am lucky to have lived my entire life in the Detroit area, and this series is, in many ways, my love letter to my home city. So thank you, Detroit, for being so inspiring.

Finally, I want to thank my readers. Thank you for loving and rooting for Molly. Thank you for the lovely reviews, comments, Facebook messages, tweets, and emails. I am so grateful for every single one of you, and I hope the time we spend together in these pages is as fun for you as it is for me.

Colleen Vanderlinden
Detroit
February, 2014

CHAPTER ONE

My name is Molly Brooks.
Vigilante.
Godslayer.
Abomination.

At least, that's what they tell me. Along with platitudes like "what doesn't kill you makes you stronger."

Well. We'll see about that.

So far, it was true enough. I'd had my soul shattered when my first husband, Nain, died. I'd teetered on the brink of death after a demon tried to blow me up, watched the man I love waste away from a plague sent to my realm to punish me.

Each time, I got stronger. I got angrier. So strong and angry that I'd sometimes been afraid of myself.

But what about the things that *do* kill you? What does it do to you, to die and come back?

With my luck, it's probably not good, I thought as I

made my way across the rocky ground toward the cave I'd seen after waking.

Not waking. After coming back to life. I'd managed to kill myself destroying the gateway between my world and the world of the gods. Why did I bother? Because war was brewing, and it was my fault, and my world would be punished for it. So, I'd done what my parents and the Fates told me to do, and I destroyed the gateway to save those I love.

The bastards never told me it would kill me, though.

When I entered the cave, I was pleased to find that it was not only empty (gods knew what weird creatures I may have found there) but also that the opening was just big enough for me to get through, crouched down, and then opened into an only slightly larger space. Large enough for me to stand up, to sleep on the floor, but not much bigger than that. The black stone that the mountains were made of was the same stone I'd seen throughout the Nether, in homes and sculptures, tabletops and other items. I'd never thought to ask the name of it.

I sat down, leaning my bare back against the rough wall of the cave. I'd never thought to do a lot of things. At times, I hadn't thought much, period. I frowned, leaned my head back and closed my eyes, more tired than I expected to be. The short walk from the place where I'd revived to the cave had taken a lot of energy. Not quite up to peak form yet, I guessed.

Coming back from the dead, regenerating a body, apparently takes a lot out of you. Which was a whole crazy thing I really didn't want to think about too closely. I'd never even considered that it could work that way, that, as a god, or the child of gods or whatever, I could lose my body completely and re-form in the Nether. Nain had done it, thanks to a whole lot of my blood in his veins. I was starting to suspect that it was more than blood, that it was life, or energy, or the soul or whatever the hell you wanted to call it.

Freaky shit.

I started to doze, in between thinking about what I'd do differently this time around. Before, my trademark had been smashing first and asking questions later. I'd thoughtlessly charged into buildings, not knowing what waited for me. Destroyed beings whose deaths only came back to bite me in the ass. I tried to tell myself that action was necessary, but the fact was that I just hadn't been smart enough. I'd charged headfirst into my relationship with Nain, when I knew, now, that everything I'd ever wanted in a relationship, Brennan had been all along.

My eyes shot open. Brennan. Oh, no. Was he mourning me? I put my head in my hands. Damn it. Would he know I was still alive, somewhere?

I hadn't even been able to see him that last day, after E had dragged him from the Nether. Was he okay? Had he made it? My gut clenched at the thought. I closed my eyes, and focused, hoping against hope that I'd feel something. Anything.

I felt it instantly, once I pushed the panic aside. There. I breathed a shaky sigh of relief. My connection to Brennan, the one I'd made after he'd been healed from the shifter plague, still existed, as bright, warm, and soothing as always. Once again, I couldn't feel my connection with Nain, but remembered it well enough to know that it felt more to me like a searing inferno. I'd stupidly believed, in the beginning, that that inferno, the passion, meant that Nain and I were supposed to be together, that two beings of the Nether, bonded, just made sense.

I knew now that what makes sense is being with someone who makes you happy, who feels like home. Nain being back had strangely enough only made me more sure that Brennan and I were the real thing. With them both alive and well, the only one I wanted was Bren.

I laid down, curled up on myself. It was a moot point, now, unless I figured out a way to get back to my own realm.

I need clothes, I thought blearily as I dozed off again.

♦ ♦ ♦

When I opened my eyes, it took me a while to remember, again, where I was and how I got there. And it just depressed me and pissed me off all over again. My eyes adjusted to the dark interior of the cave, and I saw something move.

I froze.

I continued to look as my eyes adjusted more, and, eventually, I could make out the dark shape of what looked like some kind of huge animal, so large it blocked most of the meager light coming in the cave entrance. It sat, still as a statue. Dog? Wolf? Its round eyes glowed a stormy blue in the dark.

I barely breathed. It looked like it would really hurt if it decided to start attacking me.

I sat up slowly, readied myself to throw flames if I had to. I hoped my powers still worked the way I remembered them.

The animal tilted its head, inspecting me. In that moment, it reminded me of Eunomia, and I thought of her with a pang. She was trapped in my world, much as I was trapped in hers. I watched the creature, and it watched me. The more my eyes adjusted, the more sure I was that it was some kind of large dog or something. Suddenly, it turned and padded out of the mouth of the cave, leaving me alone.

I got up and walked toward the cave entrance, trying to see the animal better, but my foot hit something on the floor, near where it had been sitting. Something soft. I bent down and touched it, timidly, half expecting it somehow to turn into something that would rip my arm off.

Cloth.

I picked the bundle up, and found that a long sleeved top, a pair of pants, and a soft pair of leather boots had been left.

As nice as it would be to not walk around with all my parts on display, I felt more than a twinge of apprehension. Somebody knew I was there. And if somebody knew, then the element of surprise I was counting on was lost. I picked the shirt up, fumbling with it, and noting that it had two large slits in the back, which I was able, after some awkward maneuvering and quite a bit of swearing, to push my wings through. I eyed them warily as I pulled my pants on.

How the hell was I going to walk around in my own world with these goddamned feathered monstrosities?

I pulled the pants on, then the boots. Everything fit like a glove, as if they had been made for me. The shirt had some kind of built-in corset thing that I managed to awkwardly lace up, and the pants almost fit like a second skin, which was definitely not something I'd gone for in my clothing choices back home. The boots went up to just below my knees, fitting my calves and ankles perfectly. The leather was supple, almost velvety.

A knife might be nice, I thought, but then I remembered that I had no need of mortal weapons. At least, I hoped not.

I extended my hand, focused on bringing my sword into being. It appeared effortlessly, but it, like too many things, it was no longer the same. The hilt was still dark black metal, but the blade, the one that had leapt with blue flames, was different now. The blade itself was longer, thinner, and the flames were black.

"Well, that's creepy," I murmured. "We're going for a very angel of death type look here, aren't we?" And then I realized I was talking to myself and that it probably wasn't a good sign. I looked at my sword again, at the black flames leaping along the blade, then I shook my head and focused on making it disappear. It did.

From inside my cave, I could hear the sounds of battle raging in the Nether, as it had since I'd revived. Booming, crashing. Distant shouts. Almost constant thunder and lightning. Every once in a while, the sound of a horn blowing. The occasional scream. The smell of smoke hung heavy in the air, and my skin prickled due to the amount of power being tossed around by the gods as they fought. Really, it was stupid. The gods couldn't actually kill each other. I guessed that, when they were injured badly enough to die, they just regenerated the way I had. The only being who could actually kill a god and make him or her stay dead, was me.

I'm special that way.

I crept out of the cave and looked around. Everything looked the same as it had when I'd awoken. Amethyst sky overhead, sharp black mountains behind me cutting the western horizon. I looked up at the millions of whitish-purple stars that dotted the sky. They were always there, no matter what time it was. When I'd first started coming to the Nether, I'd purposely tried coming at different times, trying to get a sense of day versus night. Eunomia had finally explained to me that there was no difference, that the Nether was endless night, and I'd smiled. Night had always been my time.

Looking up at the sky now, I just felt empty and lost. I missed the sky back home, even the gray clouds that Detroit wore in November like a cloak. But every once in a while, you'd get a brilliantly sunny, bright blue sky, and you'd remember what beauty was.

I shook my head and looked around. I could see the city in the distance, where Hades' palace and everything else was. The Nether was vast, but few ventured beyond Hades' reach. The mountains, the eerie forests that surrounded the city, were inhabited by creatures great and small, creatures I'd only ever read about in stories, and some that I never would have been able to imagine.

I glanced around again, looking for the mysterious creature that had, I had to believe, left the clothing for me. Not a trace of it. I racked my still-groggy brain, trying to guess, from my stupidly limited knowledge of mythology, which of the gods might have a giant dog thing at its command. It wasn't Cerberus; I'd seen that beast outside of Hades' home. Even if it had been, I wouldn't have felt any better.

I knew I needed to be smarter now. And the smart thing, at this point, was to trust no one. My parents had proven themselves to be liars, hiding my true parentage from me up until they couldn't keep it a secret anymore. I wondered if they'd known closing the gateway would kill me. If they had... then they won for shittiest parents *ever*. My aunt had tried to kill me, and I had to wonder how much the other aunt despised my existence, considering how much venom had been spewed my way. Every god, now, had a reason to want me dead for closing the mortal realm to them.

Well. Dead again, I guess.

I wondered if I'd come back from a second death. I didn't intend to have to find out.

The only thing I knew was that I'd have to be careful. I'd have to think instead of smashing first. No more taking things on faith. No more prophecies, family bullshit, or entangling alliances. All I wanted was to end the stupid war and figure out how to get home.

There had to be a way.

I ended up making my way back into the cave, and dozed on and off for what felt like a long time. There really was no way to tell, in the Nether, how much time as I knew it had passed. All I knew was that my body was still weak and every time I even thought of using my powers I ended up with a throbbing headache.

Dying *sucks*.

So however long it took, I eventually woke up finally feeling as strong as I should. I could feel my powers thrumming through me, and when I called fire into my palms, it came effortlessly. I breathed a sigh of relief, and it turned into a rumble from my stomach. Food. Food would be good.

I made my way cautiously out of the cave and headed toward the woods, scanning the area to make sure I saw anyone or anything that could pose a threat before it saw me.

The woods were silent. The black and gray trees rose into the sky, and dead leaves crunched under my feet. I tried to walk quietly, taking slow, cautious steps. I didn't even know what I expected to eat in those woods. Chances were that anything I found in the Nether's forests would either make me sick or cause me a lot of pain, somehow. But I had my strength and energy back, and now I was freaking hungry.

I froze as the giant animal from my cave sauntered in front of me. I recognized its stormy blue, glowing eyes. My jaw dropped, and I had to fight tears back from my eyes when I realized what I was looking at.

It wasn't a wolf. Or a dog. It was an enormous black cat, fur shining in the meager light, long tail lashing back and forth as it watched me.

"Well that's just fucking mean," I muttered, swiping at my eyes in frustration. The animal looked so much like Brennan when he was in his favorite form it took everything in me not to approach the damned thing and wrap my arms around its neck. Instead, I just stared at it, and it watched me. It had a dark brown satchel in its mouth, and it approached me and dropped it at my feet, then backed up a few steps and looked back up at me, waiting patiently.

"It's probably a bad idea to accept gifts from strange cats, here of all places," I said to it, and backed away. It walked forward and nosed the satchel toward me again. "Go away, cat," I said, backing up some more. I didn't want to turn my back on it, but I also didn't want to be indebted to this creature and whoever it served anymore than I already was. Clothing was one thing. I wasn't going to intimidate anybody in my birthday suit. But beyond that? No way.

The cat heaved a large sigh, walked forward, and nosed the satchel toward me again. I stood, crossed my arms, and glared at it. My glare was somewhat legendary. It had made demons piss themselves, vampires remember their manners. It had ended fights between street thugs and arguments between opposing werewolf packs. I was pretty proud of it, really.

The cat just gave me a bored look and glanced down at the satchel again.

We stood there, the cat and I, in a bit of a stalemate. After a while, it sat, still watching me in a bored manner, but clearly not intending to leave until I'd opened the satchel.

"You're so sure there's nothing in there that's going to kill me, why don't you open it?" I muttered.

The cat heaved another annoyed sigh and used its sharp teeth to pull the satchel open. Then it picked the bag up from the bottom and dumped the contents onto the forest floor. A small loaf of bread. Some fruit that kind of looked like apples, but was a dusky purple color. A bottle with liquid of some kind in it.

The cat looked at me again, then glanced down at the food.

"Who sent you, cat?" I asked it. Since, obviously, the damn thing could understand me. And for just a second or two, maybe, I could pretend it was Brennan I was talking to. And it hurt, because trying to feed me was exactly the type of thing Bren would do. I looked away from the cat, blinking tears back from my eyes again.

The cat stepped toward me and I watched it warily. It gently butted its large head against my thigh, and looked down at the food again. And then it sauntered away, and I was alone, as if it had never been there at all.

I sat on the ground, picked up the fruit, and brought it to my face. It smelled like a fruit salad, like a mix of watermelon and grapes and other sweet things. I gathered the fruits, the bread, and the bottle and put them back into the satchel. I put the strap over my shoulder and continued my walk through the woods. I didn't know how long I'd be operating out of the cave, and knowing the area immediately surrounding it, including hiding places that could be used by me or someone who wanted to surprise me would be important.

During my walk, I found a small trickle of a stream with water that looked fairly clear. A few wild bushes with some type of berries on the branches grew not too far from the stream. I had no idea whether the berries were edible or not, of course.

As I started making my way back toward the cave, the sky erupted in thunder and lightning, again. Rain started falling in fat drops that splattered when they hit my face. I quickened my pace as the storm started picking up in intensity.

By the time I reached the cave, my clothing and hair were soaked through. I was not walking around the Nether naked again. So I sat against the wall of the cave, and curled into a ball, trying to feel warm. Everything was cold, and damp, and I was starving and lonely and I had no goddamn idea what to do next or anything else.

I was starting to feel pretty miserable when movement near the mouth of the cave caught my eye, and the giant cat walked in. It settled itself next to me in the cave, curled up next to my hip like some kind of over-sized house cat. But it was warm, and I wasn't alone for the moment, so I could hardly complain.

How pathetic. I'd spent twenty-four years of my life totally alone, and now I couldn't stand even a day by myself without becoming all depressed and weepy.

Just for now, then. Tonight, I'd be weepy, I told myself. And then tomorrow, I'll be a badass again. And I hugged my knees and listened to the rain beating outside the cave, and I thought about home.

CHAPTER TWO

When I woke up, I was alone in the cave again. It was for the best. I really didn't need the emotional punch to the gut I got every time I saw that damn cat.

I needed to decide what to do next. Did I approach Tisiphone or Hades first about ending the war? Could I even trust them? I sensed that they both cared for me; emotions don't lie. But you could care for someone and still be a liar, and they were gods, and they'd already lied to me about so many things, so... yeah. Probably not.

Which left me, *where*, exactly? I stood up and stretched, flexing my wings along with my arms and legs. I needed this war to end as soon as possible so I could try to open the gateway again. It was in the gods' best interest to let me do that, because their power was severely limited without access to the mortal realm. Eunomia had explained it to me. The gods were strongest in their own realm. Beings like my father, a creature of the Nether, were at peak strength there. And beings like Zeus, from the Aether, drew their strength from their realm. But, no matter whether they came from the Aether or the Nether, they needed the connection to the mortal realm to be at peak strength. Something about the energy in my world, and how they were incomplete without it. It didn't make much sense to me. I was stronger in the Nether, usually, than I was at home, and, now that I was stuck there, I wasn't feeling any ill effects of the loss of contact with my world.

Well. Other than the obvious heartbreak and losing everything that had ever mattered to me, of course.

But gods were prideful, arrogant, stubborn assholes and most of them kind of wanted me dead. And if they didn't want me dead, they wanted to use me somehow. From the gods I knew, that was pretty par for the course.

Except for Asclepias, I reminded myself. He'd never asked me for a thing in return for helping the shifters, and he could have. And when he'd joined Hades' side in the war, fighting against many of his fellow gods of the Aether, it had surprised more than a few. He wasn't political, from what I'd learned of him. He was definitely not a fighter. So for him to specifically choose a side, and choose against Zeus… that was kind of a big deal.

Okay. Maybe Asclepias would be the first one I approached. Of course, that would mean exposing myself to one of them, and if he turned out to actually be just like the rest of them, then I'd given up my element of surprise. Since no one had come hunting for me yet, I had to believe the cat or whatever it was wasn't in a hurry to see me dead or captured.

It was the "captured" part that freaked me out the most. Chances were good I could come back from the dead again, probably. I'd been held captive once before. I could live several hundred lifetimes and still wake up in a cold sweat, remembering what it had felt like to be that helpless. And with gods as captors…no. I didn't even want to think about it.

I ventured out, carrying the satchel of food the cat had left for me. I still hadn't been brave enough to try any of it, and my stomach growled. The good thing about the Nether was that all of the power emanating from it fed me. So while I had physical hunger to deal with, at least I had no hunger for power, or fear, or pain, the way I did back home if I'd gone too long without feeding. Home, I'd sated myself by feeding on the fear and pain of the troublemakers I hunted.

God, I missed being the top of the food chain.

I made my way toward Hades' city. The ever-present sounds of battle still permeated the air, though Zeus had finally let up on the rain in favor of almost constant rumbling thunder. I didn't enter the city itself, but stayed to the woods that surrounded it, watching, listening. As I approached the edge, I heard nearby sounds of battle and shrank back a bit, angling myself to get a better look. Two satyrs held off a trio of sprites, and they all cursed at each other as the fight raged on. It would have been kind of mesmerizing to watch, these mythological creatures engaged in battle, had it not been for all of the blood.

Satyrs and sprites weren't gods. They could die at one another's hands, and their deaths would be permanent. I was about to step forward and stop it, figuring I could use my mind powers on them to make them forget me if I had to. At least, I hoped so. I took a step, and then I felt something, and completely forgot what I was even doing.

A pulsing, wild energy signature that was so similar to Brennan's that it made my heart race. I froze, looked around. Knew it was impossible that it was him, but my stupid heart dared to hope anyway. I took a breath, produced my sword, the satyrs and sprites forgotten.

A figure came out from behind a nearby clump of trees. A lithe figure with long sandy-blond hair, wearing brown clothing very similar to what I wore. She held her hands in front of her in a gesture of peace, kept her eyes on me.

Artemis.

I knew her from afar. Tisiphone had pointed her out to

me one time as we'd walked through the Nether. I'd never interacted with her in any way before this. She was another Aether god who'd joined Hades' side in the fight, even though her brother, Apollo, was solidly allied with Zeus.

She smiled at me. "Your pulse went mad when you sensed me. Did your shapeshifter mate ever tell you that the scent of your adrenaline is nearly intoxicating?"

I kept the sword out. "What do you want, Artemis?"

"Why did you react so strongly when you sensed me? I wonder if you even know why, yourself. How perceptive are you, Fury?" She approached, circled me where I stood, studying me, never quite getting close enough to make me feel overly threatened, but still closer than I would have preferred.

I didn't answer. Watched her, poised to respond to any sudden movements she made. Artemis was a strong fighter, a hunter of renown. I wasn't surprised that if one of them had to track me, it had been her.

She finally stopped circling me, stood and crossed her arms as if she was satisfied about something. "Relax. If I wanted to harm you, I could have easily done so while you were regenerating on the mountainside."

"You've been following me all that time?" I asked, my heart sinking. I hadn't even known.

"Not the whole time," she said, and then she let out a low whistle, and two huge black cats, identical, came out of the surrounding forest. They sat on either side of her, and watched me. "There is a war going on, and I can't be here without drawing too much attention to you. Why haven't you eaten the food we gave you?"

"I don't trust it. Or you. Or them," I said, gesturing to the cats.

"Why did you respond to my presence so strongly?" she asked again. "Be assured that I already know why. I'm just asking to find out if you do."

I stayed silent. Brennan had already been put in danger twice because of our relationship. I wouldn't let it happen

14

again. She seemed to sense what I was feeling.

"I would never hurt the shapeshifter you have claimed, Mollis," she said softly. "I know you have no reason to trust or believe me. And that is smart. But I'd never hurt him."

"Why not?"

She smiled again. "We should get away from the city. It would be too easy for them to sense you here." And with that, she turned and started walking through the woods, toward the mountains. I took a breath. One of the cats stayed and watched me, waiting expectantly, and, in the end, I followed her. I was not stupid enough to put my sword away, though.

We made our way deep into the forest, and even the sounds of battle faded a bit. Artemis stopped when we reached a small clearing, and she sat down on the leaf-littered ground. I sat several feet away on a fallen tree trunk, and watched her. "Answer my question, please," I said. "Why wouldn't you hurt him?"

"Answer mine first. Why such a strong response when you felt my power signature?" She picked up a leaf and started crumbling it with her fingers, brown bits of leaves falling to her lap like confetti. The giant cats both looked on, sitting still as statues.

This was annoying, and it was clear I wouldn't get any answers from her until I answered the question. "You feel like him," I finally said.

"Explain," she said, nodding.

"All shapeshifters have a similar energy signature. Kind of wild feeling, almost bursting with hyperactivity."

She nodded again. "And?"

"Brennan's is that, but a little different. His energy has this strong, steady pulse to it. It just feels so much *more* than anyone else's," I finished, focusing on sensing for her. She was calm, pleased.

She nodded in approval. "You are as perceptive as I'd hoped you would be. Though you likely attributed his 'moreness' to some ridiculous romantic notion or simply believing that he was just that much more powerful than other shifters."

I ignored the "ridiculous romantic notion" comment. "Well. He *is* more powerful than others."

She smiled. "Obviously. How many shifters do you know who can shift into any animal they choose?"

I watched her. "Just one."

"And how many do you know who can take the form of one of those?" she asked, gesturing at one of the giant black cats.

"Just one," I repeated.

"Well. Now you know two." And the air shimmered around her, and where the goddess Artemis had been sitting, now sat a majestic, enormous black cat, blue eyes glowing as it looked at me.

"I am going to assume this is not some kind of coincidence, then," I said, once I was sure my voice wouldn't waver.

Artemis shifted back, and sat there, calm and still. "There are no coincidences. Not where immortals are concerned, anyway." She paused. "Want to hazard a guess?"

"He's not your son," I said. "He knew his parents."

She shook her head. "No, not my son. He is my great-times-a-few-hundred grandson."

I just watched her. "Care to elaborate?"

She smiled. "How much do you know about me?"

I shrugged. "Not much. Huntress, goddess of childbirth and virgins and the wilderness. Though my limited knowledge usually mentions bears or deer as your favorite animals, not cats. And nothing about shapeshifting."

"Before they started calling me Artemis, I was known as Bastet by the ancient Egyptians. Cat, warrior goddess and symbol of motherhood. Some of the Greeks called me Ailuros, which they basically thought of as Artemis in cat form." She shrugged. "There is an element of truth to most of the stories about me."

I watched her. "So. Brennan," I said, hoping to get back to what I actually wanted to know.

She sat still a moment. "I was hunting, oh, a few thousand years ago in mortal time. Jungles, this time, even thought I preferred forests where I could find the bears and deer I liked so much. But this time, I was in a jungle, and came upon a sleek black cat. Not as large as me, in that form, but close. Upon getting closer, I recognized him for what he was."

"Shapeshifter?" I guessed.

She nodded. "He shifted, and he was just as amazing in his human form as he was a cat. And things happened from there." She smiled, remembering. "I am not a woman who particularly needs the company of a man to be happy. I am fine in the forest with my bow and nature for company. But that man... thousands of years later, I still remember how good he felt."

"TMI, I think," I murmured, and she laughed.

"Anyway, I left him, because obviously I had no intention of staying. But I had a little something to remember him by. I gave birth to my son. I would have kept him in the Aether with me, happily, but when he came of age he wanted to learn more of his father's world. I gave him my blessing, and let him go. And my line has continued to this day, your mate being the youngest."

"Are there others?"

"A few. Only the oldest child in each family inherits the traits of my line. The rest of the children in the family may very well be shifters, but they will not be like your Brennan."

"So it's passed from the oldest child in a family, to their oldest child. What if they produce no offspring?"

She grinned. "They always produce offspring. Surely you've noticed how energetic–"

"Okay. I get it. Enough," I interrupted, and she laughed.

She watched me, warmth in her eyes. "Your child will be amazing. All of my power, plus Hades and Tisiphone's? I can't wait to meet him or her."

I blushed, looked away. "Uh. I'm not sure that's going to happen."

"Why not?"

"Have you noticed that I closed the gateway? I'm here, and he's there."

"You intend to open the gateway. I think you'll succeed," she said simply. "And the good thing is, even if it takes you a while, you'll have plenty of time together later."

"Yeah?"

"Of course. My line is exceptionally strong, as you already know. My descendants are also blessed with long lifespans."

"His father and mother both died young."

"They were killed. It happens. I'm talking about natural life, old age, all of that. He'll live a good long time, as long as he stays smart and on guard."

"I am pretty sure he never lets his guard down," I said.

"As it should be. Which brings us back to you, lovely girl."

I watched her, waited.

"I am removed, but I am very fond and proud of my descendants. And I know that, not only are you mated to my grandson, but you also brought Asclepias in to heal him when he would have died. You were ready to tear the Nether apart when you found the Guardians had kidnapped him. And, just to top it off, you raised a demon army and then left them in your realm, where they serve and protect him."

"I didn't really intend for that to happen," I admitted. "Just luck. I'm glad they're on that side, with Brennan, rather than here."

"Precisely. And from what I've heard, your imp army is nearly as devoted to him as they are to you."

"Brennan is nicer than I am," I said, trying to brush it off.

"So, you've saved his life, and you still protect him, even when you can't be there. All I want is to help you here, to keep you safe, to let you accomplish what you need to in order to get back to him. I want him to be happy. For that, he needs you."

"This is too good to be true," I muttered. "You came in on Hades' side of the war. Why?"

She looked at me like I was crazy. "Because his was the side defending you, of course," she said. "My brother is very unhappy with me, by the way."

"I'm sure," I said. "I still don't trust you."

"Good. You shouldn't trust anyone here. But I will swear to you, nonetheless, that I honestly do want to help you. That I will do whatever I can to keep you safe, for my grandson. I have no interest in politics. I want to get back to the hunt. War bores me."

"This is so fucking weird," I said under my breath.

"Not so strange," she said. "You already knew he was different. You just didn't know why." Then she smiled. "I could not have chosen a better mate for him if I'd tried," she said, and she nearly squealed with delight. "Tell me about him."

I shook my head. "What do you want to know?"

"What is he like?"

"He's brave. Strong. Loyal. He has this ridiculous, boundless amount of energy. He's cocky, and bossy, and he takes care of me in a way I've never imagined anyone would. The first time we met, he challenged me to a fight. For fun." I looked up at her. "Maybe he gets that from you."

She grinned. "Probably."

I met her eyes. "Know this. I don't care what pretty words you say right now. If you mess with him somehow, if you hurt him, or bother him, or even look at him funny once the gateway is open, I will kill you myself. Slowly, painfully, physically and mentally, and there will be no coming back once I'm done with you."

I held her gaze a while, both of us refusing to look away.

"I like you," she finally said. Then she grabbed one of the fruits out of the satchel I'd been carrying and took a big bite. After a few minutes, I followed suit.

◆ ◆ ◆

When Artemis and I parted, I didn't end up going back to the cave. She'd been helpful. Showed me where to gather edible fruit. The things she'd given me had not made me sick. In fact, I felt good. The fruit tasted like watermelon and strawberries. Delicious.

I missed coffee. Add it to the list of thing I missed about home.

So she'd been helpful, but I was not falling into my old routines of trusting and then being screwed over. I wouldn't go back to the cave. Not right away, anyway. I knew she'd be able to find me if she really wanted to. She could track me. She and the cats all had my scent now. But I would not sit in one place and make it easy for her if (when?) she decided to betray me.

So I walked the woods, and I watched the battles that raged, from a distance. Zeus really enjoyed his lightning. Buildings in the Nether smoked. Fires were an almost constant thing, accompanied by the screams and shouts of the demons and other creatures caught up in the gods' war.

I wandered. Not lost. I was learning about the Nether. Where I could hide, where I could find food. The best vantage points to watch Hades' home. I watched the gods in battle, taking note of their battle styles, their weaknesses. That was one of the many things I'd learned from Brennan, back when he'd trained me to fight: everyone, no matter how strong, has a weakness. Learn what it is, and you can beat anyone. I had mine, without a doubt. And the gods had theirs, too. Zeus was cocky to a fault, used to being the biggest one, intimidating with the lightning. Sure, lightning would hurt. Couldn't be any worse than being caught in a bomb blast and losing your skin and a few limbs. I wasn't afraid of that. Apollo charged, sometimes with a lance, sometimes with a huge battle ax. So many opportunities for someone smaller and faster than him to get inside that huge reach and stick him through the gut.

Not that I planned on doing that. Of course.

So I watched, and I thought, and I planned. And in the midst of it, I had a moment of clarity. There was a loose end out there that needed to be tied up, now. Hermes and Enyo had not been in on the little secret of my lineage. Not at first. Where would they have gotten the idea, years ago, to go after me? The Nether at large didn't know about me until the day I'd walked through the gateway and confronted a bunch of demons.

I thought back to the that last day, the day I'd closed the gate. Persephone had sprung it on me, that I was not Cithaeron's daughter, but Hades'. And I'd confronted Hades with that knowledge.

"Hades," I said. "Please forgive my tardiness. I apologize." *Dad*, I thought at him.

He barely reacted, though I did note a tiny grimace. *My wife talks too much. We will discuss this later*, he thought at me. "Not a problem, my dear. Hermes here was early."

Who else knows? I need to know. Now.

I settled my gaze on Hermes. I would heed Persephone's warning. I didn't like her, but she was shrewd, and if she saw fit to warn me against him...

21

*Me, my wife, your mother, Cithaeron, and
you. That's it.*
Cithaeron knows?
*Your mother had some explaining to do. As
did I with Persephone.*

A short list. Enyo, and, later, Hermes, had learned
about me from someone. That list was a pretty good place
to start. Considering that my mother's sisters hadn't even
been told about me (not by her, at least) I didn't think
Tisiphone had blabbed to anyone. Hades knew that my
existence and what it meant made everything more
complicated. If nothing else, my father was practical and
calculating. He would not have talked about me, choosing
to play things close to the chest until he had use of me.

Cithaeron was a mountain god. Trapped in the mortal
realm, now. He was even less interested in political bullshit
than Artemis, from what I'd heard.

Which left Persephone. Who had never, ever liked me.
Who was outwardly respectful and affectionate toward
Hades, but harbored a simmering anger toward him.

She'd known. And she'd made sure I knew about
Hades, and steered my attention toward Hermes.

How could I have been so stupid? I'd believed the "oh,
I'm worried about Hades" shtick she'd fed me. She wanted
me to focus on Hermes. She wanted him gone. Before he
did what Hermes did, and made a deal. Before I learned
where it had all started.

I ran through it all in my mind, looking for flaws in my
reasoning. Cithaeron was still a possibility. I didn't know
him. But I knew Persephone, and she was a calculating,
angry woman who hated my guts. She did love my father; I
could sense that. It was what kept her at my father's side,
despite the way they'd gotten together, despite the fact
that my father had slept with Tisiphone, and made me.
She'd known it, and whispered it to the right goddess,
Enyo, who wanted power and respect, and Enyo had

brought Hermes in, because he could get to my realm easier, where he could use his pet demon, Astaroth, to track me down and capture me so they could use me. And when Astaroth failed, they knew I'd find my way there somehow. And I had.

It just hadn't worked out quite the way they'd hoped.

What did Persephone get out of it? My death, of course. That would have been welcome. Revenge on Hades and Tisiphone.

Why did I have to die before I finally started thinking?

Okay. So I knew. Now what? How far did her rage go? Was Hades in danger now? There was a war going on. Lots of confusion, craziness. The perfect time to make a move against Hades. They couldn't really kill him, obviously. Not without me wielding the blade. But they could weaken him. Capture him. Not that I cared, really, all that much. I didn't know my father. Between the two of them, though, I'd much rather have Hades in charge of the Nether than Persephone. Hades could be reasoned with.

Maybe.

Shit. Time to go visit my stepmom.

CHAPTER THREE

I made my way to Hades' palace. It wasn't hard. The streets, usually bustling, were mostly empty as sane beings tried to stay out of the chaos of battle and everyone else partook in the bloodlust happening on the battlefields. They fought in the sky, on the ground. It was loud, and chaotic, and freaking terrifying. But it made it easy to sneak up to the front door of Hades' palace. I turned the knob. Locked. Well. There went my element of surprise.

I lifted my hand and knocked once, lightly. A demon answered the door, and his eyes widened in surprise when he recognized me. I held a finger up to my lips.

"Who do you serve?" I asked him quietly, meeting his gaze.

"You, my Lady. Of course."

"Excellent. Then stay silent about me."

He nodded, saluted me by pressing his fist to his heart. He opened the door wider, and I walked past him. My status, as the daughter of the Lord of Death, still held some sway after all. The demons had pledged themselves to me, both because of my birth line and because I'd bonded to a demon. It didn't seem to matter to them that

I'd moved on. The fact that I'd done so at all was a big deal, and something they took as a sign that I was better than the gods they'd been serving.

I'd take it. Every bit of it.

As I walked through the halls, I greeted several demons, each who either saluted or dropped to a knee at the sight of me. I ordered each of them to keep quiet, asked where Persephone was.

"She is in the music room, my Lady," a female demon finally said.

"And my father?"

"Battlefield," she said.

I nodded, thanked her, and she saluted me and went on her way.

I made my way to the music room. The soft strains of piano music met my ears, something haunting and lonely, something full of sadness and loss. I tried to ignore the way it made my heart ache as I peeked into the room. Persephone sat at the piano, long, thin fingers rippling over the keys. Her head was bowed, and when I sensed for her, I felt a tornado of emotion: sadness, anger, loss, fear. She did not feel me, engrossed as she was in the music. All I could think about was how much I'd lost because of the creature sitting at the piano.

I walked across the stone floor, the soft treads of my boots soundless as I neared her. I held my hand out, and my flame sword appeared at my side. I reached her, grabbed her hair and put my sword blade to her throat in one smooth motion. She gasped in surprise, the music stopped, and I felt something beautiful from her in the sudden silence.

Fear.

It fed what I'd always considered my internal demon, the part of me I'd gotten from my parents, the part that lusted for fear, pain, anger. The part of me that liked to cause pain, that reveled in knowing I was feared. It was so easy to get lost in it, seductive. It was so much stronger in the Nether, so much harder to resist, already. So easy to let it take over, to submit to the whispers that if I just gave in, I'd be the most powerful being in existence. That the world was mine to take, and it all started here. I could have it all.

"Hello, Persephone. How is my favorite evil stepmother today?" I asked quietly, and I could hear the coldness in my own voice. "Did you miss me?"

"I thought you were trapped in your own realm," Persephone said, a slight tremor in her voice. Her fear still washed over me, along with her ever-present dislike of me. To her credit, she stayed still and calm.

"That would have been nice for you, wouldn't it?" I asked, pulling the sword back, releasing her hair.

"That's not what I said," she said, turning around on the bench and looking at me.

"So when exactly did you tell Enyo about me?" I watched her. Sensed for her. Anger. Guilt. Irritation.

"Years ago. Not long after you were born, probably," she said quietly.

"So she could come after me?"

She huffed out an irritated breath. "No. You won't believe it, but no. I was angry. I was hurt. My husband, such as he is, created life with someone else when he couldn't create it with me. I vented to someone who was a friend at the time."

"You were friends with Enyo?" I asked, still watching every move she made, refusing to be surprised.

"We gods have been around longer than you can imagine. Most of us have been friends and enemies with each other at one point or another. For a time, Enyo was one of my closest friends." She looked up at me. "I did not know she would do what she did with that knowledge. Believe me when I said I never wanted you to come here. I wanted you to stay hidden. I never wanted to know you, or have you become part of our lives."

"Gee, thanks."

"You're welcome."

I watched her. Took a deep breath. "I really wanted to kill you when I came in here," I said. I could feel my power settling down, the hunger that her fear had awakened now abating a bit.

"I could tell," she said dryly. "You would be in the right if you did. It was ultimately my fault she found you."

"Do you want me to kill you?" I asked, raising my eyebrow at her.

"Not particularly, no. I just know that, should you decide to, I'll be dead no matter how hard I tried to fight you." She paused, shot a dark look in my direction. "This is why they hate you so much. We can all feel it. When you walk into a room, it is as if Death itself walks there. How do mortals live with the constant knowledge that they are destined to die?" she asked, shaking her head.

"They tend not to think about it too much. They think about the day-to-day, the next lover, the next house, the next promotion." I shrugged. "They're probably a lot smarter than the gods in that way. Or their lives actually have some meaning, other than simply trying not to die off."

"Touche'."

"Truth."

She rolled her eyes and crossed her arms. "How did you end up here?"

I sat down on the sofa near the piano. "I'm not sure." I wanted to keep my resurrection close to my chest. I had a feeling knowing I'd come back from death when I was supposed to be mortal would only freak everybody out more. "But lucky for you I did, huh?" I asked.

She just glared at me, clamped her mouth down as if she'd decided saying what was on her mind was probably a bad idea.

I grinned at her. "At least you hate me for a good reason. I'm the living, breathing proof that Hades fucked around on you."

"Oh, thanks ever so much for that sensitive reminder of our relationship," Persephone said, crossing her arms.

"Sure. The love between us is mutual, believe me." She shook her head again and we sat in silence for a few minutes. "How is the war faring for our side?"

"These wars are so stupid. Both sides are pretty much equal in power, so it's a constant stalemate."

"They're just fighting to fight," I said.

"Of course. They know there won't actually be a winner and loser. Zeus and Hades will go at it until they get bored, and then things will go back to the way they were," Persephone said.

"And they'll cause a lot of destruction in the meantime," I murmured.

She nodded. "I would not want to be in your world right now. You see how bad it looks here? Last time they fought, one of the World Wars in the mortal realm was the result."

"Which one?" I asked.

"How should I know?" she said, annoyed again.

I took a breath. It would feel really, really good to punch her in her overly-gorgeous face. But I wouldn't. "It needs to end."

"This one will probably last longer. They have you to fight over now. Hades and Tisiphone protecting their cherished little daughter, everyone else wishing you were dead. The quickest way to end it would be for you to die, really."

"I can totally see what my father sees in you, Persephone," I muttered, and she laughed.

"I'm not saying anything you don't already know, abomination."

I tried not to show my annoyance at the word. It was true, as far as it went. "No. But I have no intention of dying."

"Pity."

I was about to answer when I felt Hades enter the

house, and a few minutes later he was stalking into the music room.

He stared at me.

"What the Nether are you doing here?" he asked, voice raised, anger and fear rolling off of him in waves.

"Hi dad. Nice to see you, too," I said.

He growled. "This is the worst place for you to be. You are supposed to be in your realm, protecting the mortals. Why are you here?" he shouted.

"I don't know. I closed the gateway and got trapped here. The war needs to end, now."

He laughed, a cold humorless laugh that I'd often heard from myself in times of stress. "Yeah? Try telling Zeus that. And even more so once he realizes you're here. Damn it!"

"He won't realize I'm here until I want him to," I said. "I've been here the whole time, and the only reason you realized I was here was because I came to pay mommy dearest a visit."

"Why?" Hades asked, finally sparing a look at his wife, avoiding my eyes.

"Did you ever stop to wonder who told Enyo about me, when there were only four of you who knew about me, and she wasn't one of them?" I said quietly.

I watched Hades. Felt for him. And there was no surprise from him. Guilt. But not surprise.

"You knew," I said softly.

"I knew," he admitted. "I'm dealing with it."

"Meaning?" I asked him, glancing at Persephone.

"Meaning," she said, voice full of venom, "that I am a prisoner in this house, that my mind is completely tied to him so that I can't even have a single thought without him knowing it. He knew you were here with me, because he's in my mind."

Hades looked at me. "She can't be trusted. I know this. I'm dealing with it."

"I could kill her. Or you could send her to my mother," I said.

Hades met my eyes. *I love her. I'm a fool, but I love her. I'm dealing with it.*

If she steps out of line again…

He gave a terse nod. *Then you'll do what needs to be done.*

I looked away from my father after a minute. Everything in me told me to kill her now, no matter what Hades wanted. But I also knew I needed my father firmly in my corner if I wanted to end the war as quickly as possible and open the gateway.

"We need to end this so I can go home," I said after a few minutes. "You are probably ripping my world apart."

"Probably," he agreed. "I've never seen Zeus so bloodthirsty. I'd be more impressed if it wasn't me he was so intent on bleeding."

"So you're saying you don't think he'll just say 'okay, I was done anyway'?"

He snorted. "Not likely, no." He watched me. "Just let it play out."

"Not acceptable. People in my world are probably dying because of you gods and your bullshit, and I'm trapped here and can't protect them."

"What are you going to do? Kill everyone who doesn't agree with you?" Hades asked, laughing.

I met his eyes.

He stopped laughing.

"If I have to. Yeah, I will."

He was shaken. My father was afraid. Of me. He tried to hide it, tried to appear calm. He took a deep breath.

"I'll try to get Zeus to meet with me about a truce," he said, shaking his head.

"Do that. Do not tell him I'm here."

He nodded. I watched him. His fear made him untrustworthy.

"I want a piece of your mind, the way you have Persephone's," I said.

"What?" he asked me, raising his voice, anger rising amid his fear.

I just watched him. "Should I take it, or will you give it to me?"

He watched me. "If you can figure out how to do it, then I won't fight you." Smug bastard. He reminded me of Nain, just then.

I rolled my eyes. Concentrated and made my way into his mind. As soon as I got in, I really wished I hadn't.

Shoving my way into Hades' mind was like wading into a swirling abyss of death and agony. The second I entered, I was assaulted with his memories, his thoughts. And if I'd ever thought I was kind of dark, I looked like a freaking teddy bear next to what I saw in Hades' mind. Death, judgment, retribution, dealt by him, or by the Furies, over and over and over again. Men and women in clothing from every era, from every nation and every culture on Earth, their worst deeds and punishments.

Hades remembered them all.

They were part of him, just as the punishments I'd dealt in my short time working as a Fury were part of me. The memories of those I'd punished were with me, every second of my life, sometimes floating to the forefront of my thoughts at the strangest times, surprising me with terror in the middle of peace.

Not that there had ever been much peace. But still.

It was enough – just those few seconds in Hades' mind — to make me want to curl up in a corner and sob. I don't have time for weakness anymore, I reminded myself. I steeled myself against the assault of his memories, tried focusing. I was here to get a hook into his mind, the same way he did into Persephone's. Because he couldn't trust her.

And I didn't trust him.

Especially not now. Not when he was fighting me to keep me from getting a hold. I'm his daughter, right? You'd think he'd want me to be sure I could trust him.

So I worked, and before long, I was rewarded with a throbbing headache and so frustrated I was about to scream. Every time I thought I had gotten a hook into his mind, a piece of it for myself, it slithered away from my power, and I had to start over again.

Hades laughed, and I worked harder.

You, he said in my mind. *So sure of your power. Remember this, little girl. You have power. The difference between you and me is that I actually know how to use it.*

And then I felt him change tactics. More than just defending his own mind, he was making his way into mine.

Should have done this a long time ago. You're too unpredictable, daughter.

Oh, hell no.

So I stopped trying to get into his mind, and I worked at strengthening my own defenses. He pushed harder, and I focused harder.

You can't hope to actually prevail here, he thought in my mind. *The idiocy of youth.*

I didn't answer, just focused on maintaining my mental shields.

I don't know how long it went on. I could feel Hades getting frustrated, watched him and Persephone as I focused on keeping my mental shields intact. Waiting....

And, there it was. Hades sprung forward, slashed the ebony staff he usually carried out toward me. I ducked it easily, and he swung it back again, trying to catch me at the knees.

I held my shields, produced my sword.

You really want to do this?

He stared at the sword, took in my wings, and I felt surprise from him. Then it passed, and he hit out at me again. I met his staff with my sword, and the impact produced a dull "thunk" of sound. For the next while (I have no idea how long) the only sounds in the room were the thunk of sword hitting staff, the sounds of Hades and me breathing, grunting.

He was getting frustrated. I slashed out at him again.

I focused a little harder. And then I smiled, added a final bit of strength to my own mental shields.

"Hey, dad, guess what?"

He just glared at me, tried to strike me again.

"You're more experienced, but only one of us has a mind strong enough to destroy the barriers between worlds. You seriously think I can't keep you out of my head?"

Now that my mental shield was built, his attempts to get in felt feeble, pathetic. I laughed at him, felt his rage in response.

"Fine. Stop," he shouted. He stepped back, pulled his staff in front of him in a defensive, rather than fighting posture.

I stopped. Kept my sword at the ready, but rested it at my side.

"I am not giving you a tie to my mind, Not happening, Mollis. We can keep fighting over it, or we can figure out what to do next."

"I don't trust you. You have just as much reason as everyone else to want me gone. Maybe more. You've lied to me, over and over again—"

"It's what he does. The original Father of Lies," Persephone interrupted quietly.

I rolled my eyes. "I really don't give a fuck about your little lovers' spat. He's going easy on you, and I should have killed you already." Then I looked back at Hades. "So you can choose. Let me have a tie to your mind, the way you do with Persephone, or I consider you an enemy from here on out."

He looked at me, shook his head. He was irritated. Angry. So angry that, if I were anyone else, I'd be pissing myself just then. I just gripped my sword tighter.

"You are my daughter. You need to know that I meant what I said before. Tisiphone and I made you, and you are a thing of beauty. You're powerful. Unrelentingly noble," he said, a bit of a sneer in his voice. "There is nowhere for nobility in our world. We're gods. Not a damn one of us is trustworthy. And you being here instead of where you're supposed to be threatens everything we are."

"I know."

I nodded. Gathered my strength, keeping a calm, blank look on my face.

I blinked.

And I slammed myself, full force, into his mind, crashed through his well-built defenses, and he screamed. He tried pushing me out, but I was already there.

And I was surrounded by death. Instead of fearing it, I embraced it.

Formed a connection to it. I felt the moment I'd formed a connection to Hades' mind. It was like having an angry, complaining voice at the back of my mind. Incessant.

Eh. I'd get used to it.

I pulled out of his mind. He'd crumpled to the floor when I'd assaulted his psyche. I knew from experience, from having Nain and then the Puppeteer in my head, that there was definitely an aspect of physical pain involved when your mind was attacked that way. I felt a moment of regret, brushed it off.

"Thanks, dad," I said. Then I glanced at Persephone, who was watching me with a mix of awe, fear, and loathing on her face. I gave her a sarcastic bow and left.

I walked out of Hades' home, barely registering the bows and salutes of the demons there.

I didn't know much about my father.

But what I knew was enough. He would not stand for the indignity of being overpowered that way. Add him to the ranks of gods who would actively try to hunt my ass down now.

As if it could have ever been any other way.

I walked down the front walk, away from Hades' palace, and with each step, I felt my power settling down to normal levels. And with that, sanity.

What the hell had I just done?

I stopped in my tracks.

Holy shit. I just attacked the freaking Lord of the Dead. My father. The one being who'd actually promised to take some action to end the fighting so I could open the gateway again.

If I could even do that. I couldn't think about that now.

I turned and looked back at Hades' house.

I knew my father well enough to be afraid of him. Just as he knew me well enough to be afraid of me. I took a breath to steady myself, and walked back up toward the house. Either we would kick each other's asses now, or I'd have to wait for him to surprise me later. The older I got, the more I hated surprises.

I lifted my hand to knock, but before my knuckles made contact with the dark wood, the door opened. I looked up into Hades' face.

"Let's walk," he said, and I nodded. He closed the door behind him and gestured toward the left. There was a pathway that led to the riverfront. There was a weird garden there, full of plants I would have never imagined, the types of things that looked like, at any moment, they would reach out and grab you.

Since this was the Nether, that wasn't entirely impossible.

We strolled through the garden in silence for a while, Hades' hands clasped behind his back as he walked. The two of us, walking side by side, probably made for a bizarre picture, all pale skin and black feathered wings, Hades towering nearly two feet taller than my scrawny frame.

"I'm sorry," I said softly. He glanced over at me, raised an eyebrow.

"Well. That's something you don't hear often in the Nether."

"I am. I lost myself," I said, my voice barely a whisper, afraid as I was of the words and what they meant. Hades stopped walking, looked down at me. He was silent, waiting for me to continue.

"I lost control. It's screwing with my head, being here. I draw all this power, and it almost makes me forget anything but wanting more of it. How the hell do you live here like this?"

He took a breath. "It is not as bad for us. You know that as creatures of the Nether, we draw strength from it. We're at our most powerful here in our realm."

I nodded. "But you stay in control. Is it just an experience thing? Will I get used to it?"

He shook his head. "They call you an abomination. They're not wrong."

"Thanks, Dad," I muttered.

"They mean it as an insult. That is not how I mean it. An abomination is simply something that should not be. And as much as I cherish you, and I *do*, whether you can believe me or not, you were never meant to be." We resumed walking and eventually reached a stone bench. He gestured for me to sit, and I did. Once he'd settled himself, he continued. "You have all of my power. All of Tisiphone's power. And while the two of us, individually, are fine here, the combination of our power coursing through you is understandably too much." He looked at me, pushed a stray strand of hair behind my ear. "Your mother told me how often you came close to losing control in your duties as a Fury. That fiery outburst after you killed Hermes was you losing control again, yes?"

I nodded.

"Does that happen in your world?"

I shook my head. "Only when I'm really, really angry or desperate. Usually I'm just trying to protect someone, and destroying isn't at the front of my mind. Here, it's like all I want to do is destroy things the second I try to use my powers." I plucked at my pants, not knowing what to do with my hands. "You don't seem surprised."

"I'm not surprised the Nether affects you so. I am surprised you're here at all. You were supposed to be in your realm."

"I know. That's where I want to be, too." I explained everything. The pain as the gateway closed, the blackness that enveloped me, and reviving on the rocky mountainside in the Nether, new and unmarked. About hiding.

He took my hand, clasped it between both of his. "There was nothing, in any prophecy or anything else, that indicated you would be trapped here. I swear it to you. If I'd known, we would have found another way. We would have fought them, side by side, or figured out how to stall Zeus and Ares."

I believed him. The piece of him I held in my mind now didn't indicate any falsehood on his part.

"Who else knows you're here?"

"Just you and Persephone. And Artemis," I said.

"Ah, I figured," he said, smiling. "Artemis is a good one."

"You knew who Brennan was, when you came to me in my realm and agreed to ask Asclepias to save him," I said, watching him. "You didn't just do that for me."

He nodded. "I know how Artemis is about her descendants."

"And she'd owe you a favor."

He squeezed my hand. "Well, I knew I had a daughter I wanted to protect."

We sat in silence for a while. "I really am sorry. Here, let me—" I was ready to sever my tie to him, when he took my face between his hands.

"Don't. Leave it, Mollis. If that's what it takes to give you a tiny bit of peace here, then keep it. I was a fool for fighting you over it. Stupid, selfish, proud. Just keep it."

I nodded, looked away so he wouldn't see the tears I was trying to fight back.

"We need to get you home. Your world needs you, and you need it."

"We do."

"I will do as I promised. I'll speak with Zeus. He's so hardheaded, and he has Ares whispering in his ear all the time, urging an escalation in the fighting. If I can get my idiot of a brother alone, we may end this."

"Nothing is ever that easy," I said, refusing to get my hopes up.

"No. But we'll make it happen."

"I can't open the gateway until it's over. I won't let them fight in my realm. Things are probably already bad enough, if they're even a fraction as bad there as they are here."

He nodded.

"I want you to try to keep something in mind."

"Don't break into your mind anymore," I said.

He let out a short bark of a laugh. "Yes, that would be a good thing to remember. You're lucky you're my only child and I like you. Don't do it again."

"I won't."

"But what I really meant was this: you are at your best, at your strongest, when you are protecting something you care about. Your mind is clear; your power is focused. You are unstoppable. When you protected me from Hermes and Enyo, when you refused to cause my death...that was your true self. And you know it."

I didn't answer. Looked out over the river. It didn't move at all, its glassy surface completely undisturbed. It was eerily peaceful.

"But what I saw in you in there just now," he said, gesturing toward the house. "That was fear."

"I hate being here."

"I know. But your fear will undermine you if you let it rule your actions. You have so much at stake. I understand. But you need to be better. You need to master your fear, or you're going to find yourself in much worse situations than having your father mad at you."

"I will. I'm so f– ... messed up right now. And I know I can't afford to be."

Hades tried to hide a smile.

"What?"

"The big bad godslayer is worried about cursing in front of her father," Hades said.

"Cram it, pops."

He laughed, then. "Come on. No more sleeping in caves. The demons will practically piss themselves in excitement to find out you're staying here."

I took a deep breath, and nodded, and when Hades took my hand and led me back toward the house, I let him. I just had to hope I wasn't making yet one more boneheaded mistake.

◆ ◆ ◆

Hades and I walked back into the house and into his office. I sat down in one of the leather chairs across from his desk, and he sat behind it. I watched him with some weird sense of irritation and jealousy.

I was used to being the one in the big chair behind the desk now. I frowned.

"What was that?" Hades asked, raising an eyebrow.

I shook my head. "Thinking about how much I've changed in the past year or so. It's nothing."

Hades was about to respond when Persephone poked her head into the office. "The abomination is still here?"

I winked at Hades, turned to look at my stepmother. "I'm living here now! We can hang out. Maybe you can teach me how to play the piano. We'll bond."

She looked as if she'd just gotten a whiff of something awful. "Are you serious?"

I just smiled. Hades remained silent, though I could sense that he was enjoying himself immensely.

"She's staying here?" she asked Hades again.

"Yes, my daughter is staying here for the foreseeable future," Hades said, emphasizing the word "daughter." "And she will be treated with the respect due any of my guests."

She just stared at him. "Haven't I been punished enough? I already said I was sorry, Hades."

I turned back to my father, trying to hide my laugh. The expression on her face, the absolute horror at the idea of living in the same house with me, was just priceless.

Hades was better at keeping a straight face than I was. "It has nothing to do with punishing you, my love. She needs a place to stay, and I think it would be good for you to get to know Mollis better."

"I… you… I will not spend any time entertaining your brat, husband," she said, sneering the last word.

"Aw. And here I thought we'd bonded a little when I decided not to kill you," I said, meeting Persephone's eyes. *Not that I wouldn't enjoy doing that*, I said in her mind.

"And she just threatened me. Lovely," Persephone said.

"That's between the two of you. I really don't care," Hades said, rifling through the papers on his desk. "Just be nice. When she asks for something, make sure she gets it." He paused. "Oh, and she's kind of on edge here in the Nether. You'll probably want to avoid pissing her off."

Persephone just glared at Hades. "Should I bow down before her when she passes me in the corridors as well?"

"Don't be silly. A curtsy is fine," I said, and Hades suddenly became very interested in one of the documents on his desk.

She gave me a look that would have made any sane person terrified for their life, then swept out of the room, slamming Hades' office door behind her. My father erupted in laughter, and before long, I had joined him.

"Did you see her face?" I said, erupting in another gale of laughter.

Hades rested his face in his hands, his shoulders shaking with silent laughter. "You are terrible," he wheezed.

After a while, we both managed to compose ourselves. Then Hades muttered "curtsy" and we both started laughing again.

"I am going to be sleeping in one of the guest rooms for quite a while, I think," Hades said, shaking his head.

"Probably for the best," I said, and he nodded.

"Well. We've already angered my wife, so let's just keep going. I just summoned your mother. She should be here so we can all figure out what to do now."

"Oh, you are just evil," I said.

"I love my wife madly, but she's a pain in the ass," Hades said, leaning back in his chair. "It's been this way our entire marriage. It's just how we are."

I shook my head. My father could have just about anyone. Powerful, good-looking. Kind of a nice guy if you hadn't just pissed him off somehow.

Oh well. Not my problem. Well, it kind of was, but it's not like I could do much to change it.

We sat, Hades asking questions about my friends back home, and me answering in as few words as possible, because if I talked about them a lot, I knew I'd lose it. I wanted to keep it together, and it was already really, really hard to do that. The Nether's annoying effect on my powers, plus the fact that Hades and I in the same room always made my powers act weirdly. I drew off of his constant supply of rage. It wasn't something I tried to do. It was automatic.

"Do your powers act weird around me?" I asked him, interrupting his questions.

"What do you mean, weird?"

"I'm pretty much feeding off of your power when I'm around you. And I can't stop it. It happens every time I'm around you. It's making me kind of nauseous."

"Oh. No, I can't do that. That's related more to your mother's side."

"The mindflaying thing comes from Tisiphone?"

"Right. I like pain, anger, fear, just as the demons do. I crave those things, and when I'm around them, I'm stronger. But to be constantly feeding from those around you, to be able to mentally rip into them and devour whatever you need...that's more a Fury thing."

"Why?"

"Well, think about it. You've worked as a Fury. The things you saw would have broken you, made it impossible to go on with your work. Unless," he said, "you could also draw plenty of strength from the ones you were punishing. It's almost a symbiotic relationship: you punish them, and they feed you."

"Except that only one of us benefits from that relationship," I pointed out.

He smiled. "Well. There are advantages to being a god."

I shook my head, felt Tisiphone's presence nearby. A few seconds later, she stormed into Hades' office. Her normally immaculate uniform was torn, slashes as if from a sword across her stomach and arms. Her eyes were on me, shock thundering over me.

"What are you doing here?" she asked, completely ignoring Hades' greeting.

CHAPTER FOUR

As quickly as I could, I explained, and she slumped into the leather chair next to mine. "What a mess," she said. "They need you in your realm."

"I know. I want to try opening the gateway," I said.

"The second you do that, the fighting will spill over into your realm. Ares is chomping at the bit to incite more war. The humans would be all too easy to influence, and he'd gain power from it."

"I know. That's why I can't fucking do it until the war ends. We need to stop it."

"I told Mollis I'll try to talk to Zeus. Without Ares around," he added.

"You won't get within shouting distance of him," Tisiphone said, shaking her head. "Ares won't let that happen. And Zeus is invested in this. He's angry that so many of the gods of the Aether joined our side—"

"Shouldn't that be an indication to him that he's on the wrong side?" I said.

"It should. But Zeus never admits he's wrong," Hades said. "And I've tried to talk to him telepathically. He refuses to even acknowledge me that way. He's such a horse's ass sometimes."

"Sometimes?" Tisiphone asked, raising her eyebrow.

"Good point," Hades conceded.

"Okay. So talking is out. Is that what you're telling me?" I said.

"We'll still try to make it happen, Mollis," Hades said.

"We don't have time to screw around here," I said. The words were barely out of my mouth when a thundering blast made the house shake.

"What the fuck was that?" I asked, standing up, my sword appearing in my hand.

"The bastard just threw a lightning bolt at my house," Hades growled.

Persephone came running into the office, then. "What the hell is he doing?" she said. "He's never attacked us here before." Her words were punctuated by another blast, and this time the house shook even harder. I could hear the demon servants shouting to each other about putting out fires.

"Hey, do you think he knows I'm here?" I asked as another blast hit the other end of the house. Everyone turned at once to look at Persephone.

"Oh, sure, blame me. I can't tell anyone anything, imbeciles," she said, glaring at Hades. "He'd know."

"I'd know," Hades agreed.

"They can probably feel her," Tisiphone muttered. "The amount of power she's throwing off is making me dizzy." Indeed. I could feel my power spiking in response to the attack, the tension in the room, and having both of my parents and their rage present, feeding me.

"Okay. So they know I'm here," I said, hearing the snarl in my own voice. "Let's go out and play."

◆ ◆ ◆

I started walking through the door. My power was

responding to the insanity around us. Another bolt hit the house, and I heard a few demons scream in pain from that area.

"Are you stupid?" Persephone asked, her voice more high-pitched than usual. "You can't go out there. He's throwing *lightning* at us. What are you going to do?"

I turned to glance at her. "Make him stop. Obviously."

And then I left Hades' office, stalking down the long hallway that led to the front door. Except that the front door was now a charred mess. The demons who were putting the fire out turned to look at me.

"We would be honored to help you, my Lady," one of them growled, thumping his fist to his chest in the way the demons and imps had of saluting me.

"And I thank you for that," I said, my voice barely sounding like my own. "But you know as well as I do that death is your only reward should you go out there now."

"It would be a glorious death," another said.

"Not today. I may need you more later," I said, and kept walking. They watched me walk past. I was aware, dimly, of Tisiphone and Hades following me. Another impact shook the house.

"My house," Hades muttered.

"Yes, we all weep for the destruction of your monstrosity," Tisiphone said.

Hades didn't answer. We walked the rest of the way in silence, emerging in the front courtyard of Hades' palace. Zeus hovered in the air about a hundred feet away or so, white wings flapping lazily as he readied another blast.

I was about to confront him when my eyes settled on something else.

Three Guardians, standing not far from where Zeus was hovering.

"You didn't get them all?" I growled, glancing at my mother.

"We have been hunting for those three," she said. "Now we know why they were so hard to find." She watched me, a look of understanding on her face. "We'll face Zeus. Do what you need to do."

I nodded, stalked toward the Guardians. Another of Zeus' bolts hit, fairly close to me, but I ignored it, my focus completely on the three beings in front of me.

Eunomia's sisters. Who had betrayed everything they were supposed to stand for and helped Hermes and Enyo in their stupid plot to control me.

Who had abducted Brennan.

And tortured him, from what I'd gleaned from Tisiphone right after, during the crazed trip back to the gateway.

"Hey!" I shouted, stalking faster toward them. My voice echoed across the mostly-empty street leading to Hades' palace. They were already looking at me, of course. Fear, hate, rolled off of them. One of them went so far as to hiss.

I tossed fire at her effortlessly, and she went up in flames, screaming. One tried to run, but I unleashed a barrage of mental knives (I hardly ever used them, because they were so gruesome; one of the powers I'd stolen the night Nain had died) and she fell to the ground, bleeding, screaming. The best way to describe it is I can cut someone from the inside, out. I don't know how it works, or why.

Right then, I was just happy I had the power to make her hurt. As each of the first two Guardians died, it was easy for me to get into their thoughts, to sift through them, find the day they'd taken Bren.

I watched what they did to him, as I stalked toward the third, who was backing away, then taking flight, a look of absolute horror on her face.

They'd beaten him.

Broken his bones.

Sliced his body.

Taunted him with a lifetime of the same, all in the hopes of drawing me out, forcing me to comply with Hermes' demands.

And he hadn't given them the satisfaction of screaming. It pissed them off. And they'd taken it out on Eunomia when she'd busted her way in to save him.

The third Guardian rose into the air. I threw fire at her, but it missed, and she banked to the left. My power coursed through me, almost painful, augmented by my anger that she was getting further away from me.

I glanced at my wings.

Flapped them a few times, testing them, and was shocked when I actually rose into the air.

You can do it, Mollis, Hades said in my mind. *Trust your instincts. Don't think about flying. Just let your body do what it wants.*

I took a breath, eyes on the rapidly shrinking form of the Guardian as she flew further away.

Damn, she was fast.

I stopped thinking of anything but destroying the creature before me. Barely noticed as I rose into the air and started following her. Someday, I'd marvel at the idea that I was flying. Right now, there was only one thing on my mind.

I flapped harder, hurtling myself forward faster, not taking my gaze off of my prey. I was catching up to her, each flap of my monstrous wings bringing me closer to her, and she knew it. I felt her panicking. She banked hard to the right, and I nearly lost control trying to follow her at that speed. I turned too sharply, found myself turning, flailing. It took a few panicky seconds to right myself, and then I glanced around, hoping I hadn't lost her in my stupidity.

There. I saw her ducking into the forest, undoubtedly hoping to lose me in the trees. It wasn't a bad plan, really. She could finesse her way between the branches with her shorter, nimbler wings. I didn't have a chance in hell of flying through there with my wingspan.

I put on a final burst of speed. My wings ached with it, but I ignored the pain, pushed myself forward, harder, faster. She was just lowering herself into the forest, falling below the very tops of the trees.

There, the branches were still thin enough for me to break through.

I flapped three more times, hard, and hurtled myself into her. She screamed and we fell, hard, a couple hundred feet to the ground.

I made damn sure she hit the ground before I did. We pounded into the forest floor hard, a plume of leaves and pine needles, soft soil flying up on our impact.

She screamed as her wing snapped beneath us.

"Please stop," she said, voice weak. Pathetic. "Stop. Don't kill me. Take me to the Furies. Please. I'll go quietly."

"Why did you do it?" I asked her. I stood up, feeling much more spry than I should, given the way we landed. I looked down at her, and my sword appeared in my hand. Her eyes flicked over it, and the fear and pain coming from her was so good I could have lived off it forever. Perfection.

I shook my head, trying to clear it of the effects of the Nether. "Why?" I repeated.

"You should not be," she said weakly. "Hermes promised us he would find a way to end you."

"Did he tell you he was going to try to use me to usurp Hades and Zeus? Or did your pal leave that part of his plan out when he sold it to you?" I heard the snarl in my voice, and watched with an underlying sense of glee as she recoiled from me.

"He did not share that with us. I swear."

"You attacked your own sister over this, when she tried to save the mortal you took," I said.

"She was compromised. Guardians do not get involved in the lives of mortals. She has lost her way," she said, and, even through her pain, I could feel her disgust for Eunomia.

"Maybe she just finally found her way," I said. I gripped the sword harder, my knuckles ached from the tension in my hand.

Gods, I wanted to end her. Slowly. Painfully. Seeing what they'd done to Brennan, the other two I'd taken out got off too easy.

I could do that. So easily.

"Stand up," I growled.

"My ankle is broken," she whined.

"Ask me if I give a fuck," I said, yanking her up, and she screamed in pain, and I made sure to knock into her broken wing as I released her, making her scream again.

So I'm not above cheap shots. As if this is a revelation.

"I'm taking you to my mother. And she'll punish you. And, every once in a while, I'll be visiting you, too," I said, and was rewarded with a tidal wave of fear. "Just imagine the pain I could cause locked in a room alone with you," I said. Then I reached out and grabbed her arm. "Walk."

She did. Whimpering, limping. We weren't far from the edge of the forest. I could still hear the occasional boom not too far off, screams, shouts. Smoke filled the sky, the smell of wood and flesh burning.

Once we were out of the trees, I grabbed the back of her tunic (making sure I hit her wing as I did it), and rose into the sky. I spotted my mother at the edge of the battlefield with my aunt, and I flew to them. I dropped the Guardian at their feet, and she screamed in pain again, calling me a few less-than-nice names as she writhed on the ground.

"She's all yours," I said to my mother, meeting her eyes.

"You didn't kill her," she said, glancing down at the still-writhing form of the Guardian.

"She deserves much worse than death," I said. "I wish I'd kept the other two as well."

Tisiphone nodded. "This one will get special attention from me, daughter. You have my word."

"Thank you." My aunt walked toward the Guardian, stopping only to give me a quick hug as she passed me, then she lifted into the air, the Guardian dangling from her grip by her non-broken leg as they flew off. I watched them for a second, then turned to my mother.

"Hades and Artemis are keeping him busy. Apollo is refusing to fight, saying Zeus is taking it too far."

"Has he joined us?" I asked, watching Zeus as he shouted and readied another bolt.

"No. But Artemis believes he will."

I nodded. "Where's Ares?"

She shrugged. "Not here. Which is really strange, considering that whole God of War thing."

"That can't be good," I muttered.

"I agree," Tisiphone said. "Do you want me to see if I can find him? Or stay here and fight?" she asked me.

"Let's just try to work on Zeus now. He's going to burn the whole damn Nether down if we don't stop him."

She nodded, and we both flapped our wings, lifting into the air. "Go that way," I said, pointing to the left. "Circle around. We'll meet a mile or so behind him."

She gave one final nod and flew off, and I went in the opposite direction, calling my sword forward again.

Maybe I could spot where Ares was lurking, in the meantime.

As I flew, I scanned the ground beneath me for any sign of Ares. As I did, I finally took a second to marvel at the fact that I was flying.

And then, I remembered that I was freaking *flying* and I hated heights.

I felt my stomach twist. My hands started sweating, and looking down made me want to puke. I closed my eyes, shook my head. Just keep flapping, I told myself.

Yes. It is unlikely that a fall from just about any height would actually kill me. I knew this. I also knew that even if it didn't kill me it would still hurt like a bitch.

I chanced a look down again. Bad idea.

I landed (which was an adventure all its own. Now that I wasn't in rage mode, I was actually thinking. Thinking and landing were really not a good combination for me.) I tried to mimic the way I'd simply settled down to the ground when I'd landed near Tisiphone earlier. Instead, I came in too hard, lurched, tripped, and fell.

I laid there for a minute, trying to get my breath. This was stupid. Afraid of heights. I'm a god. I'm a *killer* of gods. I looked back up into the sky for a while. Well, at least I knew I could do it when I had to.

But, right then, I didn't have to. And I sure the hell didn't want to.

I stood up and started walking in the direction I'd indicated. Tisiphone would easily beat me there, but that was fine. I needed the time to get my head straight before I did something stupid.

After a bit of a stroll, I saw Tisiphone standing, looking around, a worried look on her face. When she spotted me, she ran up to me. "What happened?"

"Huh?"

"Why aren't you flying? What took you so long?" she asked, her worry washing over me, another layer of irritation. I just shook my head, waved the question off.

"Mollis?" she asked me.

"Nothing happened. What about you? Any sign of Ares?"

She watched me for a minute. "No, no sign of him. The only thing that could make him miss a scene like this," she said, and I could hear the distant booming of more of Zeus' bolts, "is planning something worse."

"Maybe this wasn't planned," I said as we started walking toward where Zeus was.

"Probably not," she agreed. "Zeus is trying to show you how powerful he is."

"Am I supposed to be afraid?" I asked, and she laughed.

"I think that is the plan, yes," she said, and I shook my head. "It would work against most of us, actually. Those lightning bolts hurt."

We had come within about a hundred yards of him. And I smiled. I could tell the instant he sensed me. Anger, disgust, concern flowed from him. "Watch this," I told my mother.

I kept walking toward Zeus, and he turned to look at me. His face was a mask of rage. He looked like a freaking giant; the same height as my father but with a lot more bulk.

"You know, you could have just knocked nicely and asked me to come out and play," I called across the distance between us. "I've been looking forward to some quality time with my uncle."

"I am no family of yours, godslayer," he roared, and lifted his hands to ready another bolt.

"Aw, come on. We're just one super dysfunctional group of inbreds, aren't we? How's Dionysus doing? I hear my aunt has been having some fun with him while he's in custody."

That did it. Zeus roared and, in a flash of white light, hurled a lightning bolt at me. I jumped away, ended up flying up to avoid it. I landed, kept walking, grateful that I'd managed to land on my feet that time.

"Your aim sucks," I said. "Go ahead. Try again. Even you can't miss at this distance." I stood about twenty feet from him now. "Typical privileged asshole. Never has to practice being good at anything, because you just bully your way through life. Taking what you want, throwing temper tantrums when someone bigger and badder than you comes along."

He laughed then, malice evident in his eyes when he looked at me. "Yes, little Fury? Are you the bigger and badder we're talking about?"

I drew my sword, watched his face as he looked at it, examined the black flames licking along the blade. "I know something else about you, Uncle Zeus," I said, enjoying the disgust he felt when I used the name. He just glared at me. "I know that I'm much, much stronger here than you are."

And then I rose into the air, flying toward him. He readied a bolt, tossed it, and I had to spin out of the way to avoid getting hit. Once I steadied myself, I dove toward him.

At that instant, Ares appeared next him, and, in the blink of an eye, they were both gone.

I stopped in mid-air, looking around. Tisiphone flew up next to me.

"Where did they go?" I asked her, still scanning the area.

"Back to the Aether, most likely," she said. "Let's make sure."

I nodded and we flew, side by side, surveying the area. From that height (I tried really, really hard not to think about that) I could see fires dotting the landscape, demons and other creatures working to put them out. I could see Cerberus sitting near the tall stone walls of the Pit, a very visible deterrent to anyone who was considering escape. Hades' home was no longer in flames, but now one entire wing of it lay in charred ruins.

"He's not here," Tisiphone said, and I nodded. We made our way back toward Hades' house, where Hades, Persephone, and Artemis, as well as her two huge cats, were standing in the courtyard.

"I really think I want something more classic this time around," Persephone was telling him. "Remember when we had a beautiful limestone castle? And that drawbridge? I adored that version."

Hades stood, arms crossed, nodding. Resignation on his face. I nearly laughed. He was in the doghouse, (mostly because of me) so Persephone would get her way this time around. It was kind of funny watching the Lord of the Dead get pushed around by his wife.

They all turned to Tisiphone and I as we landed.

"Nice job driving him off, daughter," Hades said.

I nodded. "I was going to try to talk to the asshole, but he wasn't in the mood," I said.

"It is unlikely he'll talk to you," Hades said.

"He may have, if Ares hadn't swooped in and pulled him back to the Aether," Tisiphone muttered, and I nodded.

"Did he, now?" Hades asked, a thoughtful look on his face.

"They're not stupid. Zeus is weaker than I am here," I said. Hades stared at me.

"He is?"

"Of course. All of you are weaker than me here. It's kind of weird."

"You don't have to point it out. Rude," Tisiphone said, shaking her head.

"You didn't used to be more powerful than me," Hades said. "I didn't really notice it before, but you are. And more so than when you first showed up at my home. How is that possible?"

I shrugged.

"Immortals are so blind sometimes," Artemis said, sitting down on one of the stone benches.

"So says a goddess," Hades said, raising an eyebrow at her. "But continue, by all means."

"Hades, when is the last time a mortal prayed to you?" she asked.

"I don't see how that's --"

"How long?" Artemis asked again, interrupting him.

"Too long," he said quietly.

"That goes for most of us. I'm lucky enough that I still

have the occasional woman praying to me. I'm still able to feel that burst of strength that comes with belief," Artemis said. Then she looked at me. "Tell me, lovely girl: how often do mortals pray to you?"

I just looked at her. "Um. I heard of a few people doing it. Why?"

"Do you know what it feels like when someone prays to you?"

I shook my head.

"Imagine a burst of warmth on a cold day, enveloping you, strengthening you. It seems to come out of nowhere, but when you feel it, you never, ever want to let that feeling go," she said, a softness to her features that seemed out of place there.

I stayed silent for a while. The feeling she'd described was usually what seemed to chase away the madness that came over me in the Nether. I'd come to rely on it in my short time there, figured it was just my more rational side asserting control again.

Artemis was watching me closely. "You have felt it," she said. "Often."

I nodded. We all stood in silence for a while.

"Out of all of the immortals here, only one is worthy of the prayers of the men and women of the mortal realm," Artemis said quietly. "We have all faded away, become myths and stories. Mollis strengthens over time, because belief in her grows."

I shook my head. "How? Why? I'm not even there anymore."

"People pray when things get bad," Artemis said gently. "They pray to you to do what you've always done: to save them."

"Crap," I groaned, sitting down next to her and resting my head in my hands. "And I can't save them because I'm stuck here."

"You have a plan, and it's a good one. We'll end this and get you home, somehow," Tisiphone said. "And chances are good that things are improving in your realm anyway."

"How?"

"Zeus and Ares know you're here now. That will take some of the attention off of your home. They'll still feel the effects of war, but there won't be a determined effort to try to punish them. Not as much, anyway," she explained.

I nodded. A yawn escaped my mouth, and I quickly tried to cover it.

My mother noticed, smiled. "I think we could all do with some rest."

"Mollis, we still have plenty of rooms," Hades said, and I nodded my thanks.

"If she's staying here, then I stay as well," Artemis said.

Hades watched her. "She is in no danger in her father's home," he said.

"Of course not. But I am not willing to chance my future descendant on you and the shrew," Artemis said.

Hades gave her a forced smile. "Fine. You can take the room next to hers, then."

We all filed in and I fell into one of the soft beds, after noting that Artemis' two huge cats sat in front of my chamber door. As always, they made me think of Brennan, and he was the only thing on my mind as I drifted off.

CHAPTER FIVE

It didn't take much effort to fall asleep. Chasing down and getting vengeance on the Guardians, then facing Zeus was enough to knock me out almost immediately.

I really wasn't a fan of sleep. I never had peaceful sleep or dreamless nights. My subconscious runs on an auto-loop of nightmares I've lived.

Being alone on the streets after I'd run away from one of my creepier foster families when I was seven.

Being held captive by a demon when I was a teenager.

Destroying that demon.

Brennan under the Puppeteer's control.

The night Nain died.

Watching Brennan barely hang onto life. Except in my nightmares, I was never able to save him.

My mind went through them all, and I tossed and turned, woke up briefly, drifted off again, only to replay them all again.

Through the haze and fear, through the suffocating terror, I felt a warmth, a presence that pulsed with power.

Familiar. Beloved.

Comforting in a way nothing in my life ever had been. Soothing.

The nightmares ceased, and nothing other than that presence existed. I held onto it like a life preserver.

Brennan. He was with me, somehow, and just for a while, I felt like I was home. The only time in my life I'd ever slept in peace was when I'd slept by his side. Something in him kept the terror at bay. Kept me sane.

I've lived through enough crazy shit to know that the impossible is sometimes much more possible than we think. And I knew the way I know anything that Brennan's presence was with me in dreams. As much as I wanted to talk to him, feel him, hear him…his presence in my dreams was more than I ever would have dared to hope for. And I could sense him. Happy, realizing he was feeling me, too. Sad. Longing. Love. I pushed as much emotion as I could into our bond, or whatever it was, hoping he could feel it.

And he did.

The connection between us burned warmer, and I spent the rest of the night just being there with him, in dreams.

I felt when he was pulled away, when he woke up. I opened my eyes and looked at the ceiling, wishing I could hold onto that feeling a bit longer. Having him with me, even just that little bit, made me miss him even more.

I had to get home.

I tried to go back to sleep, hoping to feel him again. But it was over. However we'd managed it, it was over now.

I took a deep breath, tried holding the memory of his warmth in my mind, and got out of bed.

♦ ♦ ♦

I showered and dressed in one of the uniforms my mother had left for me, the traditional clothing of the

Furies: tailored black pants and a top, leather boots. I braided my hair over my shoulder and made my way out into the sitting room, where I could hear Hades, Persephone, and Artemis talking. The two huge cats were patrolling the exterior of Hades' home, along with Cerberus. I could sense them moving around.

"And there's little miss abomination," Persephone said from her spot near the fireplace. She had a book open on her lap. Hades and Artemis sat on a long sofa, each at an end. Hades shot a glare at Persephone, and she smiled sweetly back at him.

"Aw, Persephone. We should hang out some time. Have a little one on one time," I said as I sat on one of the other chairs. "Or are you going to just cower by my dad every time I'm around?"

"Not all of us are barbarians," she said. "Every problem doesn't need to be solved with blood and death."

"No, but it sure is satisfying," I said, my gaze steady on her. I felt a spike of fear from her then, and she shifted uneasily in her chair.

"You're just going to sit there and let her threaten me, Hades?" Persephone said, glaring at my father.

He shrugged. "You started it."

Artemis hid a laugh, winked at me.

"Oh, shut up. You're no better than she is," Persephone said to Artemis. "With your hunting and wild, coarse-mannered ways."

"Persephone, that may be the nicest thing you've ever said to me. Thank you," Artemis said, and now it was my turn to laugh.

Persephone made a very unlady-like gesture at Artemis, then picked her book up again. "Ready to end this sham of a marriage yet, Hades?"

"Never. You know you'd be lost without me, sugarplum."

She raised her lip in a snarl at him. "In your dreams."

"That's not what you said last night," Hades murmured.

"Oh, ugh. TMI, seriously," I said, shaking my head. Hades and Artemis both laughed at my obvious discomfort. Persephone just glared at me.

"Good sex isn't everything," she snapped, and I winced.

"It sure doesn't hurt," Artemis said, laughing.

"She says this now. She plays this whole 'Hades kidnapped me and dragged me to the Nether' sob story. Ask her who made the first move," Hades said, a small smile quirking at the corners of his mouth.

"You. Wish," Persephone muttered.

"Yeah?" he said, smiling at his wife. I had a feeling this was an old routine with them, something rehashed over and over, one of those things that every couple who's been together a long time shares.

"She was picking flowers in a field in the mortal realm. I was going through at the same time, on my way to meet with Zeus over something. We just happened to be in the same place at the same time. Fate."

"Bull dung," Persephone said.

"And I saw her, and at the same moment, she looked up and saw me. And she couldn't look away."

"Well, you are terrifying to behold," she said.

"Thank you, my love," Hades said, and Persephone shook her head, though I did note the tiniest of smiles on her lips. "I stayed on my horse. Who approached whom, hm?" he said to Persephone, and she rolled her eyes.

"She came up to me, and we talked. I knew Demeter, of course, and I knew she had a daughter with Zeus."

"Isn't it kind of gross to be married to your niece?"

He gave me a bored glance. "We are gods. We were the first things in existence. Things like that do not apply to us."

"We are not like the mortals you're used to," Persephone said. "Hades and Zeus are 'brothers' only in that they and Poseidon were created at the same time. Three of them, to rule the sky, the seas, and the earth. Three parts of a whole. Hades is *not* my uncle," she said.

"I've never heard it explained that way before," I said. "Does this mean I shouldn't call Zeus 'Uncle Zeus' anymore?"

"Oh, not at all. Keep doing that. He seems to love it," Hades said, and I laughed.

"To continue," Hades said, and I gestured zipping my lips. "I stayed on my horse, and Persephone came swaying across the field toward me, all long flowing hair and sinuous curves. And I knew I wanted her, immediately. Which is amazing in and of itself, because I never wanted anyone. I have always embraced solitude."

"So that's where I get it from," I murmured.

"And she started talking to me. And we talked for a long time, and I forgot all about my meeting with Zeus. And then she looked around, and she looked up at me, and what did you say, my dear?"

"Shut up, Hades," Persephone muttered.

"Come on. Refresh my memory," he said, grinning.

"I told him to show me the Nether," she muttered.

"And a few other things, if I recall correctly," Hades said, and I stared at Persephone.

"You hussy," I said, laughing, and Artemis erupted into gales of laughter.

Persephone glared at me. "I didn't tell him 'take me to the Nether and keep me there forever.' That was his own brilliant idea."

"By the time she wanted to leave me (and that took a while, if I recall) I knew I needed her. And then Demeter came raging into the Nether, demanding her daughter and angry that Zeus apparently wasn't bothered by the idea of me and his daughter." He paused. "Coming into my home and threatening me is generally not a good idea. So I told her I was keeping Persephone, and she'd never have her back."

"Which was news to me, because I had every intention of going home after our little tryst," Persephone said, folding her arms.

Hades smiled at his wife. "To appease both of them, I made a deal that Persephone could spend half of each year with her mother, if she wanted. How many times have you taken me up on that offer, darling?"

She glared at him. "Twice."

"In the eons we've been together, she's only taken advantage of it twice. So whether she'll admit it or not, she's madly in love with me and hates it when we are apart."

"You keep thinking that, imbecile," Persephone said, going back to her book, but not before a small smile cracked her icy facade.

Damn it. I almost liked Persephone after watching the little exchange between her and my father. After a while, I excused myself. I wanted to talk to my mother and aunt about the possibility of opening the gateway. Since the Furies had been largely responsible for guarding it, they might have a bit more insight into what it might take to bring it back. I had a feeling a lot of it would be instinct, the way it was when I'd closed it.

I walked, and realization struck. Not "opening" the gateway. There was no gateway anymore; I'd destroyed it. I would have to create a gateway.

Well, shit.

How the hell was I supposed to do that? Could I just undo what I'd done before? Do it in reverse or something? And even if I could, I sure the hell didn't want the gods to have a bunch of gateways into my world anymore. They couldn't be trusted. If there was going to be a way into my world, there would be one way, and I'd be in control of it.

I was sure they'd just love me for that.

Assuming I could do it at all, of course.

When I got to the building where the Furies lived and worked, I let myself in and my eyes were immediately assaulted by the Furies' unique decorating sense. Hot pink, neon yellow. Lots and lots of purple. My mother and aunt had apparently adored the 1980s. Their house looked like a Cyndi Lauper video come to life. Big bad, dark, vengeance-seeking Furies crushing on Richard Marx. Clearly, the afterlife was in awesome hands.

The house was kind of a "U" shape. One wing was the private living area, which was 80s chic. The other wing was where the Furies worked, and that was about what you'd expect: dark, cold, and filled with the scent of blood and an overwhelming sense of desperation. As a whole, the building wrapped around a central courtyard, and that's where I found my mother and aunt, along with Athena, who I'd only ever seen in passing. She was another Aether god who'd joined my parents' side in the war when Zeus had decided to attack.

The three immortals were sitting on the low wall around the edge of the courtyard. Between the wall and the house were planting beds. My family can't garden for shit, apparently. Most of what was in the beds was dead or near death.

As I walked into the courtyard, my mother rose and hugged me, and my aunt greeted me with a smile.

"Mollis, you remember Athena," Tisiphone said, and I nodded, holding my hand out to the completely intimidating goddess of wisdom. She was tall. Muscular. Her face was plain at first glance, but once you really looked at her, she was completely awe-inspiring. Her sharp gaze seemed to see everything, and her face was pretty much expressionless, like those white marble sculptures you see in a museum. She wore white leather from head to toe: boots, pants, a jacket. Her silver-white hair was cut into a severe bob.

Yeah. This was a woman I wouldn't want to cross. She watched me wordlessly as she grasped my hand, shook it firmly.

"It was foolish to close the gateway without knowing what would happen. Why would you trust the word of the Fates?" she asked me in greeting.

I crossed my arms over my chest. "It had nothing to do with listening to the Fates. I needed to keep my world safe from the war that was brewing between the gods. Since they were fighting over me, I considered it my duty to keep my world as safe as I could."

"You didn't expect to be trapped here," she said after a few moments of studying me.

"I didn't."

"And now that you are?"

I shrugged. "I'm going to find a way to create a new gateway. After the war ends. Which needs to happen soon, because I need to get home."

She smirked. "And you think you can do this?"

"Yes."

She shook her head. "The gods do things at their own pace. You can push all you want, and all you're likely to do is end up making the war last longer."

"I'm not pushing. I'm waiting," I said, annoyed to even be saying the words. I am not the world's most patient person. "Hades is going to try diplomacy. And though everyone's telling me it won't work, I'm trying to behave and let it go. If diplomacy fails, then I might have to do something stupid."

She studied me. "Your mother tells me you can fight."

"I manage all right."

"Against mortals. Creatures from your own realm."

"Demons. Vampires. Shapeshifters," I said, irritated. "Killed a god or two, in case you'd forgotten."

"And you are prideful, and arrogant. You faced gods who underestimated you. None of us will make that same mistake now. Will you come out victorious when faced with a foe who knows what you are, and what you are capable of? When you can't surprise them?"

"Arrogant? Seriously?" I asked her. My mother and aunt were staying out of it.

"You charge into situations as if there is no chance of failure. That is arrogance, Mollis Eth-Hades," she said, glaring at me. "And you need to be smarter. We fear you. Don't give all of us a reason to hate you."

"Don't you already?" I asked her.

"No. I think you are worthy of the power you wield. But you are weak. You have no idea what you're doing."

I didn't answer. It wasn't like she was saying anything I didn't already know.

"Athena has offered to train with you, while you're here," Tisiphone said.

"Why?"

"Because you cannot afford to get complacent. I will teach you humility, Fury," Athena said.

I nodded. "Fine. Is there anything any of you can tell me about the gateway that would help me create a new one?" I asked, turning to my mother and aunts.

Tisiphone shrugged. "To be honest with you, we never really thought about the gateways themselves much. They were there, and we used them. The only thing I know is that they were impossible to detect from your side, unless one belonged in the Nether or Aether. It kept mortals from wandering into our world, and kept the demons and other creatures out of your realm, once we enhanced them to only allow gods through."

"Who was responsible for strengthening it?" I asked her.

She grimaced. "Hermes. Which is how the demons apparently started getting through anyway."

"Why Hermes?"

"Because of his ability to travel the realms with no loss of power, he was uniquely suited to working on the gateway from both sides, strengthening it. And then it was up to us and the guard demons to be the last line of defense. Of course, he didn't bother telling us that he would make sure to weaken it behind our backs so his demon servants could cause chaos in your world, trying to take you."

I sighed. "Great. None of you considered confronting Hermes about his sucky defenses when demons started going through?" I asked, irritated.

Megaera looked embarrassed. "We never considered one of our own. This entire situation has reminded us that there are plenty of cancers among us. I don't think any of us will look at other gods the same way again."

"We are just as petty as the mortals," Athena said, agreeing.

"I think some of you are getting bored," I said.

Tisiphone was watching me. "You're probably not far off in that regard, daughter," she said.

"Well," Athena said, "I can assure you that *I* am growing bored. Are we going to train or stand around gossiping?"

"What, now?"

"Yes. Now," she said, taking off her leather jacket. She wore a sleeveless top underneath it, showing off her muscular arms.

"So?"

"Let's spar. I'd like to see what you've learned up to this point."

I nodded, barely had time to prepare myself before she launched herself at me, a full assault complete with punches aimed at my face, kicks aimed for my stomach, knees. I managed to duck her punch, mostly out of pure panic, and she barely missed my stomach, but caught my hip with a kick that felt like it would have gone straight through the soft flesh of my gut had I not flinched aside.

She punched out at me again, and I ducked.

Okay. This bitch was crazy.

"Child," she sneered. "Learn to focus. It shouldn't be that easy to surprise you." And then she kicked out again and I grabbed her foot, flipped her down onto her back, and she landed with an "oof." I knew better than to revel in that small victory; Brennan had taught me better than that. I readied myself for her attack, and it came quicker than I could have expected. She jumped up, at me, elbow to my throat. This time, she connected, and I bent double, unable to breathe around the bruising of my windpipe. She used that to her advantage, brought her knee up, smashing my nose with a sickening sound. I felt bones shatter, blood pouring from my nose and mouth. I fell, and she kicked me in the side, then pulled my hair, made me look up at her.

"You just lost. And I haven't even worked up a sweat," she hissed. "You need to be better, Fury."

Then she let go of my hair, and my head fell onto the dirt. I still couldn't catch my breath. "Once you've stopped writhing around like some kind of worm, we'll continue," she said.

This was probably the point where a normal mother would have stepped in on her child's behalf, urged a break or something. Or, you know, kicked the ass of the one who'd just made her daughter bleed. My mother offered Athena a cup of tea instead, and they sat there talking quietly while my body repaired itself and I got my breathing back to normal.

You know what I could do without? Feeling the bones in my face knit themselves together again. Shards of broken bone shifting beneath my skin, moving like sharp little maggots as they reformed my cheekbone.

I've never said that self-healing wasn't a disgusting process. It's just really, really useful.

I sat up once I felt able to, watched blearily as the goddesses drank their tea.

I put my elbows on my knees, breathed.

"Ready to go again?" Athena asked me, and I nodded, stood up.

She approached me, looked me over. "You're small. Rather on the scrawny side, really."

"Thanks."

"Your strength lies in using that to your advantage. Any time you hit something, as you know, you cause more damage than someone of your stature usually would, because your powers allow you to hit harder than a mortal would be able to."

I nodded.

"But other immortals have that same advantage, as I've just demonstrated for you." She made a motion as if she was going to punch me, and I readied myself to block it.

"I'm not going to hit you this time. Watch." And she extended her arm, to just before she would have hit me. "Look at where our bodies are. Look at my reach in relation to you. Look at how many vulnerable areas I leave open to you when I raise my hand against you. Ribs, breasts, underarms. A punch to any of them will hurt enough to throw an attacker off. A stab, and you're on your way to victory. If you're able to recognize these weaknesses, take advantage of them, you'll be far ahead of most opponents. It's not all about chopping heads off all the time."

"It's fun to chop heads off, sometimes," I said, studying her body, trying to see what she was showing me.

"Of course it is. Quite satisfying at times, really. But you need to focus on reducing the threat against you, weakening your opponent before you go for the kill. Keep them off-balance. Keep them on the defensive. That is your job." Her silvery eyes met mine. "Discipline, Fury. You need to learn it. Focus."

I nodded.

"Again."

We fought. I lasted longer the second time before Athena totally destroyed me. I recovered, and we did it again. After the fourth time getting my ass kicked, I stayed down, spitting up blood. "That was better. You're still fighting stupid, though," Athena said as she sat on the ground next to me. I hadn't even messed up her hair.

My mother came and sat with us, and I picked myself up, wiped my mouth with the sleeve of my shirt. There was already blood all over it, anyway.

"Great," I said. It still hurt to talk. She'd broken my jaw with that last punch. I'd thought Nain was brutal when he fought me. He was a puppy compared to Athena.

"Daughter," Tisiphone said, and I glanced up at her. "You need to focus during these sessions."

"I need to get home. This is doing nothing to get me there."

"And when you do get there? What are you going to do? Have you even thought to ask about the gods you've trapped in your realm?" Athena asked, annoyed.

"Who? Cithaeron? I knew about him."

Athena gave a disdainful laugh. "You are clueless."

"Then why don't you enlighten me," I said. Yes, I was aware she could easily kick my ass for my rudeness. Old habits die hard. Then I looked at my mother. "Who did I trap there?"

She took a breath. "A few minor beings who won't do much more than annoy people."

"Except for the two who will do much, much worse than just annoy the mortals," Athena said.

"Who?" I asked, my stomach turning.

"You've heard of the spirit daemons, yes?" Tisiphone asked, and I shook my head. She sighed. "Your education has been sorely lacking."

"Sorry," I said in irritation.

"No, it's my fault. Your father and I should have been teaching you once you started visiting the Nether." She paused. "The spirit daemons are kind of a step between gods and mortals. They are powerful in their own right. They are what we consider lesser gods. Not as powerful as us, maybe, but unique in their power. Each of the spirit daemons feeds and feeds off of mortal emotions or qualities. So we have spirit daemons such as Aidos, the spirit daemon of respect and modesty, or Nomos, the spirit of law and order. But the flip side of that is that we also have malignant spirit daemons. They tend not to do damage themselves, because they don't need to. They whisper, influence the mortals to act in accordance, and the results strengthen the daemons. And the stronger they get, the more influence they have."

"Shit. I'm guessing I didn't trap the spirit of happiness and rainbows in my realm," I said.

"No. When you killed Enyo, two of the spirit daemons who were close to her decided to go to your realm, lie there in wait for you, and get revenge on you for her death. We learned this from two of the Guardians we caught," Tisiphone said.

"Who?"

"Eris, the goddess of strife and discord. And Deimos, the spirit of terror."

"Lovely," I groaned. "I need to get home. Now. Has Hades set up that meeting with Zeus yet?" I asked my mother.

"He is trying. He's waiting for an opportunity. Ares refuses to leave Zeus' side, and with him there, any attempt at discussion or peace is hopeless," she said. "Artemis has tried arranging for a meeting as well, but he seems even angrier with her. He views the Aether gods who have joined us as traitors."

"Which we are *not*," Athena said. "He forgets that we are all gods and that he doesn't automatically deserve our support. Especially when he's behaving like an ass."

I stared straight ahead. I'd never even considered what could be trapped there, with the people I loved. My stomach twisted when I thought of the chaos and destruction those two spirit daemons could be causing.

I excused myself after a while and started walking back toward Hades' palace, the revelation that I'd trapped ruthless beings who also (of course) had grudges against me in my realm, with those I loved, weighing heavily on my mind. I had to find a way to get home. I was thinking that maybe I could appeal directly to Zeus. I'd have to try to be polite, which was always hard.

I was so lost in thought that I didn't register the power signature nearby until it was right on top of me.

I turned just in time to see Ares.

"Hello, Mollis," he growled.

And before I could react, his sword swept across my neck, and the world went black.

CHAPTER SIX

I woke, emerging from the darkness slowly.

The first thing I remembered was my name. Then, more. A smiling man with a blond beard and slate blue eyes. Lost girls, criminals, vampires, demons. Love, loss.

Gods.

Nether.

It all rushed back to me, nearly suffocating in its intensity. My life.

A lingering ache in my neck shook my groggy mind awake, and I opened my eyes in a panic.

I was chained to a rough stone wall in a dark room. I was weak. It had taken all of my power to come back again.

And that wasn't even the worst of it.

Ares sat in a comfortable-looking leather chair, not five feet from me. His elbow was on his knee, his chin propped in his hand, and he watched me avidly.

"That was different," he said. "You remind me of a hydra. Very unsettling, seeing something you beheaded start growing a new one before your eyes. There I was, dragging your body into the forest to bury you, and you started regenerating. It was a disgusting process to watch, really."

I stayed silent. Tried to assess the room. Ares. Son of a bitch. A sword lay across his lap, still coated with my blood. I tried to move my body. Nothing. I was conscious, but nothing below my neck was in working order yet. My powers were practically non-existent; all of my energy had gone to re-building my body. Again.

I tried not to freak out too much about that. Twice dead, now.

I'd think about it later. I had to get myself free. Something about living the life I'd lived ensured that I'd never been the type to hope that a knight in shining armor would come riding in to save me. There was one thing I knew for sure, and I'd known it for a very long time.

I wouldn't be saved unless I saved myself.

I still couldn't move. I was useless at the moment, so weak that even the simple act of opening my eyes and looking around had made me dizzy.

"Takes a lot out of you, doesn't it?" Ares asked in a mockingly sympathetic voice. I didn't answer. Tried to think. Manacles at my ankles and wrists. Fire, maybe, though I had the feeling melting them would be nearly impossible. I could try to just smash my way out of them. I was good at that, if I built up enough power.

I couldn't believe I'd stumbled right into this. Damn it.

He was still sitting there, watching me.

"You're trying to figure out how to get out, aren't you?" he asked, humor in his voice. "Weak as a baby, and you're thinking about escaping the God of War himself. Little fool. I've killed more beings than you can even comprehend. I've inspired untold numbers to do the same to their enemies. But you... you are going to be especially satisfying."

I felt a flicker of my power returning, tried to stay calm to give it a chance to build.

He watched me a while longer. "Did you feel anything

when you killed my sister?" he asked, and his voice was deceptively soft, deceivingly gentle. Beneath it lurked more than a trace of malice. A taunt.

"Probably nothing different than Enyo would have felt if she'd gotten me first," I said, my throat raw, dry, still aching. I guess having a blade sever it would do that.

"Am I supposed to have mercy because it was self-defense? You should not even be. Were you not an abomination, my sister would still be alive, no matter how grievously you injured her. And you," he said, the volume of his voice rising in his anger, "are supposed to be a mortal. So why. Aren't. You. *Dead?*" He roared the last word, and I looked at him, not wanting to admit that I wondered the same thing.

"Let's see if you can come back again, shall we?" he asked. And then he stalked toward me, sword raised, and I felt the blade pierce my chest, scraping past my rib bones, driving into my heart. He pushed, harder, until the sword was stuck into the stone wall behind me. The last thing I saw was his face, a mask of rage, before my body convulsed one last time and everything went black.

"How annoying," Ares said as I opened my eyes. I looked down at my chest as memories of my life returned. I was crusted over with blood, but Ares' sword was gone and my chest had healed completely. I didn't get much of a chance to respond before he brought an ax down on my head, and I felt my skull split, bone shattering under the impact. Blood oozed into my eyes, and I saw nothing but red before I died again.

I'd come back again. I knew it the second I regained consciousness. Instead of making the same mistakes, I stayed slumped, eyes closed, hanging from my manacles. Eventually, he would notice that I was breathing, and he'd undoubtedly come up with another way to kill me. The only chance I had of getting out of this was to regain my power and then either smash my way out or see if I could use my mind control powers on Ares.

The good news was that my body or soul or whatever seemed to be becoming acclimated to dying. I could already feel a little of my power flowing through me, and I almost cried in relief. Alongside the power was rage, pure and beautiful, and I held onto it like a life preserver.

My power grew, and I started to have hope.

I should really know better by now.

"Back again, eh? Well. I may as well enjoy your death this time," Ares said mildly. "Torture, after all, is part of war."

And it began.

I was conscious through things I never could have imagined, pain worse than anything I'd ever been through (and I've been through some pretty rough shit). He wanted me to scream. He wanted me to beg, to cry.

All I did was bleed, and I nurtured the hatred and rage that flowed through me. And, finally, I let death claim me again.

When I woke again, I felt my power building almost immediately. I sensed. For once, he wasn't in the room with me when I woke. I had a bad feeling about that. If the God of War was taking a break from torturing and killing his prize, it could only be because he was spurring things on in the war between the gods.

I kept my eyes closed, my body still, just in case. Now. This would be my time to make him hurt. Make him bleed. Make him wish he'd never laid eyes on me, let alone been foolish enough to cross me.

My power rose, quickly. A few more minutes, and I'd have enough to at least blast the motherfucker the next time he came at me. I would hear him scream in agony. I would flay his body. I would wear his bones as jewelry. I would devour every bit of his godly power and lay waste to the world of gods.

I would survive. Just a little more. A little more time. A little more power, and I would make him bleed.

But this is me, and I am not a lucky woman. I heard the door clank open, and he stalked up to me.

"Are you kidding me?" he shouted, and he punched me in the face, hard. I forced myself not to react. Punching was fine. Yes, it hurt. A lot. I felt my cheek bone shatter on the first impact. But if I could withstand it for just a few more minutes, I'd have enough power to hurt him back.

He punched me again. And again, each punch sending the back of my head crashing into the wall behind me. Each punch only increased the rage I felt, increased the amount of power I felt roaring through me. A quick look at him between punches told me he was becoming completely unhinged. Fear rolled off of him. Hatred. Rage. He kept shouting about how I was supposed to be mortal, as if shouting it enough would make it true.

I tried to gather my power.

And he brought his sword out, and when his sword met my neck, I could have screamed in frustration. Instead, everything just faded to black again. For just a moment, right before I died, I swore I felt Brennan's warm presence with me again, and I went out feeling the one thing I wanted most.

It went on. All I knew was that Ares killed me fourteen times, and the memory of each of my deaths stayed with me until I had one thought and it was vengeance.

I came to faster each time he killed me, and it was completely freaking him out. He didn't leave my cell anymore. It reeked of blood and decay, and Ares' anger and fear permeated the air.

I could use that. Hopefully.

I woke up after my most recent death, in which Ares had eviscerated me, to find him standing in front of me, looking deranged. He still held the knife he'd used on me.

My innards, or, I guess my old innards, still strewn on the floor around me.

God, his fear was good.

It fed me, and my power rose quickly. I was cold, and all I craved was his death.

Except, when I killed him, he'd stay dead.

"You're supposed to be mortal. Why the hell won't you stay dead?" he asked, and his voice was wavery. A muscle at the corner of his eye ticked.

"Clearly, I'm not mortal anymore, dumbass," I muttered. "So killing me is a waste of time. I'm the only truly fucking immortal thing here."

In retrospect, that was probably a dumb thing to say.

He knew (I was able to read his thoughts clearly now. Either his fear and growing insanity had weakened his ability to shield his mind, or I was getting stronger) that keeping me weak meant killing me, but that each death saw me reviving faster. And I was becoming a little harder to kill with each death.

They still hurt like a bitch, though.

He went into a frenzy of stabbing and slashing, cursing, and soon, everything faded away again.

When I surfaced again, I wanted his death so badly I could taste it. Thoughts of devouring his still-warm heart, of wearing a coat of his leathered flesh, of making him watch as I fed his entrails to Cerberus... these are the thoughts I had as I came to life again. I felt sick, tried to shove them away. Aside from the constant pain, the terror of having my life and power snatched away when they were just out of my grasp, these thoughts of violence and cruelty were more and more present. And while I knew they were justified, they still scared me.

A few times, I came back and had no idea who I was; failed to recover my memories before he killed me again.

I lived in fear now (when I was alive, that is) of losing myself completely. What if this thing I was during my worst moments became all that was left of me?

I shook the thoughts off. There would be a time and place to think about my mental state. This definitely wasn't it. I needed to find a way to escape before I worried about whether I was off my rocker or not.

I sensed for Ares. He was not with me, for once, though I could hear voices just outside of my cell. I listened, straining to figure out who he was talking to. I tried to stay still and calm. My power was growing by leaps now. Yes.

"What are you telling me? You can't kill her? The God of War can't kill one insignificant girl?"

I tried to place the voice. I knew I'd heard it before, but my mind was still groggy.

"You haven't been listening! She keeps coming back. They lied to everyone. She's no mortal. And she gets stronger," he said, and I reveled in the fear in his voice. "She's like a rabid pit bull. She won't let go. And once she rips into me..."

"What in the Nether is a pit bull?" the voice asked, and I placed it, then: Dionysus.

How the hell was he free?

Oh, fuck. This was bad. Who else was out? My aunt? The Nosoi?

Damn it.

My power increased in relation to my anger. Nearly there.

"She needs to breathe, doesn't she?"

"What?" Ares asked.

"Air. She needs to breathe air," Dionysus said, irritation in his voice.

"Of course."

"Well. There's a weakness. I'm sure you'll figure out something."

"Why don't we try to use her? I want the gateway open. She's the only one who--"

"Are you insane, man? You just told me she's getting stronger, and she undoubtedly hates you. You think you can use her?" he gave a derisive laugh and I heard Ares growl.

Then it got quiet. "She is awake," I heard Ares mutter. Damn it. I tried to focus, silently pleaded with my power to grow faster. I sent a prayer, begged the Universe or whatever beings were out there that granted wishes to just let me out of this. I'm not usually the praying type. Desperation. My power sang within me. Maybe, this time. Hope started to swell within me along with my power.

"Take care of it. I don't want to hear any more about the abomination. My father has promised me Hades' place, once we complete the next phase. She cannot be alive to interfere, Ares."

"Why don't you kill her, then?" Ares asked.

"Fine. Let me show you how it's done."

Almost.

And Ares and Dionysus stalked into the room. I let loose my power, blasted fire at Ares, and he screamed. So intent was I on punishing my tormentor that I stupidly forgot about Dionysus.

And ignored the fact that he now carried Ares' sword, and was stalking toward me. I didn't even notice him until he hefted the sword..

And then I was gone again, but at least I smelled Ares' flesh burning as I died.

CHAPTER SEVEN

When I woke up, the first thing I felt was a heavy weight on my chest. The second thing I felt was dirt in my mouth, and it made me gag immediately.

The next thing I noticed was that I couldn't breathe.

It was cold, and opening my eyes made no difference. There was no doubt about it.

The bastards had buried me.

I started to panic, tried to force myself to be calm. My hands were chained behind my back. I couldn't move anything.

With no air, I felt myself fading away again, along with any hope I had of getting home.

I came back, again and again and again, only to suffocate and die again.

Was this the rest of my existence? Coming back only to suffocate and die? There was no air. No time for me to rebuild my powers before I faded away again.

At some point, I stopped panicking when I came back. I took the brief moments available to me to think of Brennan. I mourned the children we'd never make, the fact that I'd never again wake up with his warm body pressed against mine. I'd never see his smile again, or the way his eyes sparkled when he teased me. I felt tears forming, my chest aching with something other than lack of oxygen. And then, I died again.

It just went on. Unlike when Ares had been murdering me, I had no hope now. I could not get myself out of wherever he'd buried me. I couldn't move, and I suffocated too quickly to regain any of my powers. I could have blasted the soil around me with my rage, if only I'd had the power to back it up with. I'd tried calling out to Artemis and my parents with my mind, but I had no idea if it worked. And, even if it did, I had no idea where Ares had buried me.

Each time I woke up, I felt a little more of who I was, die. I held on to Brennan's memory, because he was the only thing worth hanging onto. I sent another silent prayer: I'd give anything, anything at all, if it meant getting a chance to make my way back to him. And I died again.

My next few resurrections were flashes of memory, bits of my life, re-lived.

Nain, lifetimes ago, telling me "The stuff you can do....you don't even know what you're capable of yet. You can make bad things happen, and you have no idea how bad you could be."

Brennan: "Some things just can't be controlled. And that's when instinct takes over."

Eunomia: "Do what you do best. Destroy them."

Brennan: "You're not the monster you think you are." And me answering: "No. I'm much worse."

Hades: "You are at your best, at your strongest, when you are protecting something you care about. Your mind is clear; your power is focused. You are unstoppable."

Brennan: "I love you. I gave myself to you a long time ago. Because, no matter whether you can love me back or not, you're mine in a way no one else ever has been or ever will be. Your essence, *you*, are so much a part of me that when you're in pain, it hurts me. When you're hungry, I want to feed you. When you're cold, I want to make you warm again."

I had no doubt anymore that I was not so much a body that was home to a soul, but a soul that wore a body. And my soul belonged to someone, and there was not a chance in any realm known to the gods that he would ever give up on me.

And I needed him. He was worth fighting for. I craved his warmth, the way he soothed me.

I'd be lying if I said I didn't also crave revenge. The screams and terror of my enemies.

I came to each time now faster, stayed awake longer as long as I didn't let myself be taken over by panic. Something was happening. I began to focus, not so much on the suffocating sensation of the soil of the Nether, but on the feel of the Nether itself surrounding me: its power, which had welcomed me, surrounded me, empowered me each and every time I'd stepped through the gateway from my realm and come home to its embrace.

I'd feared that power. Worried about losing myself in it.

Now, I surrendered to it, sensing, somehow, that it was the only way to save myself and get back to the one thing I couldn't live without.

I stopped fighting. Not because I wasn't still enraged and determined to make my way home, but because the Nether itself was soothing me, cocooning me.

Empowering me.

My grave became a womb, my death merely a rebirth.

The Nether became my lifeline, and I held onto it. The power suffusing the very soil around me, the languid pulse of its energy, like a mother's heartbeat.

I absorbed its power, felt it flow alongside my own, alongside the powers I'd taken from others. I felt my body strengthen. I felt peace settle over me, even as I plotted my revenge.

Child of the Nether.

That was me, in more ways than one. The Nether is powerful. Cruel. Unforgiving. Vengeful.

I felt its power suffuse me, and I thanked it.

There is a price, I felt, more than heard it tell me.

No price is too high, I told it. All I could think of was destruction. And then, getting home.

It will be so, child of Mine.

And I focused, and gave thanks, and my power built within me.

I felt the soil rumble, just barely, around my stiff, frozen body. Stones shifted beneath me, pushing sharply into my back.

It was a start. I faded away again, knowing freedom would be mine.

When I woke, I let my power build, released it in a burst, felt my body tumble within the soil as it heaved beneath me before I lost my grip on life again.

Once again, Brennan was with me. I wept when I revived again and felt him, warm and steady. I pushed as much love as I could into our connection, and felt him respond in kind.

Our connection flared, stronger, brighter, and I smiled as I died one more time.

One more time.

The Nether showed me things as I floated in and out of life. Things I could do that I'd never even considered. Ways to make my enemies pay. Ways to make myself stronger. Cocooned within it, I learned, finally, everything I'm capable of.

I could have laughed. And I gave thanks again that out of all the beings the Nether could have chosen, It shared Its secrets with me.

I let my power build again and released it in another burst. Felt my body dance with flames that did not burn me, felt soil and rock blasted from my body.

And, just above me, the sweet promise of fresh air.

I focused hard, felt the soil of the Nether shift again.

Cool air hit my face, and I tried to drink it in in huge gulps.

Unfortunately my lungs were full of soil and who knows what else.

I rolled over, threw up mud, blood, muck. I heaved, and it hurt, but I let it hurt.

I was alive.

I was free.

Once I was empty, I rolled back over onto my back, stared up at the amethyst sky of the Nether. There was a price. I could feel the Nether in my soul, another connection, running alongside the connection I had with Brennan. Where his felt warm and strong, the Nether felt cold.

It was a good cold.

It gave me life.

It would help me harness my rage. And I would be the terror I was always meant to be.

I laid there a while longer, exalting in the feel of fresh air surrounding my filthy body, the sensation of breathing. My eyes adjusted to sight after so long in the dark. As I rested, I felt my power building, filling me, finally, after too long barely straddling emptiness. I let it build, and I laid there, and thought about all the things I would do, now that I had another chance. Part of me was gone, destroyed by the things I'd experienced since Ares ambushed me. I didn't know if I'd ever get it back. There was an emptiness in me that hadn't been there before, and I didn't know what that would mean. I felt cold, inside and out. Partly because of the Nether living within me, partly because of everything I'd gone through.

I'd make it work. That's what I do, I told myself as I stared up at the sky and enjoyed the sensation of breathing.

Once my power had built enough, I pulled my arms apart, hard, snapping the chain between the manacles on my wrists. I brought my arms to the front of my body, for the first time in who knew how long, and my shoulders and back protested at the change of position. I sat up and stretched my arms, flexed my wings. A bit more brute force, and I was able to snap the iron from my wrists and ankles. When I finally stood on shaky, trembling legs, I felt like an infant standing on its own for the first time.

I stood, and breathed. I closed my eyes, sensed for Brennan's connection. Still there. Still warm, and strong. I focused for a moment, let myself feel him. Let myself focus on what really mattered so I wouldn't lose myself in what came next.

I was the child of prophecy. My coming would destroy the world of the gods.

Not that I would kill them.

Well.

Not all of them anyway.

I held onto Brennan's warmth, memories of the best moments of my life (which had been with him, coincidentally) for as long as it took to center myself. Then I opened my eyes when I felt centered again.

I looked down at myself, at my blood-crusted, muddy, torn and shredded clothing. At my filthy skin, lank hair.

I needed a shower badly. And clothing. But there was no time, and I had things to do. My enemies didn't rest, and neither could I.

I focused, and the next time I looked down, I looked as strong and together as I needed to. Immaculately crisp black uniform and boots. Glistening wings. My long dark hair flowed down over my shoulders. Enchantment, and nothing more, a trick the Nether had taught me as I made my way back to life. I could still feel the crud and mess on my body. But I could damn well at least look like I had my shit together.

I looked at my clothing again, and smiled. Then I focused again, and there I was: Jeans, black long-sleeved top, and Chucks. If I was going to be me, then I was gonna be me all the way. As I looked at my shoes, I noticed a smooth black stone near my left foot. I picked it up, tucked it into my pocket.

I held out my hand, and my sword appeared in it. I looked around, listened, sensed. There was no thunder, no screaming, and I recognized this part of the woods as being not terribly far from where I'd first resurrected. I walked toward where I knew my father's home was.

As I got closer, the fact that the streets were mostly deserted was the first thing I noticed.

The second thing I noticed was that demons and these weird flying things that kind of looked like cherubs patrolled the tall iron gate around Hades' home, which was still in the same charred, dilapidated state it had been in the last time I'd seen it. The gate was closed; something that I'd never seen before.

As I got closer, the patrolling guards saw me.

I felt their responses, even before I saw the hungry grins spread across the faces of the demons. The cherub things started to shout and charge me, but the demons intercepted, battling their Aether counterparts to keep my path unobstructed. One of them opened the gate after knocking his opponent out.

"Pleasure to have you back, my Lady," he said in a deep growl. I nodded at him and he saluted me.

"Who is in there?" I asked him.

"Pretty much all of them."

"Good." I glanced around. "Keep them off my back, will you?"

"It would be an honor, my Lady," he said. He smiled, bowed, and went away to fight some more.

I walked to the front door, pulled the heavy charred wood slabs open. Two of the demons were at my back, and as cherub guards from inside the house came at me, they both intercepted and destroyed my would-be attackers. I ignored them all and continued on to Hades' formal reception area. It was kind of like a throne room, I guess. Except that in his receiving room, no one, including

Hades, ever sat. They stood. Mostly because comfort was for the weak. Also, if they had to stand, they'd be reminded that no matter how big they were, my father was bigger and scarier.

They could feel me. I smiled again, and my demon guards laughed when they saw it, cut down more of the Aether guards. They each pulled open one of the double doors that led into my father's throne room, and I strode through.

Yes. There they were, indeed. Except that my father's throne room was changed. There was now a gaudy golden throne on the dais, and Dionysus' wormy self sat on it. I scanned the room. My father, mother, aunt Megaera, Artemis, Apollo, Asclepias, Athena, Aphrodite, and a few others sat along one wall, chained (manacles were part of the décor, meant to accommodate those waiting for Hades' judgment) but looking defiant. My aunt Alecto, traitorous bitch, was using her powers to keep the captured gods under control. We Furies are the few beings in existence who can control the gods, thanks to our ability to do really nasty things with their minds. As I entered the room, I saw my father and mother exchange a glance, and Tisiphone smiled. Chained with them, surprisingly, were Zeus and Hera. I surveyed the rest of the room. Several of the Nosoi. A few other minor gods who had been captured by my mother and aunt. The Guardians I hadn't killed.

And, standing to the left of Dionysus' pretender throne, Ares.

He stared at me.

And he trembled.

And fear flooded me, from him.

A few of the Guardians rushed me. I waved a hand at them and they simply fell to dust. Then it was Alecto's turn, and she met the same fate.

"Anyone else? I can do this all day," I said, and my voice thundered through the room. The assembled gods winced.

I strode up to the dais. Smiled sweetly up at Ares. "Boo," I whispered, and he jumped as if I'd slapped him. I laughed, and I knew well how cold and evil it sounded. My power soared within me, augmented by what I'd gained from the Nether.

"Please, don't kill me," Dionysus begged. "It was his idea," he said, pointing at Ares, who looked at him like he had lost his mind.

"Oh. I'm not going to kill you," I said, my voice still at a thunderous volume, enhanced by the power of the Nether. "Not when you can be of use."

CHAPTER EIGHT

I waved my hand, and Dionysus went hurtling through the air out of his pretender's throne. He crashed into the stone wall opposite where the gods were chained, and he fell limply to the floor.

"Though by the time this is all over, you'll wish I'd had enough mercy to end you."

It was right about then when the immortals in the room started to freak the hell out.

Not that I could blame them, really.

The Guardians I hadn't killed, the ones freed by Ares and Dionysus, tried to run. As much as I wanted to destroy them, I really wanted them to spend eternity being punished. I forced the thought into their minds to kneel, and they stopped where they were and did it. One of them even started to plead with me.

Cute.

The demons swarmed into the room, started rounding up the Guardians, the spirit daemons who'd been allied with Ares and Dionysus. I'd let my mother and aunt deal with them, too.

Ares and Dionysus tried to run.

Such a couple of badasses, when I was chained and helpless.

"Stay," I thundered, forcing the order into their minds, and they obeyed. Everyone else in the room froze as well, but that had nothing to do with me.

Well... it did. But not the same way.

"Who has the key for the chains?" I asked, gesturing at the gods who were chained against the wall.

"Ares does, my Lady," one of the demon guards answered.

"Give it to the demon. Now." I said, and my voice still thundered. Ares hesitated. "Or I will take it from you," I said, saying each word slowly, deliberately, almost daring him to defy me.

He flinched, dug the key out of his pocket, and handed it to the guard, who handed it to me. I glanced over at Ares and Dionysus again. "Don't move," I ordered, and they both froze.

I approached the captives. Walked up to Zeus, specifically, at the end of the chained row of immortals. "And how did you end up in this situation, Uncle? I thought you promised him a throne."

Zeus looked up at me, a mixture of fear, hatred, and gratitude flowing from him. "I saw that my sons were out of control. While my brother and I fight, we both understand that there is a balance to our existence. My sons were going too far, and I was too stubborn to see it. By the time I smartened up, Dionysus had already decided that I was unfit to lead as well."

"I will free you," I said to him and Hera. "But there is a price."

They both looked up at me and nodded.

"The war ends. Now."

"Yes, Mollis," Zeus said, and it clearly pained him to give in to my demands.

"And I get a piece of your mind, so I know if you ever decide to betray me."

Zeus stared at me, his mouth opening and closing like a fish out of water, his face turning red. Hera answered for him. "Yes, Mollis." Zeus turned to look at his wife, and she glared at him. "Don't be a fool, Zeus."

Zeus just glared sullenly at me. "Very well," he finally said.

I stepped back, looked at the assembled gods. "That is the price of your freedom. It is the price of access to my realm. A piece of your mind, your soul, bonded to me. I will know if you intend to betray me or harm anyone who matters to me. I will know where you are. You will answer to me."

I glanced toward my parents. My father was staring at me. Tisiphone smiled. "I'll need a word with my parents before I free the rest of you," I said. I could feel my power wavering a bit. I needed to get away for a few minutes and recharge. Holding the enchantment to make myself look together was harder than I'd thought.

I knelt down next to Tisiphone, then Hades, and unlocked their chains. *Can Megaera be trusted?* I asked my mother.

Yes. She can be trusted, daughter.

I nodded, unchained my aunt as well. "Watch over them, please," I told her, and she put a fist to her chest, the same way my imps and demons did. Then she stood in the center of the room, where she was able to see all the captives, both those who had been on Dionysus' and Ares' side, and those they'd taken prisoner. She knew, as I did, that none of them could be trusted.

Not yet, anyway.

"To your office, father?" I said quietly, and he nodded, then he bowed to me, and my mother did the same.

My parents aren't perfect. Not by a long shot. But they knew what I needed most just then, and their show of obedience sent exactly the message it needed to: I called the shots.

I glanced at Ares and Dionysus, then at two of the demon guards. I nodded toward the shackles my parents had left, and the demon guards saluted me and dragged the two gods over to them, secured them against the wall.

"We will be right back," I said. Then I glanced at my parents and we left the room, headed across the hall to my father's study. I closed the door behind us, and the enchantment fell as my power wavered.

Tisiphone let out an audible gasp, and I felt Hades' rage flow over me.

Tisiphone put her hand over her mouth, her eyes filling with tears at the state I was in now that the enchantment had fallen. "Mollis?" she whispered, staring at me.

"I'm really, really unkillable," I said, the only explanation I could give without losing my mind.

"Ares," my father growled, and then he stormed from the room. A few moments later, I heard screams from the throne room. Ares, becoming more garbled and pain-filled the longer it went on. I knew, from my connection to Hades, that he'd had the guards unlock Ares. He was quite enjoying beating the living hell out of the God of War.

Like father, like daughter.

My mother was watching me, the silence only interrupted by the occasional scream from Ares. "Tell me," she whispered.

"I've been beheaded, stabbed, had my skull split, been gutted, burned, strangled, suffocated, dismembered. I've been buried, and come alive only to die again and again in my grave," I finished, astonished by how emotionless I was able to sound. Tears rolled down my mother's face. Sadness, terror, rage, love, guilt all flowed through her.

"Precious girl," she whispered, and then she came to me and folded me into her arms, holding me tightly. "I am so sorry. I am so grateful you're back with us."

"I need you and dad to have my back in this," I said.

"You need to show the other immortals that things have to be different now."

Hades entered the room as I finished speaking, and I stepped back from Tisiphone, glanced up at him. His fists were bloody. Splatters of blood flecked his face, his arms.

"You will have anything and everything you need from us, daughter," Hades growled, bowing to me.

"Did you leave anything for me?" Tisiphone asked him, and he smiled.

"Of course. I left you Dionysus."

Then it was my mother's turn to leave the room. I understood that this was something they needed. They both blamed themselves for my existence and the shit I'd gone through because of who I was born to. They felt helpless, and that was not a feeling they were especially accustomed to. They really didn't like it, and rage was their only outlet. My father and I stood watching each other as we listened to Dionysus scream and beg my mother for mercy.

"That's a foolish thing to beg a Fury for," Hades murmured. I nodded in agreement.

After a while, Dionysus's screams faded, and Tisiphone came back. Hades looked her up and down.

"How do you stay so clean when you do that?" Hades asked her.

"Furies don't need to touch a being to hurt them," I reminded him, and my mother nodded.

"I was in his mind," she said softly. "I saw... I saw what they did to you, my darling girl. If I could have killed him, I would have."

"But you will do it," Hades said, looking at me. "They don't have long."

I shook my head. "No. I won't kill them."

"You meant that?" Hades asked in disbelief.

"I did. They will live eternally, trapped, and I will use their life force to strengthen me."

"You can do that?" Tisiphone asked, a mixture of pride and fear coming from her.

"I can," I said simply.

Hades was studying me. "You are different," he said.

"I'm sure dying and resurrecting a few dozen times would do that," Tisiphone said.

"That's not what I mean. I mean... you feel different."

"You feel like the Nether," Tisiphone said, after going very still and studying me.

"Because I am the Nether," I said. "At least, part of me is." I didn't really feel like going into it, and, for the moment, I think maybe my parents were too freaked out to hear it anyway. "Anyway. I'm going to do this. And I'm going to get home. But I'm going to make damn sure that the risk of one of the immortals hurting my world is as close to nonexistent as possible before I create a new gateway. Things will not be the same."

Hades was about to say something, hesitated, shook his head. He took a deep breath. "The gods will answer to someone. This should be entertaining," Hades said, smiling, though he was sad, too.

"They will. Those are my terms," I answered.

"Then it will be so," Tisiphone said. I nodded. My power had rebuilt itself during the short break, and Ares' and Dionysus' fear and pain at the hands of my parents had strengthened me. I glanced at each of them, meeting their eyes. Then I focused, and brought the enchantment up again.

"I need a bath so bad right now," I muttered once it was back, and they both nodded. I felt relief from both of them, now that my true state was disguised.

If there was ever an overarching theme of my existence, that was it, wasn't it? Please don't show us who you really are. You're too freaking bizarre to deal with.

Except for Brennan. I felt some peace settle over me, thinking of him, then I set my features into the stern gaze of someone who was meant to rule.

I left my father's study, my parents following behind me. When I entered the throne room, fear hit me, and it was sweet. Ares and Dionysus were chained to the wall again, both bloody and still in agony.

All right, then. My parents were pretty decent at messing people up.

I glanced around at the rest of the immortals, paced back and forth in front of them, met their eyes as I passed. "Here are the terms of your freedom. You will be linked mentally to me. There will be no place to hide. There will be no secrets from me, and your lives are no longer solely your own. You want freedom? That's the cost. Take it or leave it."

My parents and aunt stood a few feet behind where I was pacing, hands clasped behind their backs, backs straight, like soldiers at attention. My gaze fell on Ares and Dionysus. "Except for you two. You're fucked." They both flinched back from my gaze.

"I accept your terms, niece," Megaera said, and I met her eyes. She came and knelt before me, put a fist to her heart, head bowed. "I am yours." I made my way into her mind, which she opened to me immediately. I made the connection to her, took a piece of her soul, just as I had with Hades.

"It will be so," I murmured. "Thank you. Rise." She did, and met my eyes, and smiled.

It is good to have you back, my darling girl, she said in my mind, and I nodded, then gestured toward the immortals, and she nodded and started unlocking their chains, one by one.

And it began. Artemis and Asclepias each came to me, knelt as I bonded them to me. Apollo, Persephone, Demeter, and Hestia followed. Persephone acknowledged me with a glare, but knelt and didn't fight when I bonded to her.

After them, a god I didn't know walked up to me, knelt before me, head bowed, dark hair falling over equally dark eyes.

"I don't know you," I said quietly to him.

"Hephaestus," he said, looking up at me. "It's good to meet you, finally." His voice was a deep rumble. He didn't speak loudly. Didn't need to.

I just looked at him. Well, that was a different attitude, anyway. Hephaestus was kind of what you'd expect a god worshiped by blacksmiths to be: big, burly, barrel-chested. Jet-black hair and eyebrows, dark eyes. He looked like the kind of man who worked hard, a fisherman or a steelworker or something were the best comparisons I could make from my own world. Which I guess fit, considering. I tried recalled from what little mythology I remembered (stupid, huh? Not to have learned more..) that Hephaestus' limp was due to a birth defect, which had caused Zeus so much embarrassment, this fact that one of his children could possibly be defective, that he'd banished Hephaestus from the Aether. Which only added to my opinion that Zeus was a major asshole, and not to be trusted no matter what he said to me. The limp had done nothing to make Hephaestus seem less powerful, though the myths I'd read had said he was the brunt of the gods' jokes because of his "deformity."

Further evidence that the immortals are a bunch of bastards: even a "deformed" god could have been a model or something in my realm. Bunch of shallow idiots.

I entered Hephaestus' mind, which he'd opened completely to me. I did my best to ignore his thoughts, memories as I made the bond to him. I'd forgotten he was Aphrodite's husband. I kind of pitied him. She was not my favorite being. Stuck up, haughty.

And I had a feeling she probably didn't like me much, either.

Once the bond was made, I told Hephaestus to rise, and he did. He nodded once, bowed, then joined the other gods. Aphrodite followed her husband, glaring at me and refusing to speak, but opening her mind nonetheless. Then Hera knelt to me.

Finally, the only ones sitting against the wall were Zeus, Ares, Dionysus, and another god I hadn't met before. Megaera freed him next, and he came to me.

"Poseidon?" I guessed, and he nodded. He had a flowing red beard, long red hair. He was built like an Olympic swimmer, which made sense, considering. "Nice to meet you," I said.

"Likewise," he said gruffly. "You strive to protect the mortal realm."

"Of course."

"I may return there once the gateway is opened to us again?"

"As long as you behave yourself, yes," I said.

"I have no quarrel with you," he said. "Do what you must. I miss my oceans." He knelt before me as all the others had, and I connected his mind to mine. When it was done, he joined the rest of the freed gods.

Which left Zeus. I told my aunt to leave him. I wanted to make a few things clear first.

I went to the Lord of the Aether, sat in front of him on the stone floor. He watched me suspiciously. He was angry. Enraged, actually. Afraid.

"Gods were not meant to be ruled," he said, glaring at the others.

"Maybe not," I agreed, "but this is the only option you have. I have no intention of messing with your way of life the way you messed with mine."

He watched me, and I let that sink in.

"You want to stay and rule the Aether? Then do it. My rules are pretty easy. I own part of you, so you can't betray me or the ones I care for. You do not fuck with the mortal realm. And in return, you get your life and your freedom. Simple, really. And, maybe you'll even get a little more out of the bargain."

"What, more?" he asked, trying not to seem interested.

"Wouldn't it feel good to be worshiped again?" I asked softly. I knew the other gods could hear. The energy in the room intensified, as if everyone was holding his or her breath. "To be relevant? To be something more than a bunch of stories in a dusty old book?"

"What are you saying?" he asked, some of his anger receding now.

Gods were so fucking easy.

"You've undoubtedly caused a mess in my realm," I told him, and, by proxy, the rest of the gods. "We all know your war spilled over into my world. And that, because of its connection to me, Detroit probably took the brunt of your bullshit," I said, and he nodded in confirmation. I wasn't really sure how it worked. Something about my energy, faith in me or whatever being strong in my area, so any bad things manifested by the gods' war in their realm would become physical in that area of my world. Hades had tried to explain it to me once.

"So I can guess that things are bad back home. And I know that, because I can still feel them praying to me," I said softly. "The mess is probably too much for even me to handle. And I have more than a few things I need to take care of when I return home. What do you say to walking among the mortals again?" I asked him. "Help them. Serve them. They deserve that."

"You love them," Zeus said, staring at me in disbelief.

"Of course. And so should you. Because they're strong, and weak, and complicated, and, for the most part, pretty goddamned decent. I think you'd be good for them, and they'd be good for you."

"I... we're not as strong there," Zeus said, though it was evident he was just posturing now. He was practically salivating at the idea of being relevant again.

"Does it matter? You're strong enough to be of use. And it's not like anything there can kill you. Except me, of course," I said.

"Are you threatening me?" Zeus asked.

"I don't need to resort to threats when I have facts on my side," I said. He sat, silent, and I knew it was mostly his pride he battled now.

I watched him patiently, waiting for a decision either way.

"And if I don't accept your terms? Will you kill me?"

"I won't kill you. But I think you'd maybe prefer death," I told him.

"Well. At least you're honest," he said grudgingly.

"I try to be. You could do a lot of good, Zeus. You had the sense to try to stop Ares and Dionysus. You know right from wrong, and you aren't so lost to your own ego that you can't be reasoned with."

"His ego is plenty large enough," Hades muttered, and I sensed irritation from Zeus.

"Look who's talking," Zeus said. Then he turned back to me. "You have a deal. I accept your terms, godslayer."

"I only slay those who deserve it," I said as I unlocked his chains. "Don't cross me, and we won't have any problems, Uncle."

I bit back a grin at the irritation that coursed through him at the word, as well as at the fact that he knelt to me, bowed his head.

I made my way into his mind, forged a connection, and dismissed him. I faced the gods who had accepted my terms. A mixture of pride, fear, anger, happiness, relief, affection came from them as they watched me.

Time to demonstrate the price they'd pay if they ever betrayed me.

I turned to Ares and Dionysus. They glared at me while cowering from my gaze. It was an interesting combination.

I dug into my pocket, pulled out the stone I'd brought with me from my grave. Black, shiny. Warm to the touch, though that would change. I closed my eyes, reached into the depths of all the Nether had taught me as I died and resurrected within it. I looked down at the stone again. Flat and round, about two inches across. Uneven in thickness. So small and innocent, considering what it would become.

I settled my gaze on the two gods who had been responsible for my torture.

"Death, for me, was a temporary thing. I died at the hands of these gods a total of thirty-seven times, both in my grave and out of it." My voice was soft, but the chamber was so silent you could have heard a feather falling to the floor. "Because of what I am. Because of the circumstances of my birth. Because I will not just disappear, and I cannot be used. Because, no matter what else I am, I am the only truly immortal being here."

"Death can be comforting. It can be a long-craved silence in an otherwise insane life. It can be the comforting embrace of nothingness. Once upon a time, I craved death. But I can say now that it was none of that for me. I have too much to live for. I hated death." I paused, looked up at Ares and Dionysus. "But what you have ahead of you is much, much worse."

I set the stone on the floor in front of where they were chained. I would have just liked to have done what I needed to do and be done with it. But these were immortals, gods, and I knew that, if nothing else, they loved a bit of theatrics. They also needed things spelled out for them, very, very clearly. I took a deep breath, hoping the Nether hadn't been fucking with me when it showed me what to do.

"For the crimes of torture, murder, and betrayal, I sentence you, Dionysus, to an eternity in a prison made entirely of the Nether. May your soul empower me to save innocents with the same unrelenting focus you displayed when you put your greed ahead of family and honor. It will be so." My voice had raised in volume as I spoke, and with the final words, Dionysus let out a long, keening wail, and, as we all watched, he seemed to dissolve into nothing more than a silvery mist, which hung uncertainly in the air for a moment, and then swirled toward the black stone, settling into it, imbuing it with the soul of the god of wine and ecstasy, the son of Persephone and Zeus. I could feel Persephone's acute mourning behind me, her shame, her anger as her son ceased to be.

The room was silent as I gathered myself, readied my power to complete the spell again.

"God of War," I said, and Ares looked up at me, defiant to the end. "Your hatred was turned on me because I caused the death of your sister, Enyo. I can respect that. If anyone took those I loved from me, I would go into a murderous rage, too. In that way, at least, we are the same. The difference between us is that I have never enjoyed being cruel. The glee you felt the first several times you killed me... that is something I can't stop thinking about."

I paused, looked down at the stone that would soon be his prison. All I really wanted to do right at that moment was curl into a ball, preferably with Brennan, and pretend nothing else existed. But I couldn't do that, until I did this.

"For the crimes of torture and murder, I sentence you, Ares, God of War, to eternity in a prison made purely of the Nether, where your soul, so full of anger and discord, will help me fight for those who can't fight for themselves. It will be so."

He glared at me until the moment his body became silvery-black mist, until he fell apart. Unlike Dionysus, he refused to scream, refused to show how much it hurt, how afraid he was.

But I could feel it. I felt it all.

As his soul settled into the shining black stone, I stood and stared at it. It pulsed with power. Dark, angry, potent power. And I was responsible for it. It would serve me.

I didn't even want to look at it, let alone touch it.

I took a deep breath, pulled myself together, and bent to pick up the stone. It was ice cold now, and would remain so. I could feel their presence. But, more, and the whole reason I'd done this: I could feel their power,

COLLEEN VANDERLINDEN

already making mine grow, making it easier for me to uphold the enchantment hiding the blood and mess I wore, easier for me to feel everything the gods felt, easier for me to hear their thoughts, bonded to me as they were.

It would make it easier for me to create a gateway, so I could go home, which was all that really mattered.

I held the stone tightly in my palm, felt the curves of it, cold against my skin. I turned to the immortals. "And that is the fate of anyone who dares to betray me. Any questions?"

There were none.

CHAPTER NINE

After that little scene, I think the gods and I were all pretty ready to be rid of one another.

I told the Aether gods they were free to go home if they wanted, but they all opted to stay in the Nether. Hades' home was filled with gods, though Persephone had had the sense to room them in the other wing of the palace, away from me. The only ones in my wing were Hades and Persephone, and Artemis, who, even more now, refused to leave my side.

I went to my room, locked the door behind me. I dropped the enchantment; no reason to hold it anymore. I knew that Artemis' cats sat outside of my door, and that Cerberus sat outside, just below the balcony off of my chamber.

I looked down at the stone still clasped in my hand. This was now my burden as well as a source of power. If it fell into the wrong hands, Ares and Dionysus might find themselves free somehow. I wasn't willing to risk that. Sighing, I brought up the enchantment again and left the room. The shower would have to wait a while longer.

I walked to the other wing, asking a demon along the way which chamber was Hephaestus'. Once I knew, I headed there, knocked twice on the door. He answered after a few moments.

"Yes, Mollis?" he asked once he saw me.

"May I come in?" I asked him.

He nodded and stepped aside. Artemis' two cats had followed me, and they sat outside the door. Hephaestus gave them a glance, then raised his eyebrows questioningly at me.

"It's a long story," I told him, and he nodded.

"What can I do for you?" he asked, getting right down to business.

I held the stone out, and he grimaced at the sight of it. "I need this on me at all times, for obvious reasons. I was hoping you could make something so I could wear it somehow."

He looked at it thoughtfully. "You could wear it on a chain. Wouldn't be hard to make a setting for it. Or a ring, maybe."

"Maybe a chain? I'd prefer to wear it in as discreet a way as possible."

He looked at it a bit more. "Chains can be grabbed, snapped," he said, thinking aloud and shaking his head. He looked at it a while longer, then he glanced at me.

"Arm band."

"Huh?"

"I can fashion a band of iron or silver, with a secure setting. And we can fit it to you so you can wear it here," he said, pointing at my upper arm. "You could wear it all the time under clothing. You want to make sure the stone is secure, that it doesn't pop off. The setting could come up to cover the edges of the stone, so most of it is encased in metal, surrounded by the band itself."

"I intend to wear it everywhere. Shower, sleep..."

"Silver, then. Iron will rust," he said, nodding. Then he glanced at me. "I don't suppose you have tools handy?"

I shook my head. "I think we'll have to visit your realm for that."

"All right. Artemis seems intent on protecting you, based on the kitties," he said, nodding toward the door, "which is kind of funny, considering. When you're ready to go, you and Artemis come and get me. I'll be here."

I sensed for him. No hatred. No fear. Respect. "Why don't you hate me?" The words slipped out before I could second-guess it. I was tired, I told myself. Stupid to show that kind of vulnerability to a stranger.

He watched me for a moment. "I know what it's like to be reviled because of the way you're made. You know how to rise above it, queenie?"

I grimaced at the nickname. "How?"

"You decide you don't give a shit who likes you, and you go forward and live your life. Yeah?"

I nodded. He glanced again at the stone in my hand. "I won't lie to you. Watching Ares end that way was damn satisfying. If I didn't already like you before based on everything I heard, I fuckin' worship you now."

I couldn't help it. I laughed, just a little, and shook my head. "It's a creepy thing."

"It is. But I can't think of a better punishment for those two," he said. "I don't know what all they did to you, but I'm guessing it wasn't good."

"It wasn't good," I affirmed.

I left shortly after that, telling Hephaestus I'd be back soon.

Shower.

I needed a shower so badly I was about to scream.

The cats trailed me back to my rooms, and I shut the door behind me, letting the enchantment fall again. I went into the bathroom, turned the shower on as hot as it would go, and stripped off the remnants of my crusty, bloody, filthy clothing. I looked at them in a pile on the floor, then picked them up and took them back into the bedroom with me, tossed them into the fireplace, where they ignited immediately. I stood and watched them burn, wishing the memories would disappear as easily. When they were nothing but ashes, I walked back into the bathroom and stepped into the searing hot shower. I set the stone on the ledge of the bathtub, and stood under the water, watching rivulets of brownish gray grossness sluice down my legs and disappear into the drain. For a long time, I just stood there, and let the water do its thing.

I closed my eyes, fighting back the fear, the terror of the memories of my deaths. If I started thinking about it, I knew I'd fall apart. And adding to that, I had a jumbled mess of thoughts and emotions from the immortals I'd bonded with. My mind was a noisy, chaotic place. It was like being locked into a tiny, windowless room with a bunch of people you despise, and they just won't shut the fuck up for even a second. Overwhelming. Irritating at every level.

It worked the way I needed it to. When one of them had a strong emotion, it seemed to flare in my mind, drawing my attention to them. Hera and her anger, shame over the things Ares had done. Zeus with his wounded pride. At the moment, the thought I kept catching most often was "what happens now?" They were worried, tense, angry.

Having them in my mind was enough to make me want to start pulling my hair out.

But I'd asked for this. And if it meant that the ones I love would be safe from the schemes of the immortals, it was worth it. I'd learned first-hand how vicious, heartless, sick they could be when they wanted to. I'd take every bit of insanity. I'd learn to deal with it, so no one I cared about would ever feel the things I'd felt at the gods' hands.

I stood under the water, and hoped I'd feel clean again, and my mind wandered. When I wasn't listening to the chatter in my head, I was back in my grave again.

I took deep breaths, determined to keep myself steady. There was no time now. Someday, I'd curl up in a fetal position and freak the fuck out, but not just yet. I swiped impatiently at my eyes, at the tears that had escaped, and I took another deep breath, and I focused on the one thing that centered me when I felt myself going over the edge: my connection to Brennan.

Someday, I'd tell him how he'd saved my life, and my sanity, over and over and over again. Because while I was strong enough to handle just about any damn thing that came my way, it felt good to have a little something to hold onto during the darkest times. And he was it.

Once I felt steady again, I picked up a bottle of herbal-scented shampoo, and went to work on my blood-matted, filthy hair. By the third shampoo, the water finally started running clear, and by the fifth, I felt somewhat clean again. I scrubbed my skin hard with the washcloth, abrading it, feeling like I'd never quite get all of the filth and death off of me.

When I finally stepped out of the shower, I at least looked normal, even if I didn't feel it.

I went to work combing the snarls and tangles out of my hair, which took longer than I would have liked, then I put on my Fury uniform and started braiding my hair. There was a knock at my chamber door. I sensed.

Persephone.

I was not in the mood for her shit.

I stuffed the black stone in my pants pocket and walked through my room. I pulled the door open to find my stepmother standing on the other side. Her eyes were red, and anger and sadness emanated from her. Dislike. As usual.

"I need a word with you," she said when I opened the door.

I nodded and waved her in, then closed the door behind us. The cats still stood guard.

I folded my arms across my body and watched her, waited for her to speak.

"You killed my son in front of me today," she said.

"Actually, you did worse than kill him."

"I did," I said.

"You know I have no love for you. I wasn't especially fond of my son anymore, either. He may have been the get of that mortal that my father took, but I raised him as mine," she said, then she paused. "I wanted a child. I would have preferred one of my own, but my husband was incapable of producing life. Or so we believed," she said with a glare. "So I had the next-best thing in Dionysus, a child to raise, because his father, my father, couldn't be bothered with his upbringing. And it made me happy, for a time. And then he grew to be more like Zeus than I would have liked."

I stayed silent, watched her.

"But, as I said, for all intents and purposes, he was mine." Her gaze met mine. "And as his mother, I want to apologize to you for the things he put you through."

For a second, I was sure I'd heard wrong.

"I can't stand you. We will never, ever be friends. You said it best once when you said that you were the living, breathing reminder that Hades messed around on me. And it's true. It's not your fault, but I still hate you for that. I hate that you've turned my world upside down. I hate that you exist. Period."

She paused, took a breath as if trying to steady herself. "But no one deserves the things Ares and Dionysus did to you." She watched me. "Hades told me what you really looked like when you first came back. My husband is angrier than I've ever seen him, ever. And that is saying something. He feels guilty that he couldn't save you, guilty that he didn't protect you better. Guilty that he and Tisiphone did the one thing they weren't supposed to do, and made you, and your life has been a series of traumas. He feels helpless. And for a god, that is a completely alien feeling."

We stood in awkward silence for a few moments. "Well, at least you don't do shit behind my back. You have the guts to actively dislike me to my face," I said.

Persephone smirked. "Of course. What fun is it to skulk around in the background?"

I shook my head and opened the door. "Thanks, mommy dearest," I said. "This has been fun. Time to go now before you hug me or something."

"I'd rather kiss Cerberus, abomination," she said as she walked past me. "I'm glad you're not dead. For Hades."

"I'm glad I'm not dead too. Bye, now." Once I closed the door behind her, I shook my head and laughed a little, trying to imagine Persephone and I bonding.

I finished braiding my hair, then went next door and knocked on Artemis' door. When she answered, I explained about Hephaestus and told her where I was going and (as Hephaestus had predicted) she insisted on coming with me.

As we walked through the corridors to Hephaestus' room, I kept noticing her sneaking glances at me. "What?" I finally asked her.

"I am sorry. I failed you," she said. I knew it already, of course. Shame flooded from her. Anger.

I glanced at her. "You didn't. I was the dumbass who wasn't paying attention. I walked right into him."

"I should have sent the cats with you, at the very least."

"I would have gotten angry with you. I don't need a babysitter. Although, maybe I could have used one at that moment," I said, shaking my head.

"I'm glad you're back with us, dear girl."

"You didn't say 'I'm glad you're okay.'" I remarked.

"Because you're very obviously not okay. Nor should anyone expect you to be." We walked in silence for a bit. "But you are strong. You'll be all right," she said.

"Thinking about your grandson is the only thing that kept me together," I said, my voice low. "I will do anything to get back to him. Anything." I looked at her, and our eyes met.

"And I will do whatever it takes to help you get back to

him," she said. We walked, and the cats followed, and I found myself noticing things more than usual. The dark stone of the floors in my father's house, the same stone I now carried in my pocket. Pieces of the Nether. The art on the walls. Someone (Persephone, probably) had a thing for landscapes. Woodsy scenes, with waterfalls. I wondered aloud where the art had come from, and Artemis grinned. "Are you serious? All the best art the beings in your world ever created is in the Aether and the Nether. Gifts to the gods who inspired it. I have the most beautiful cat sculptures in my garden. You will have to visit my home some time."

I just nodded. I really wasn't planning on many social calls.

When we knocked at Hephaestus' door, he opened up, greeted Artemis with a hug, and we got ready to go to the Aether.

"How do you get there?" I asked as they each held one of my hands.

"Two ways: you can either travel over the mountains, which is a very, very long trip. Or," Hephaestus said, smiling a little, "you travel like this." And with that, he closed his eyes, and I felt myself being pulled apart, much like the time Eunomia had zipped me from the loft to the Packard Plant to guard the gateway.

Within an instant, we were standing on vibrant green grass under a golden sky.

"How do you do that? Can I do that?" I asked them, envisioning the possibilities for when I returned to my realm.

"I don't see why you couldn't," Hephaestus said.

"Takes some practice, but you'll figure it out," Artemis said. They started walking toward a large gray structure, made of what looked like stacked boulders, and I followed.

"We couldn't just do that out of the Nether and get to my realm?"

"No. Someone," Artemis said, winking at me,

"destroyed the gateway. There has to be a functional gateway if we want to rematerialize there."

"What about flying? Couldn't I just fly far enough that I'd end up home, somehow? If I can fly over the mountains to get from the Aether to the Nether, couldn't I fly far enough to get to my own realm?"

Hephaestus shook his head. "Your realm doesn't exist in the realm of the gods. It's separate."

"It kind of exists next to our world, but the two do not overlap at any point, the way the Aether and the Nether do. Hence the need for a gateway," Artemis explained.

We entered the cavernous gray building, and Hephaestus immediately went to work. Artemis and the cats (who had also rematerialized with us. I was more than a little embarrassed that they knew how to do it and I didn't) patrolled around the building, watching out for trouble. Hephaestus found a small rod of silver and went to work, melting, shaping it first with a hammer, and then with increasingly more detailed tools. He measured my arm several times.

"Any particular design you're wanting?" he asked after measuring my arm again and settling back in to work. The arm band was taking shape, and I could see the depression Hephaestus had formed in one part of it to accept the stone, which he'd also been measuring carefully.

"No one's going to see it," I said.

He stopped his work and glared at me.

"What?"

"You're going to see it, and you're the fuckin' queen of the gods, so it has to look like something."

"I am not the queen of the gods."

"No? You just made everyone swear fealty to you. What else would you call it?"

"Empress!" Artemis shouted from outside.

"Oh, shut up," I called out at her, and she laughed.

"I'm not," I said to Hephaestus again, more quietly.

"You are as far as I'm concerned, and I'm the one

making this thing. Tell me what you want." He looked at me for a moment longer, his dark gaze holding mine. "What? Flowers? Swords? Butterflies? Hearts and cherubs? Happy puppy dogs? What?"

"Leaves," I said finally.

"Leaves," he said, then nodded. "Was that so hard?" he muttered as he went back to work.

"It's not that I don't appreciate your artistry or anything," I said, trying to placate the irritated immortal. "I'm thinking in practical terms, is all."

"I know," he said. "Here's another question for you, queenie," he said as he worked.

"What?"

"You're really going to fix the gateway?"

"Create. There is no gateway anymore. I have to make a new one," I said.

"Have you considered this? You'll not be the same when you go back."

"Well, duh. I've been through some shit during my time here..."

He shook his head. "That's not what I'm saying." He worked a few more minutes, shaping the silver, and I could see the beginnings of leaves forming along the band. "I'm saying, I can feel the Nether in you."

"That was the price," I said quietly.

"Remember when we said that the realms of the gods and the realm of mortals were separate, that they didn't cross at any point?"

I nodded.

He met my eyes again. "Could be maybe they're separate for a reason. And you're going to go carrying a piece of the Nether itself with you into your world."

"What choice do I have? I need to go home. I needed to have a chance to be free and live again. There was no other way."

"I'm not saying there was. I'm just suggesting that things might not be all roses when you make your way back." And with that, he bent over the arm band, engrossed in his work again.

I watched him work, trying to shake off the worry that his words had caused. It's not like I could change it anyway. I had a feeling the Nether wouldn't respond with "Oh, that's okay. I saved your life and all, but I'll totally let you go back on paying the price." Extremely doubtful. I'd deal with it. I'd make it work. I wasn't sure why its price had been a piece of my soul, but I had been willing to pay anything. I hadn't even considered asking it what it wanted from me, or why.

I sat and watched as Hephaestus worked. The plain, hammered silver armband was becoming something much more elaborate. I was picturing maple leaves or something like that, but the god was adorning the band with the delicate leaves of the trees I'd seen in the Nether, along with leaves I recognized from my world: oak, maple, ash. They came together in a way that reminded me of leaf piles I'd jumped in when I was a kid. It was the most intricate, beautiful piece of jewelry I'd ever seen, and it seemed to take him no effort at all.

"It'll lay flat under clothing. Too bad, really. Be nice to add a more sculptural element to it," he murmured as he added detail to what looked like the final leaf. "Once I'm done with this part, we'll set the stone in, and I'll add silver over top, work that so the design blends with the rest. Only a little bit of the stone will be visible. Right?"

I nodded, and he looked back down at his work, hair falling over his eyes again. He finished, then placed the stone into the depression he'd formed in the band. It fit perfectly (of course) and he started placing additional silver over it, forming it into more leaves. By the time he was finished, the black stone was mostly covered with silver leaves, just a bit of shiny black stone peeking out between them. It looked like nothing more than an absolutely stunning and innocent piece of jewelry.

Hephaestus gave it a final polish, then held it out to

me. I held it in my hands, turning it over, running my fingers along the delicate work. I could still feel the coldness of the stone, turning the silver around it cold as well. Hephaestus watched me as I admired it.

"Okay?" he asked.

"I... it's amazing. I honestly don't feel worthy to wear something as gorgeous as this."

He grunted. "You're worthy." Then he turned around and started cleaning up, and I slipped the band up my arm. It rested perfectly just above my bicep. Made for me. It felt cold against my skin, and I could still feel Ares and Dionysus' power emanating from it. I looked up to see Hephaestus watching me. His emotions were a dull roar, a jumble of things I didn't have the energy to sort out. Respect. Admiration, for sure.

I pulled my sleeve down quickly. "Thank you."

"My pleasure, queenie," he said quietly.

Artemis popped her head into the workshop. "Done?" she asked, glancing sharply at Hephaestus.

"Done," I said.

"Ready to go back?"

I nodded, and we traveled back to the Nether. Now, I had work to do.

CHAPTER TEN

When we got back to Hades' palace, Hephaestus excused himself and went back to his room, and Artemis headed to the kitchens to get something to eat, muttering about "worthless Nether food."

I made my way toward my father's study. The door was open, and I could see my mom, my dad, and Persephone sitting around his desk.

"Dysfunctional family reunion?" I asked when I walked into the room. Persephone rolled her eyes and gave a small shake of her head. My mother laughed, and Hades (probably wisely) stayed silent.

"We're trying to figure out if we know anything about making a gateway," Hades said, gesturing to a chair.

"Wait. Aren't we all supposed to rise until she's seated?" Persephone asked with a sneer.

"No, Just you," I told her, flopping into the empty chair. I sensed humor from my mom, and she glanced at me and gave me a small smile. "You guys aren't going to start the 'queen' bullshit too, are you? I just went through that with Hephaestus."

"Well. I wasn't going to call you a queen. But it's not inaccurate," Hades said. "You forced the gods to swear loyalty to you. You rule us."

"And how do you feel about that, dad?" I asked him, meeting his eyes.

"You know how I feel about it. You're a Fury," he said.

"I want to hear it."

He shook his head. "I am not used to the idea of being ruled. I'm not overly fond of the thought. But if it had to be anyone, it's damn appropriate that it's my daughter who made the gods finally bend a knee to something bigger than themselves. I'm proud of you, and I'm enjoying lording it over the other gods. All right?"

"I think you'll find that what you promised them will bind them to you much more strongly than anything else you've done," Tisiphone said, and Persephone nodded grudgingly.

"What? Access to my realm?"

"Being relevant again. You gave them permission to be gods again. We've been blind and stupid, sitting here in the Aether and Nether, playing a game of thrones when the world we once loved was there the whole time," Hades said.

"Why did you draw back?"

Hades shrugged. He sat back in his chair and crossed his arms over his chest. "For a while, we walked among the mortals. We helped them. Or harmed them, depending on our whims. It's not like they had any say in the matter." He took a sip out of a crystal glass that held a dark purple liquid. He was seated in his large chair, looking every bit like something out of *The Godfather*. A fire crackled in the huge stone fireplace across the room.

"Not that that's a good thing," Tisiphone said, and Hades nodded, after a slight hesitation.

"But you know the issues we have with your realm. We're not as powerful there. And we've spent our entire existence stabbing each other in the back. So we all knew that we needed to be at our most powerful--"

"You can't actually kill each other," I reminded him.

"No. But we can be captured," Hades said.

"Tortured," Tisiphone said.

"Imprisoned," Persephone muttered.

"Used," Hades finished. "So it was foolish to be in a place where our power is less. Over time, we just all stayed here. Ares and others, like Artemis, made occasional trips to the mortal realm. Most of us simply became more comfortable here."

"The Furies are fine in my world," I said, and Tisiphone nodded.

"We're pretty much the only ones though. Furies and Guardians must go to the mortal realm to fulfill their duties. The others do not have the same situation."

That reminded me of the conversation I'd had with Athena and my mother what felt like an eternity ago. "What about the spirit daemons?"

"They're stronger there, because of the way their powers work," Tisiphone said, crossing one long leg over the other. My father noticed it, with some appreciation.

I really would have rather not known that. The Lord of the Nether loved his wife. But he still lusted over my mother and what they'd had together, brief as it had been.

I forced my mind back where it needed to be. It was proving very, very distracting, having them all in my head with me. "So they don't suffer any ill effects from being cut off from this world? I'm thinking of the ones I trapped there," I said.

"I know you are," Tisiphone said softly. "And unfortunately, no. It matters not at all to them that they can't access this realm anymore. Your world is their playground. So much emotion. So many minds and hearts to put to use."

"Tell me about Eris," I said.

"She is what you'd expect her to be," Hades said. "Spiteful. She enjoys violence and chaos. The more, the better. She never tires of causing discord."

"Great," I said, shaking my head. "And I trapped her there with them."

"The good thing is, like most spirit daemons, she tends to work from behind the scenes. It's just how they do things."

"What do you mean?" I asked.

"She usually takes other supernaturals into her circle," my mother said. "Witches, warlocks, beings like that. Beings with a bit of power of their own. And she whispers in their ears, gives them visions of greatness. She teaches them how to do things they never could have imagined possible. And in doing so, she leaves strife in her wake."

"One of her specialties used to be having witches infect the innocent with a kind of curse that would cause discord among those around him or her," Hades said.

"Those were bad," my mother said, shaking her head. "She managed to start a war or two with that curse."

"My wife is a genius at getting rid of them," Hades said, smiling at Persephone in a way that made her blush, just a little.

"Well. It's been a while. She hasn't needed to work very hard to cause discord in your world. You mortals excel at fighting with one another," Persephone said.

"Yeah. And you all are a bunch of benevolent angels," I said to her.

"Point taken," she said, giving me an icy glare.

We sat in silence for a while. "You said you were trying to figure out what you knew about creating a gateway. Come up with anything?" I finally asked.

Hades shook his head. "I am sorry." He took another sip from the goblet in his hand.

"Who created the original gateways?"

"They just existed. No one created them," Hades said.

"Someone or something created them. Things don't

just appear out of nowhere," I told him.

"Well, whoever it was, we have no idea. They've been around for my entire existence. Well, until recently, anyway."

"Was it the Titans or whatever it was that came before you?" I pressed.

He gave me a steely glare. "We don't talk about the Titans."

"They--"

"They were here already," Tisiphone said. "We don't know where they came from."

I sighed, dropping the subject. Apparently, this was getting me nowhere fast, and, selfishly, I really didn't want anything else to think about. I had a feeling the Titans were a can of worms I didn't want to open just then. After a few more minutes of conversation, I excused myself and went back to my room, Artemis' cats shadowing me. My patience had started wearing thin, and the emotions in the room, between my father's lust for Tisiphone and Persephone's rampant dislike for me, had set me on edge. My hands were stiff from holding them clenched in my lap as I'd gotten more and more irritated.

I shut myself in my room. Rubbed my hands together. They felt dirty all the time now. My skin prickled. I could still feel blood and filth caking my body, and it felt like I'd never be truly clean again. I could ignore it better when I was focusing on something else, even though the feeling was always there. Tired and alone, though, not having to worry about keeping up a facade of control I didn't feel, the fear threatened to suffocate me.

I went into the bathroom and washed my hands for a long time under scalding-hot water. Not that it helped. I stood there for a while and tried and failed to pull myself together. The constant rumbling of the thoughts of the gods I'd bound to me threatened to drown out all other sounds, and the Nether pulsed within me and in all the noise it was becoming harder to pick out my connection to

Brennan. I held my head, which had started pounding as soon as I'd left the Nether to visit the Aether and still hadn't stopped. I tried to take deep breaths, but doing that only reminded me of what it felt like in the ground, gasping for breath, suffocating.

I felt like I was dying again. Like I was teetering on the edge of an abyss, just about to go over. Trying to pull myself together only made it feel worse, as if my psyche was mocking me; the harder I tried to calm down, the more intense everything became.

I tried talking to myself, reminding myself that I could get through anything. That I *had* gotten though just about everything. I tried focusing on Brennan, on home, on hot coffee and a warm bed. Nothing worked, and in the end, I had no choice but to ride out the panic, to feel it, to let it obliterate every good thought I tried to have. I slid to the floor, immobilized by the terror coursing through me.

I don't know how long I stayed on the cold stone floor.

After a while, I was able to breathe without wanting to puke.

I stopped shaking, eventually.

My head still pounded. Too many voices, too many emotions. I could hardly stand it. I'll adjust, I tried to tell myself. It's only been a little while. I'll get used to it.

I decided to try a bath with some of the herb-scented bath oils I'd spotted in my chambers. I forced myself up, ran the bath water, added several drops of one that smelled a lot like lavender. I stripped, leaving the silver arm band Hephaestus had created for me snug around my bicep.

I lowered myself into the steaming water and leaned back, resting my head on the ledge of the tub. For a while, I listened to the thoughts and emotions of the gods. Zeus was pouting, but resigned. Apollo was hunting, and quite enjoying it. My aunt Megaera was working, punishing the damned. Aphrodite was mourning Ares. I'd have to watch out for her. Persephone..

Oh, ew.

Persephone and Hades were doing something I didn't really want to think about them doing.

I shoved the thoughts of the gods away, shaking my head to try to clear it of the thoughts I'd just witnessed. This was going to be more irritating than I'd thought. I was still on edge from my breakdown, still raw from the helplessness I'd felt, the way I'd had no choice but to let fear and despair claim me.

I closed my eyes, and my thoughts turned, not unexpectedly, to Brennan.

The remnants of what Persephone had been feeling still hovered in my mind, reminding me what it had felt like, in another life, to be loved. My thoughts wandered to Brennan loving me. I rested in the hot water and remembered the feel of his warm lips, the sensation of his strong, sure hands on my body. How good it felt to be filled by him.

It wasn't just a physical thing. The connection we had was so much stronger, warmer, brighter when we were together that way. I craved it. I could go the rest of my existence without food or water, but that connection, the feel of our souls entwining as our bodies writhed in ecstasy... I needed that.

Eventually, fantasies about Brennan lulled me to sleep, and, for a while, I dreamed about him and his warmth, and what it felt like to be home.

When I woke again, I pulled myself out of the bath, dried off, and climbed into the fluffy bed. As I laid there, I tried to think about how to create the gateway. I had all the power I'd ever have, between what I'd been given by the Nether and the stone powered with Ares and Dionysus. My ties to the gods, too, gave me a little extra something, in addition to the headache and general sense of irritation.

I'd destroyed it by simply focusing. I'd try that again. I knew two things now that I hadn't known the first time around: it would likely take enough power to kill me in the process, and it really didn't matter if I died, because I'd come back.

Except now, with my extra power... I was hoping to stay alive through it. Dying was not an option, really, because resurrection left me weak. And when I was weak, when my guard was down, bad things happened.

No. I definitely had no intention of letting it kill me this time around.

The ideal thing would be to have an immortal or two I trusted who would watch out for me in case it killed me. I wanted to trust my parents and Artemis. I probably could.

Probably.

I wasn't willing to risk it. I'd just have to manage to stay alive.

I rolled over, and my wings flapped awkwardly. I still hated them. The good thing was that I guessed I could probably enchant myself to hide them when I was back in my realm.

That gave me an idea.

I stood up and stood in front of the large gilt mirror in my room. I focused, bringing up an enchantment, and I looked in the mirror. No wings. Long dark hair. Creamy, but not deathly pale, skin. Normal, non-alien eyes. The way I'd looked a few dozen lives ago.

I didn't even know this girl anymore. She'd thought she was such a badass.

She was nothing.

The enchantment fell, and as it did, it wavered and showed me as I'd been after emerging from my grave. Filthy. Destroyed. Bordering on madness.

That's the real me, I thought as I forced the enchantment away completely. The blood and filth fell away, and then it was just me, glowing-eyed, winged freak, standing in an empty room.

◆ ◆ ◆

I spent a lot of my time in the stretches of

unmeasurable time that followed alternately trying to open the gateway and having my ass kicked training with Athena. I actually kind of preferred the ass-kickings. The gateway was proving to not be nearly as straightforward as I'd hoped, and fighting Athena helped me burn off some of the ever-present rage I felt gnawing at me since I'd emerged from my grave. I worked, and I fought, and I tried not to think about how home felt farther away than ever.

I had no idea how much time had passed in my realm. I hated that there was no way of telling time in the Aether and the Nether. I mean, I understood that hours, days, even years, have no meaning to immortals, but it made me feel off-kilter and kind of lost.

It had been another long stretch of failure at the gateway, and I finally gave up and made my way back to my father's house, I was tired and crabby and feeling completely worthless. I'd fought my way back from the freaking grave, and I was still trapped in the Nether, with nothing but a really noisy mind to show for it.

When I got there, my parents, Persephone, Hephaestus, and Artemis were sitting in the living room, around the fire place. There was a large, rich-looking cake on the side table, and I helped myself to a huge slice and sat down on one of the sofas between Hephaestus and Artemis.

I listened and ate. They were debating the things they'd do once they had access to my realm again, how they'd handle ensuring that they were worshiped and revered again. And I recognized it as one of those times where I should have kept my mouth shut. But I was in a bad mood and I suck at self-control.

"You know what I think? I don't think you're gods at all," I said, setting my empty plate on the table and leaning back against the sofa cushions.

I heard Hephaestus make a sound in his throat, but I didn't have a chance to focus on that, because my father started going off on me.

"Not gods, eh? In your educated opinion of gods, since you've known about us for so long, you've determined that we don't know what we are. Okay."

"Do any of you create life? Were any single one of you the beginning of anything? No. You came from the Titans or whatever the hell you call the beings that came before you. Maybe they're gods. I don't know. Maybe you can say you're descended from the gods, if gods even exist at all. But from where I'm sitting, you're just a bunch of souped-up supernaturals. There's not a damn thing I've seen in my time here that makes me believe you're anything worth worshiping."

The five of them stared at me, and Hephaestus laughed. "Finally, someone with some fuckin' sense. I've been saying this forever."

"And you're also off your rocker," Hades muttered.

"What makes you gods?" I challenged him.

"You come from beings who sentence and punish the souls of the dead, and you're asking what makes us gods?" Hades asked.

"I'm not saying I don't believe in what you do. I'm just saying that maybe you're just a bunch of super-powered freaks, too. More powerful than those from my realm, but super-powered freaks nonetheless. You have special abilities. Yours involve interacting with the dead." I shrugged.

"What? Are we missing our halos? Is that why you don't believe in us?"

"People pray to us and we respond to it, Mollis," Artemis said. "How do you explain that away?"

"I don't know. Maybe we're more in tune with mortals, somehow. They need us, and we feel it. But you're trying to sell this idea that you're gods, and so am I. I'm not buying it."

Every immortal in the room was irritated with me, except for Heph, who seemed to be rather enjoying himself.

"You're talking semantics now. What does it even matter what we call ourselves?" Persephone said, exasperated.

"Exactly. What does it even matter? Why does it bother you all so much, then, that I don't think you're gods?" I asked her, and got a stony glare in response.

"Why does the idea that we *do* consider ourselves gods bother you so much?" my mother asked me.

I sat quietly for a minute, trying to think of how to put it. "Look. You're all super-powered. Obviously. You have powers that seem crazy to anyone from my realm. But guess what? I know lots of beings who have powers that seem crazy. You're not unique in that. More powerful, sure. But not unique."

I glanced at my father, then my mother. "Once you start tossing words like 'gods' out there, it does something. You start believing the shit you're selling, that by calling yourself a god, you're somehow above everyone else. And don't deny it, because every one of you in this room, except for him, maybe," I said, gesturing toward Hephaestus, "believes you're better, somehow, than everyone who isn't one of you."

I paused again. "And you're not. You're just as small, petty, dishonest, and stubborn as anyone else. You think you're above those in my realm. But you know what? Nobody in my realm owes any of you shit. Nobody in my realm owes me a damn thing. So you can call yourselves gods, hold onto that lie. But I'm not buying into it."

"They pray to you, Mollis. They believe you're a god," Hades said. "And you can feel it when they do so."

"They can believe that if it helps get them through the night. But I know better. I don't answer prayers. If I'm lucky, I stumble around and eventually save someone who prayed for it." I shrugged. "And you're no different. I'm right, aren't I?"

I was met with a stony silence, all the answer I needed.

"You don't hear prayers. You feel when someone's thinking of you. Okay. Yay, congrats. You have a superpower that puts you at the whims of the people in my realm. They focus on you, you get a boost in power. They don't... well, no boost for you. So you're a bunch of drama queens who need to be the center of attention. And people are supposed to worship you?"

I sensed a whole lot of amusement from Heph, but everyone else stayed silent. A while later, my father and Persephone excused themselves, and, shortly after, Artemis and my mother did the same. Then it was just Hephaestus and the cats and I. I stared into the flames dancing in the huge fireplace. It made me wish I could feel warm again, just for a little while. The coldness that had pervaded my body as I waited, resurrecting and dying in my grave, still hadn't gone away. I knew it was the Nether, now living, just a little, inside of me. That, and the icy cold coming from the stone I now wore on my arm. I rubbed my hands absentmindedly and leaned my head back against the cushions.

"Well. You pissed them off good, queenie," Heph said after a while.

"I probably should have just kept my mouth shut."

"And what fun is that?" he said, and then we were silent for a while. "So, you don't believe in gods. You believe in prophecy?"

I crossed my arms, kept looking at the fire. "I don't know. I believe in the ability to see the future. I know a woman who can do that, for real. And she's not perfect but she always gets at least some of it right. Prophecy is just that, I think."

"So when you listened to the Fates and destroyed the gateway? Why'd you do it?"

I shrugged. "I figured there was a kernel of truth in it. And even if there wasn't some half-assed prophecy they were all trying to sell, I knew I needed to shield my world from this one. Zeus was already throwing lightning around. I acted fast. And probably stupidly. But I did the only thing I knew I could do at the time."

"You heard the part of your prophecy that said your coming would destroy the world of the gods, yeah?"

I rolled my eyes. "Yeah. I heard that part. And when I destroyed the gateway, everyone assumed it meant cutting you all off from your supply of energy from the mortal realm. Like I said: bunch of drama queens."

He laughed, and I saw him lean forward out of the corner of my eye. He was looking into the fire, too. "Maybe it just meant that you'd make them start to think differently. Maybe this is the beginning of them realizing they're not as high and mighty as they think they are."

"They're not going to change. They'll keep believing what they want to. But I'm not buying into it."

Neither of us said anything for a long time. "You don't buy it either?" I finally asked him.

"No. Same reasons as you, pretty much. I haven't seen anything to suggest we're that special. We're more powerful than what you'd find in your world. Different worlds, different power levels," he said, shrugging his massive shoulders.

"Are you an atheist, Heph?" I asked him.

He laughed. "Could be. All I know is this: my parents," he said with a sneer, "didn't want me because of my deformity. I was imperfect. They abandoned me in your realm. Cast me out, left me to die. Came down to it, I made it back by myself. That's what I can count on, and that's all I believe any of us can count on: ourselves." He was quiet a while. "Maybe that's why I never did hate you. Never feared you. We have more in common than just about anybody here. You don't give up, and neither do I."

"Is that why you joined my father's side?"

"I joined *your* side," he clarified, glancing at me. "My father is an absolute horse's ass. Anybody who thinks Hermes was all right and you were the villain is a joke. And anyone who hates you for what you are needs to take a good look in the mirror."

"Your wife joined Zeus," I said.

He got up, walked to the fireplace. He tossed a couple more logs on, poked at the fire for a few minutes. "My wife," he finally said, derision in his voice. "My wife has slept with just about every male immortal here, and who knows how many mortals. She never wanted me, and I never wanted her. Early on, I'd get upset that she didn't respect our marriage. It's been so long now, I don't care anymore. Doesn't matter to me either way which side she chose."

He sat back down. "Can I tell you somethin', queenie?"

I nodded.

"Once you make the new gateway, I'm thinking I'm done here. Used to be a time, I spent years on end in your realm. I was happier then. Once I'm able to, I'm going through that gateway, and I'm not coming back."

"What will you do in my realm?"

He crossed his arms across his chest. "Work alongside the mortals. Make things. Use my hands and body. Stop wasting away here like some useless relic."

"You make weapons and armor," I said.

"I make everything," he said, glancing at me. Not prideful, just stating a fact.

"My team, back home. In Detroit," I said. "If you feel like it, you could consider working with them. I'm sure they'd appreciate having someone as skilled as you making weapons for them. My friend, Shanti, she adores swords. When I got stuck here, she'd just started the next level of her training..." I trailed off, remembering.

"You miss them," Hephaestus said, and I gave a small nod. "Could be I'll look them up when we make it to your realm. Maybe for a while, anyway. It would be nice to be part of something like that."

"It is. You feel like you're really doing something worthwhile. And it's scary as hell and you want to scream in frustration, sometimes. You wonder, time and time again, how we can be so awful to one another. But when you fall asleep at night, you do it knowing someone's alive, home, because of what you did. It's the only thing I've ever been good at."

"I'm finding that a bit hard to believe."

I didn't answer for a while. "Well. I'm also good at making really bad decisions."

He laughed. "And at having a sunny outlook. Don't leave that out." Then he got up. "You gonna sleep at some point?"

I shook my head. "Later, Heph."

He gave me a wave and walked out of the room. I sat there until I heard the rest of the immortals start moving around again, hours later. There was no point in going to my bed, where I'd just lie awake either remembering nightmares or missing Brennan and my friends back home. I listened to the immortals' thoughts for a while, and I thought about what I could do differently with the gateway. There had to be a way, because there was no way in heaven, hell, or anyplace else that I was spending eternity trapped with a bunch of self-important assholes.

CHAPTER ELEVEN

A while later, I ended up making my way back outside, to the smooth black wall that stood where the gateway had been. At first, every time I'd come to the gateway, the immortals had gathered around, eagerly waiting to walk into my realm and their promised power and adoration. Their excitement and anticipation had flooded through me, distracting me, and I'd finally growled at them to get the hell away from me.

The next several times, they'd gathered around anyway, until I made them leave again.

Eventually, they stopped coming.

They started to lose hope. The promises I'd given them, about access to my realm, about being worshiped and relevant again started to feel like lies. Soon, the only ones who stayed with me were Artemis and Hephaestus. They seemed to have come to some kind of agreement about me, that one or the other or both would be nearby whenever I left my father's house. I didn't see any point in arguing with them, as long as they didn't bother me by hovering or talking too much. Artemis spent most of her time with me sitting off to the side, reading or stringing and polishing her bow. Hephaestus usually sat somewhere nearby, scribbling in a notebook he seemed to have with him all the time. I'd asked him once what it was, and he'd showed me. Sketches and designs for weapons, armor. He was always coming up with ideas for things. He was cranky, and abrasive, but he never did the saluting thing and he didn't actively hate me, and he also wasn't waiting impatiently for the moment I returned home to start the next generation, the way Artemis was. I wanted to get home, to Brennan, but babies were the farthest thing from my mind.

Now, the activity that sometimes results in babies... yeah, that was on my mind, probably more than I'd have liked. Part of the problem was that the gods are a rather lusty group. I knew way too much about their interpersonal relationships than I really wanted to. My father and Persephone were among the worst, though they weren't the only ones.

The bigger part of the problem was Hephaestus. Or, rather, the insinuations a few of the gods decided to make about Hephaestus. Artemis was the most irritating. And maybe I was a little thrown off by the fact that I actually liked the surly immortal, so the insinuations bothered me all the more.

After our little "you aren't gods" conversation around the fire, Artemis wasn't exactly happy with me. She arrived at the gateway a while after I did, and sat, not reading, irritation coming off of her in waves. I finally gave up trying to focus on the gateway and glared over at her. "What the ever-loving hell is your problem now?"

"He wants you. You know this, yes?" Artemis said. I shrugged, assuming she was talking about Brennan and wondering why she was bringing it up just then, all worked up and annoyed.

"Of course he does. He's my mate," I said, irritated.

I felt a hot bolt of anger flood over me, from her.

"Have you really forgotten my grandson so quickly, then?"

I stared at her in disbelief. "I was talking about your grandson. Who the hell are you talking about?"

"Hephaestus," she spat. "He sits here, and watches you, especially when he knows you're not paying attention. All of that agreeing with you over the gods thing. He doesn't want you to know. You don't need to be a Fury to get a sense of what he wants from you."

I rolled my eyes. "Well, I *am* a Fury, and I haven't felt anything like that from him. He's actually the calmest of all of you."

"Or he's just better able to stifle his feelings than the rest of us are," Artemis grumbled.

"You're wrong. I would know."

She waved me off in a huff, opened her book and started reading. I stared at her a while, half wanting to just have it out and half wanting to forget the conversation had ever happened.

I thought about Hephaestus, trying to figure out if I was actually missing something. And I was irritated that I was even wasting time thinking about it, because I actually had more important shit to deal with. I mean, yeah, he was always there, usually not talking to me, but a constant presence nonetheless. And we'd verbally spar every now and then, and I'd get irritated when he called me "queenie," and the other gods would look at him like he was stupid when he'd argue with me. I searched my memories, looking for signs of what Artemis said, but they just weren't there, and I was pretty pissed at her for making me second-guess the one semi-normal relationship I had in the Nether.

And I could admit, to myself if to no one else, that Hephaestus was kind of a weird combination of Nain and Brennan, personality-wise, and that was something I tried not to think about too often. I wondered if I was doing something wrong by actually liking him and enjoying his company. Was I friends with him because he reminded me of the two men I'd loved in my life? And even so, was that such a bad thing? I mean, it wasn't like I was even considering jumping his bones or anything. And, from what I could tell by owning a piece of his mind, he wasn't thinking about jumping mine, either.

Goddamn Artemis.

◆ ◆ ◆

Time passed, the strange, uncertain way it passes in the Nether, and I just grew more and more frustrated, more afraid that I'd never make it home. When the gateway issue got to be too much, I had Hephaestus teach me how to rematerialize elsewhere. It was ridiculously simple. All I had to do was picture a place, and I'd appear there. I was learning about how much of my power is really mental. There's a joke there, somewhere, about me not being the smartest chick in the world, yet having to rely on my mind to make my powers work. The only trick to rematerializing is that I have to be able to envision the place I want to go. It works best if it's somewhere I've been before. A photograph works for some of the more talented travelers, but we tested it with a picture of the inside of Zeus's house, and nothing happened. So I was limited, but at least I could do it.

If only creating the gateway was as easy.

I was at the place where the gateway should be, again, and I'd just given myself a throbbing migraine trying to make something happen. I still worked at it, though I felt blood start flowing from my nose, the way it always seemed to when I hit a certain threshold. I kept going, and my stomach turned due to the pain, and I felt like my body would split, like I was maybe, hopefully on the precipice of something. And I pushed harder...

And my power fizzled out and I slumped down to the ground, exhausted. Again.

I groaned in irritation. Really, I wanted to scream. I

wanted to throw things. I wanted to incinerate everything around me in a single fiery blast.

I lifted my head, eventually, and sat staring at the stone wall that had once been the gateway into my world. I rubbed my hands together without thinking. My head was pounding. Aphrodite was in a really shitty mood and it was affecting me. Not that I was in a great mood, but having someone else's irritation layered over my own was not something I needed.

I closed my eyes and rested my head in my hands. I felt someone approaching. Hephaestus. I heard him sit down on my left.

"Here. Eat," he said, nudging my arm with something.

"I'm not hungry," I said, lifting my head and glaring at the wall again. I pressed the handkerchief I'd started carrying with me to my nose, trying to staunch the bleeding.

"Can't hurt, right?" he said, and I gave up and took the fruit he was holding out to me.

"You know food does not actually solve anything, right?" I muttered. Remembering Brennan, how he'd always tried to feed me, with a familiar stab to my heart. He felt farther away than ever, even though I could still feel him. I could feel Hephaestus watching me.

"It doesn't. But it's enjoyable, and that isn't a bad thing, queenie."

I didn't answer. After a while I muttered, "why can't I figure this out?"

Hephaestus was quiet for a while. "I know you don't want to hear this, but maybe it can't be done."

"I destroyed it, I can damn well create a new one," I said.

We both sat looking at the wall then.

"Could be you're too tied to the Nether," he said thoughtfully. He was one of the few who knew about my "bargain" with the Nether. "Nether can't leave the Nether, maybe."

"Fuck," I muttered, wiping a hand over my eyes. "I just want to go home." I hated it, immediately, the weakness and longing in my voice.

"There's someone there waiting for you, yeah?" Hephaestus asked, and, after a moment, I nodded. Knew what he meant.

"At least I hope he's still waiting. I don't even know how much time has passed in my world."

"Unless he's a damn fool, he's still waiting," he said, continuing to stare at the wall with me. "Who told you how to destroy it?"

"Fates."

"No help at all, then."

"Nope." I sat, thinking. He'd made some sense. "So if your theory is right, I need to break away from the Nether."

"Yeah."

"Do you think you're right?"

"Yeah."

"Not to be too sure of yourself or anything," I muttered.

"I'm several thousand years old and I specialize in making shit and taking it apart again. Pretty sure I got this, queenie."

"Okay, genius. Then how do I break away from it?"

He shrugged.

"Maybe you don't want to tell me," I said, still looking at the wall, thinking of Artemis' warnings.

"Go ahead and believe that if you want to."

"Let's just drop it."

"Fine." He sat in silence for a few minutes. "But I would tell you if I knew how. We'll figure it out."

"I'm going to try again."

He nodded, stayed where he was. I closed my eyes, and tried again, envisioning creating an opening into my world, one that would come out in the place I knew best, my back yard at my house. Private, quiet. A good place for a gateway. I focused on creating it, but I tried to pay some attention to what I was feeling as well.

As much as I hated to admit it, Heph was right. The harder I tried to break through, the harder I felt the Nether holding me back. I felt so close, like if I just had a little extra kick of power, I'd make it. I finally gave up with a groan and rested my throbbing head in my palms. Heph sat silently beside me.

"You're right. It's pulling me. I try harder, it pulls harder," I said. "How the hell am I going to do this? Damn it." I stood up and so did he. I paced back and forth, thinking.

"It may be trying to hold you, but there's more to it than that. You're holding back."

"Fuck off. I am not," I muttered.

"Fuck off, yourself, your majesty. I felt you destroy a Fury and some Guardians, then watched you imprison two powerful immortals. I've seen what you can do, and I'm fuckin' telling you you're holding back now."

I tried to ignore him.

"Maybe you don't want to go back so bad. Maybe he's not worth it to you."

I glared at him. "You want to join Ares, Heph?"

"Don't make threats we both know you won't keep. It's beneath you," he said.

"I don't like immortals. That includes you."

"And yourself?"

I glanced at him, then looked back toward the wall. "You talk too much."

"I don't even say a tenth of what I'm thinking," he muttered.

"Good."

"This killed you when you destroyed it, right? That's how you ended up stuck here."

I nodded.

"Okay. Well could be you're not giving it your all because you're scared of dying again."

"Obviously, I'm scared of dying again. Doesn't mean I'm not giving it everything I can," I said.

"Why are you afraid of dying? You know damn well you'll come back again," he said, watching me. I just shook my head. He pressed on. "You know that's nonsensical, yeah?"

I kept staring at the wall. "I'm weak when I resurrect," I finally said.

He was quiet for a few moments, and I could feel his eyes on me. "Right," he said softly. Understanding. Anger, from him. A rare clear emotion.

"Angry at me or for me?" I asked him.

"For you. I hate it that Furies can do that, by the way," he said.

"Sorry."

"Not your fault. It's just really disconcerting to talk to someone and not be able to hide what you're feeling."

I almost told him he was harder to read than most, to reassure him. Ended up keeping it to myself. It was better if he thought I knew everything, every emotion he was trying to keep secret, every flash of anger or happiness.

"You know, Artemis and I would watch out for you. If you died again, she'd track you down. We'd watch over you until you were strong again."

"Or you'd be the next ones to keep me captive for one reason or another," I said softly. Then I glanced at him. "That's nothing personal. I don't trust any of you."

He watched me. "Okay. Understandable. What about your parents?"

I shrugged. "I really don't know my parents all that well."

"You have to trust someone."

"No. I don't."

We sat in silence after that, and, once it was clear the conversation was over, Hephaestus retreated to his usual place, farther away, and started scribbling in his notebook again.

I stopped sleeping. Didn't need it, and it only brought nightmares, anyway. I ate the food Hephaestus and Artemis pushed into my hands. Mostly, I sat and stared or paced back and forth in front of where I wanted to create the gateway. I'd tried over, and over, and over again. A few times, I felt close, like maybe the boundary between my world and the realm of the immortals was thinning, weakening. It could have been wishful thinking. But I had to believe that I was at least doing *something*.

My parents had come, usually separately, to check on me regularly. Tisiphone mostly gave me pep talks. This day was no different. I was pacing, and felt my mother's power signature nearby. I turned and waved at her as she neared.

"Mollis," she said in greeting, folding me into a strong hug. "Any progress?"

I shrugged. "I thought I felt it waver, but then my power broke on me. If I could just keep my focus longer..." I trailed off, shaking my head. "It feels like I'm so close sometimes."

"You'll do it. I know you will."

"I have the feeling you're one of the few who still believes I'll manage it."

"Well, I'm your mother and I know what you're made of. And since when do you care what the rest of them think?"

"I don't."

"Good. You're a Fury. It is not for them to judge you. You are not one of them, and they have no idea what it's like to be you."

I smiled a little. "Full of ourselves much?"

She smiled then. Real, unguarded smiles from my mother are a rare thing. My aunt Megaera smiled and laughed a lot, but my mom was always a lot more reserved. When she really, truly smiles, it's very easy to see the woman Hades damned the gods for.

"Of course. We're Furies."

I thought back to the discussion I'd had with

Hephaestus. "Hephaestus thinks I'm holding back because I'm afraid of dying."

"Is he right?"

"A little bit. I'm not afraid of dying. Not anymore. But I am afraid of being weak while I regenerate," I said, glancing away from her.

"And why are you ashamed of being afraid?" she asked me.

I shook my head. "Because I should be stronger than that."

"Says who? Considering the nightmares you've been through, the way your enemies have taken advantage of those periods of weakness, I think it's very smart to be concerned."

"If I die one of these times," I stopped shook my head. Couldn't even voice the things I wanted to ask, because they made me feel weak. But she knew anyway.

"Your father and I will find you. And we'll guard you until you're strong again. You know that, don't you?"

I didn't answer, and, after several long moments, she took my hands in hers, pulled me so I was facing her. When I finally looked up at her, she gave a small, sad smile. Love, sadness, pride radiated from her.

"You are not alone. I know you fear trusting anyone. But you cannot do everything yourself. Every once in a while, even the mighty need someone to lean on."

"And if we lean on the wrong person?"

She squeezed my hands. "Then we do what Furies do, and punish the hell out of them for their betrayal."

As she said the last few words, Hades strolled over to us.

"Who is betraying you?" he asked me.

"No one just now," I said, and he gave a small nod. Then he folded his arms and looked at the wall.

I relayed to him what I'd told Tisiphone about how it kept feeling like I was nearly there, and then I lost focus and it all fell apart.

"And it's usually something stupid, like Aphrodite gets really pissed off about something, or Artemis succeeds in a hunt and she's excited. It would be so much easier if..." I trailed off. "Fuck."

"I was going to talk to you about that. Aside from the difficulties you just mentioned, it's not healthy having all of us sharing soulspace with you. I've been watching you. You're more and more disoriented, especially when you don't have something to focus on. And Artemis said you wandered, forgetting your way back home last time you left this spot."

"Artemis has a big damn mouth," I muttered.

"She was right to tell me. None of them understand how it works--"

"So this was something only you could do?" I asked him, surprised. I don't know why I'd assumed all of the gods could do it.

"Yes. The two of us are the only ones. Being able to bind someone that way is very, very handy for someone who will be deciding the ultimate punishment for someone. It allows you to know not only their current thoughts, but their deepest, darkest fears. It makes punishment very efficient."

I nodded. I could see how that could come in handy.

"But I've never held more than a soul or two bonded to mine at a time. What you're doing, daughter, is going to damage you. And considering how long you've had the connections now, and how many you've bonded to you, there is a good chance some damage has already been done."

"And you didn't think to tell me this shit before I bonded all of them?" I asked him. Tisiphone was watching both of us, irritation and anger now radiating from her, for Hades.

"Would you have listened if I'd tried? You still don't trust me. You would have thought I was trying to betray you somehow, and you would have done it anyway. Yes?"

I nodded, admitting he had a point.

"Okay. Well, now you know."

"If I release them I won't know what they're up to."

"Welcome back to reality," Hades said, sweeping his arms open. "You can't know what everyone who is a threat to you is going to do. You've sacrificed your power for security. And if it comes down to one or a few of them betraying you, you may not have the power to fight back."

"Unless I break the bonds," I said.

"Right."

"The one fucking time I think ahead," I muttered, shaking my head.

"It was a good plan," Tisiphone said. "There are just too many. And you need to be able to focus."

"Damn it." I closed my eyes, focused on each of the bonds I'd made, first releasing those I trusted most: Megaera, Artemis, Hephaestus. Hades. Then the ones who seemed indifferent to me either way. Finally, I released Aphrodite, Hera, and Zeus.

"Oh, sweet silence," I murmured, and my mother gave a small laugh. My mind, which had been so crowded, noisy, and chaotic, felt like the place I'd worked so hard to make it earlier in my life. I'd honed my telepathy skills early on, shielding my psyche from the constant barrage of other people's thoughts so I could survive without losing my mind. Having the immortals sharing soulspace with me had reminded me too much of the early days after my telepathy had appeared. Thoughts, emotions would hit me out of nowhere, and I had been sure I was going crazy. It took work to separate the thoughts of others from my own thoughts, and only once I'd fully started to be able to recognize the thoughts of others for what they were, was I finally able to find some peace.

"Okay. Let's try this again. Please find me if I die," I said to my parents. Artemis and Hephaestus had joined us, and they nodded as well.

I faced the wall.

I closed my eyes. I gathered my power. It was so much easier now, without the never-ending yapping of the immortals.

And I went to work. This was it. I was going home.

I focused on my world. On what it felt like to be home. I pictured where I wanted the gateway to connect to. And as I worked, I felt the Nether pulling me, holding me back.

I ignored it. Focused harder. The same way I'd pictured the gateways before, and visualized filling them with a black, impenetrable stone, I pictured that wall thinning, just in one place.

Oh, god, I felt close. I started to feel a different type of energy, so different from the throbbing, pulsing energy of the Nether that it was very obvious that something was happening.

My head pounded. My heart raced. My body trembled under the amount of power I drew. My own power, plus that given to me by the Nether and the souls of my enemies.

It was happening.

And then I felt the Nether fighting harder.

There was a price!

And I paid it. You own part of me.

All of you. You belong to me, godling. Gave you life, made you strong. Mine. You swore it to me!

I am sorry. I did what it took to live again.

And I focused on ignoring the Nether, fighting against the way it tried to hold me. I felt the barrier between the worlds thinning.

I could practically smell the air in my backyard.

I was bleeding. Shaking. Exhausted.

The Nether screeched in protest through its bond with me. Fought back, harder and harder the closer I got.

Just a little more.

I clenched my teeth, let my power build higher. There. The barrier was breached. Now to make it permanent.

"It will be so," I groaned, and I felt my power snap. I heard a loud cheer, and then I slumped forward, only to be caught by a strong pair of arms.

"You did it, daughter of mine," Hades said as he lifted me into his arms.

"Finally. Put me down. I'm not an infant."

"You'll fall down like one if I set you down now. Just give yourself a moment," he said.

Then there was a cool hand on my forehead. "I told you you would do it," Tisiphone said, and pride washed over me, from her.

I smiled a little. Yes. I'd done it. I was going home. And I'd set the immortals free in my world, and I had no way of keeping them in line.

Later. I'd deal with it later.

I gave Hades a push, and he set me down on my feet. I took a moment to make sure I wouldn't actually fall over. I smiled as I inspected the gateway. The other immortals had rematerialized where we were, drawn by the sensation of energy from my realm flooding the area. They all stood around, waiting, looking at me expectantly.

I grinned, feeling lighter, more alive than I'd felt since I'd resurrected in the Nether. "Okay. Time to go." And I took my first step through the gateway and back into my world.

Home.

CHAPTER TWELVE

When I came out of the gateway, I was hit with both intense relief that I'd ended up right where I'd meant to (I was imagining coming out in the middle of someone's bedroom or something) and the fact that my connection to Brennan blared brighter, brought to full strength again by my return to my own world. The strength of it took my breath away, brought tears to my eyes.

I stood in my back yard, one of the few places in the entire world I'd ever felt much peace. It was evening, the sky just barely lighter in the west, stars bright above. My garage stood to the right, and the lawn was longish, but had been mowed recently enough that it still looked like someone lived there. The huge oak that shaded the main part of the yard stood tall and sturdy, its now-brown leaves making a crackly, wispy sound as the cool breeze blew through them. Red and yellow leaves littered the grass; the maple and birch tree in my yard were nearly bare.

So, autumn. It had been at least a year, then, since it had been October when I'd been pulled into the Nether.

The thought of a year passing in the lives of my friends and loved ones, a year in which they'd gone through god-knows-what, scared the hell out of me. Was everyone even still alive?

I couldn't feel my bond with Nain. What did that mean? I'd expected that to flare to life again now that we were both in the same realm again. I didn't want to think about what it might mean. If he was dead, his death was on my hands.

Again.

I turned around and looked at the immortals who had come through with me. My parents smiled, though I could sense tension in them, too. They weren't any happier than I was about the fact that the immortals would have free reign in my world now. And at least a few of them would be only too happy to pay me back for making them bow to me. I'd deal with it later.

I glanced at each of them. "Okay. You're here. Don't fuck up or I will come and find you. Bye." And with that, I kicked off, rose into the air with a few strong flaps of my wings. There was one person I wanted to see, and he definitely wasn't one of the immortals I'd spent too much time with. I focused on my connection to Brennan. He was somewhere to my south. Not tremendously far away, I didn't think.

My stomach twisted in anticipation. I was home. I'd see him again. I'd tell him about how he'd saved my life, kept me sane. As I flew, I looked down at my city. Parts of it were dark. I wondered if they'd always looked this dark from above, or if that was something caused by the war between the Aether and the Nether. It was quiet, and the evening air was cool against my skin. I looked around. I could see the Renaissance Center; the Fisher Building, glowing in the distance.

I grinned. If it were possible to hug a city, I would have been wrapping my arms around Detroit at that moment.

I was home.

I kept flying in the direction where I sensed Brennan. Not far now. As I neared where I felt him, I surveyed the area, and realized where I was, and where he would be.

I landed, and the deserted Packard Plant stood in front of me. Dark, dilapidated. A lonely place; haven for hipsters with cameras, site of one of my worst recurring nightmares. The place I'd killed Nain (or so I'd thought.) And the place where I'd lost my life trying to protect my home from the destruction the immortals would have wrought.

And the best thing in this world or any other stood inside. Confused, happy, nervous. I brought up the enchantment again to hide my wings. We'd deal with that little addition later.

I walked through the gaping entrance into the plant. He stood not even thirty feet away, near the spot where the old gateway used to be. He looked... wow. He looked better than anything had in what had felt like an eternity. Same blond hair and beard, same slate-blue eyes. Well-worn jeans, flannel shirt over a white t-shirt. And he was staring at me.

"Tell me this is real," he said, his voice low, hoarse, full of emotion.

I stopped walking, unable to trust my wobbly legs anymore. The power I'd expended at the gateway, my flight, and now seeing him was more than I could handle.

"Hey," I said, and I felt tears spring to my eyes. For once, I didn't care. "What are you doing here?"

He took a few steps toward me, stopped. He stared at me like he was sure I would disappear. "Waiting for you. I come here every once in a while, figuring that you left this way, and you'd be back here someday."

I could barely breathe. The love, and need, and happiness washing over me, from him, was overwhelming in every way. There were other things, too. Anger. Guilt. Sadness. Anxiety.

"Brennan," I whispered, and that was when he closed the last few steps between us and pulled me into his arms. His embrace threatened to suffocate me, and I didn't even care. It wasn't close enough. I put my arms around his waist, rested my face against his chest. And then I did something I never do.

I let myself cry. He held me tight, and I could feel his heart pounding, feel his chest hitch once or twice as he struggled with his own feelings. We stood, and he let me cry without murmuring all of the usual "it's okay, you'll be all rights," because he knew better than anyone that it wasn't okay and I wouldn't be all right. But I was home, and I was with him, and it was enough. He just stood, and held me tight, and I felt his love wash over me. Once I felt spent, I took a few deep breaths, forcing myself to calm down.

"It's really you," he said, and I pulled away, wiping my eyes.

"Yeah. I'm so sorry, babe."

He stared at me. "You're sorry?" he asked in disbelief, his voice still hoarse. "For what?"

"They had you. And I couldn't save you and they hurt you and--"

"No. No way. You don't have a single damn thing to apologize for," he said, cupping my face between his hands. "I've been dreaming of this moment for so long. Every moment since you've been gone." His gaze bored into mine, and then his lips met mine, and it was everything I'd remembered: warm and demanding, soft and insistent, all at the same time. I nibbled his lower lip gently as he kissed me, and he groaned, and I felt him smile against my mouth.

His hands were in my hair, holding me close, and I clung to him as we devoured each other. "I am never," one soft kiss, "letting you," another soft kiss, "out of my sight," slightly harder kiss, "again," he said, and he followed it up with a hard, hungry kiss that left me leaning against him for support, clinging to him.

When we finally came up for air, I pulled back slowly, reluctantly, and looked up at him. He had that near-crazed, hungry look in his eyes that he got sometimes when we were together, and I knew it was mirrored in my own.

"How long was I gone?" I asked him, not sure I wanted to hear.

He folded me into his arms again, rested his forehead against mine. "A little over three years," he said after a few moments.

I tried to pull away, and he held me tight. "Three *years?*" I asked him.

"Yeah."

"I... oh, shit."

"Yeah."

I stared at him, trying to wrap my mind around that. Thee years.

"How is everyone? Are they all still alive?"

"Yeah, they're alive. They're all around. There have been so many changes since we lost you, Molly," he said, and I sensed anxiety in him again.

Oh.

"Have we changed, Bren?" I asked, afraid of what I'd hear.

He reached out and took my hand, pressed it to his chest, right over his heart. "Not as far as I'm concerned. There's so much I need to tell you."

I stayed like that, my hand clasped in his. His answer made me nervous for some reason. I didn't want to deal with it right that second. I just wanted the bit of happiness I'd fought so hard for to stay as perfect as it was. I let it go.

"Okay. What about everyone else?"

"We've had some issues," he said, and he pulled me toward the exit.

"Of course," I said.

"The most pressing of which is that right now, Nain and Chief Jones are being held in the Wayne County Jail."

I looked up at him. "What?"

"Remember that underling of the Chief's? The one who was hell-bent on proving that supernaturals exist?"

I nodded. Chief Jones had officially declared the question of supernaturals closed after Nain's death and all of the enemies I'd killed in its wake. Mostly because Jones was one of us. But he had a few guys on the force who didn't quite buy it, and one in particular who had made it kind of his life's work to prove the existence of supers.

"Okay." He held my hand as we walked around to the opposite end of the plant site. "Well, after we lost you, shit got crazy. We had storms, and sicknesses, and rioting. We didn't have power here for months. And in all of the chaos, a few dumbass supernaturals decided to flaunt what they were. And that gave Jones' guy all the incentive he needed. Nain and Jones and I did a decent job of shutting down any issues that came up, so the guy was just kind of frustrated at every turn. He couldn't prove anything. And then a few weeks ago, he called the chief for back-up, saying that there was this big fight going down near Six Mile. And Nain was with the chief at the time on patrol, so he went with him. And when they got there, they were ambushed by the guy and a few of his buddies."

"They could have gotten away, if they'd used their powers," I said.

"Right. Except that they would have given him all the proof he needed. So they didn't do that. But they're still being held."

"How long?"

"Almost a month."

"Crap," I sighed. "No one's been in to see them?"

He shook his head. "We can't get in. They're in solitary."

"Have they called in anyone else? Feds or anything like that?"

"No. I don't think he knows what to do with them. He can't prove a damn thing, and you know Jones and Nain are too smart to prove him right."

"Right. Have you guys tried breaking them out?"

"We don't really have the firepower for that. Not without outing ourselves."

I nodded, a plan forming as we walked. We came around the far corner of the plant, and I stopped short. My car, my beautiful jet-black, gleaming 1970 Barracuda, was sitting there, imps standing beside it. I glanced up at Brennan, who looked a little embarrassed.

"Sorry," he said.

All right. So I had a reputation for being a little uptight about my car. Everyone has a vice. My car is mine.

"No, it's okay. What's mine is yours and all that. You didn't let anyone else drive him, did you?"

"Of course not," he said, pretending to be offended. I shook my head, and watched as Bash and Dahael, my top two imps, walked over to us. Bash had a huge grin on his wizened face, and Dahael blotted her eyes with her sleeve.

"Knew we felt you," Bash said, bowing to me and lifting a fist to his chest. Dahael was sobbing outright, head bowed. I crouched next to her, rested my elbows on my knees, my chin in my hands.

"Hey," I said to her, which only made her sob harder. She brought her fist to her chest.

"Made it back. Started to doubt you," she said as she wiped her face again.

"Well. You know how stubborn I can be," I said softly, and she laughed a little, though her slim shoulders still hitched with the occasional sob. "It was a hard road back."

She nodded. "Bad times."

"Yeah."

She did something then that she'd never done. Dahael took my face in both hands, looked into my eyes. "Be merciful, Mistress. Be good."

My stomach plummeted. "About what?"

She looked down. "You'll know. Remember the good in you. No matter how bad. No matter how angry. Be better."

Then she released my face, and stepped back, next to Bash. I stood, shaken by her words, by the anxiety I felt from Brennan. I turned to glance at him and he looked away.

"Ready to head to the loft?" he asked. "They'll be excited to see you, too."

I watched him another moment as he walked to the driver's side and opened the door for me. Then I walked toward him, and he pressed my keys into my hand. And before I could slip into the car, he put his arms around me again and kissed me breathless, desperately. There was an urgency, stress flowing from him that put me on edge, even as I kissed him back.

It was over all too soon. He released me, squeezing my waist gently before he walked to his side of the car and climbed in. I settled myself into the driver's seat and pulled out of the gravelly lot.

Despite how freaked out I was, the smell of old leather, the sound of the Barracuda's engine rumbling, the feel of the smooth steering wheel under my palms felt like home, and I couldn't help but smile again.

We drove, and it took all my focus to keep my eyes on the road instead of staring out the windows at the passing landscape. Streets I'd walked a hundred times, buildings I'd seen my entire life. Every bit of it was precious to me now in a way it never had been before. I was a jumble of nerves and emotions, and there was an underlying anger that I guessed had to do with what I'd just been through in the Nether. I shook it off, tried to focus on things that mattered.

"So, tell me more. How about Ada and Stone? Shanti? Levitt?"

I sensed relief from Brennan. He relaxed back into the passenger seat. "Ada and Stone are still together, inseparable as ever, really. They've been arguing a little lately. I think everyone could use a break."

I smiled. "They're so damn cute together."

He laughed. "Yeah. Levitt is still living at the loft. He's still out there, tracking down your lost girls and lost boys."

"He's been good this whole time?"

"Hell, yeah. Those first few months, we barely slept. Everything was crazy. Levitt was a huge help, and he's kept it up since. He was a great addition to the team, Molly. Even Nain likes him."

I shook my head. "Yeah, that's saying something. Two demons in the same place?"

"Right. Usually a recipe for endless pissing contests," he said, laughing. Then he sobered, glanced at me. "Shanti moved out."

I took a deep breath, preparing myself for the worst. "How come?"

"Remember how I told you things were really different now, with the supernaturals?"

I nodded, turned a corner onto Warren.

"One of the big changes has been the vampires. Most of the country was already organized into districts, with a vampire king or queen at the top. They kept their vamps in line, punished those who made things messy for the rest of them."

"Right. We didn't have that. Ours were all on their own, which was stupid," I said.

"Not anymore. This region finally has a vampire queen. And she's tough. Terrifying, actually. She keeps the vamps on a short leash. We've had a lot less bullshit since she came into power."

"That's good news." The vampires always were a pain in the ass. I'd be happy to not deal with them all the time.

"Yeah. It's helped us out a lot. Shanti decided to join her. She's actually one of the queen's top enforcers."

"What does that mean?"

"It means that when a vampire breaks their laws, causes trouble, Shanti gets to go and hunt their ass down and end the problem."

I smiled. "She is freaking perfect for that." Shanti had been turned against her will when she was sixteen. She had a definite issue with rogue vampires.

"She is really good at her job. Once you're settled, we'll have to pay her a visit. And introduce you to queen Rayna, too. I think you'll like her."

I nodded. Okay. So, nothing terrible yet. I'd have to get Nain and Jones free. It didn't explain the warnings Dahael had given me, or the nervousness that came from Brennan the longer we were in the car together.

"You died," he said suddenly. "Many, many times."

I took my eyes off the road to look at him. "You could feel that?"

He took a deep breath. "I felt that. Every time. And the pain you were in beforehand. Muted, because of how far you were. But yeah, I felt it. Every time you died, I was sure I'd lose my mind before I felt you come back again."

"How long ago was it?"

He looked at me in confusion.

"Time passes differently there," I reminded him. "It only feels like I've been gone a few weeks, a few months, tops. When you said it was nearly three years..." I shook my head. "Shit."

He was watching me again." It was about six months ago, the last time you died."

"And how long ago, the first time?"

"A little over a year ago."

I nodded. It was hard to wrap my mind around how much time had passed. How much time I'd spent dead and resurrecting.

"Molly. What happened?"

I glanced over at him, looked back at the road. I turned another corner, onto Woodward. Nain's building was just ahead. I shook my head. "I can't."

"You'll tell me someday, though," he said, a question in his voice. He rested his hand on my thigh, and just that touch was enough to send shivers through my body.

"I will someday. When I think I won't lose my mind," I said softly. He squeezed my leg gently, left his hand resting there as I turned into the parking garage.

I put the car into park, and Brennan and I walked toward the elevator. He pulled the metal gate down and hit the button to take us up to the loft's living area. I looked up at him, and he stepped closer to me, backed me into one of the corners of the elevator. I felt the cold metal of the wall against my arms, his warm body pressing against mine. The look in his eyes, anger, need, sorrow, made it nearly impossible for me to breathe. And then he claimed my mouth with his, and rational thought was impossible. I reached up and tangled my fingers into his hair, brought him closer, always closer, and he groaned against my mouth.

"I love you, Molly," he growled against my lips. "Always have. Always will. Please remember that."

The plea in his voice made my stomach turn. He kissed me again, then pulled back, and I let him go. I held his gaze.

"Do you feel them?" he asked me.

I sensed, felt for the other beings in the loft. Ada. Stone. Levitt. Another presence I couldn't identify. The first three were confused.

"They don't know what to think," I said, smiling a little. My stomach was still clenched, mostly because of the anxiety rolling off of Brennan. "Is there something you want to tell me, babe?"

He looked away. The elevator stopped, and he pulled the gate open. Then he waved me toward the door.

I opened it, and Ada and Stone were standing there. They'd been heading to the door. Levitt stood about ten feet behind them, a huge grin on his face.

I barely registered them, happy as I was to see them.

My attention was on the bundle in Ada's arms.

The fourth presence I hadn't been able to identify. I could now.

Shifter.

Blond hair. Blue eyes. The same slate-blue as his father's eyes actually. I could feel my mate in him as clearly as I'd ever felt anything.

Brennan's son.

CHAPTER THIRTEEN

I stared at the baby. Tiny. He was strong. I could feel that already.

Of course he was. He was his father's son after all. Guess Artemis had her next-in-line.

"Molly, baby girl!" Ada said, settling the baby into Brennan's arms. Then she folded me into a huge hug, and I hugged her back, numbly.

Oh fuck. I could barely breathe.

All of the guilt.

The anxiety.

"Be merciful," Dahael's voice came back to me.

Stone crushed me in a big bear hug next, and I tried to focus on he and Ada, both of whom were crying and telling me how happy they were to see me, asking a million questions I couldn't answer, even if my heart hadn't just been ripped out of my body.

I felt my power rising in response to my anger, my pain. And it hurt. The rise in power made me physically ill. It felt like knives stabbing every tender organ of my body.

I took deep breaths, trying to maintain my composure, keep my face neutral.

I couldn't do this.

Levitt came to me then, bowed, then shook my hand, grinning. The imps were with us, and I could see Dahael watching me closely.

They were all talking. I had no idea what they were saying. I couldn't take my eyes off of Brennan and his son.

At some point, everyone else seemed to pick up on my silence. Ada and Stone excused themselves after another hug each, and Levitt left to hunt. Brennan and I stood in the dining room, about ten feet apart.

"Well. At least you weren't lonely, huh?" I asked, barely trusting my voice.

"Molly... I screwed up. Once. One time."

"Who?"

He met my eyes. "A witch I rescued one night."

I felt a growl rising in my throat. To his credit, he didn't respond. He kept his eyes on me. "It was one time. One night stand. It happened when I was feeling low and sorry for myself. I was starting to believe I'd lost you for good and you weren't coming back. The second it was over, I wanted to die. I never, ever wanted to hurt you."

"You were feeling low?" I asked him, and I knew there was a threat in my voice. Right then, I didn't care. "Was this before or after I started dying over and over again?"

"Before. A few weeks before. And then you died that first time, and I thought the universe or whatever the hell it is was paying me back for being a fucking idiot. And then you kept dying," he shook his head.

"So why is he here? Why isn't he with her?"

"The idea of raising an 'animal' disgusted her. Screwing one was one thing, but raising one was something else. She never even held him after he was born. The midwife handed him to me, and that was it."

I didn't respond.

I looked at the baby. He was fussing in Brennan's arms,

as he had been in Ada's arms when we'd walked in. Brennan caught me watching the baby. "He's kind of fussy. I think that's common with shifter kids. Nain said I was always hyper, too. Too much energy," he said.

"What's his name?" I asked.

"Sean. I named him after my dad."

I stepped forward and held my arms out. I don't know why.

Brennan watched me. Stayed still.

"I'm not going to hurt him, Brennan," I said, meeting his eyes.

"I know."

I held my arms out again, and he settled the baby into them. I looked away from Brennan, then walked into the living room, carefully carrying the little bundle of pain.

I settled onto the sofa, then I looked down at Brennan's son.

I understood my stepmother better than I'd ever expected to in that moment. Part of me wanted him to disappear. This child was living, breathing evidence that Brennan had screwed around on me, that what we had maybe wasn't quite as perfect as I'd believed.

And yet, he wasn't. He was a person. A powerful being who never asked to be born into the situation he'd been born into.

I could relate.

As I sat looking at him, Sean settled down, big blue eyes staring up at me.

"It's the eyes. Freaky, huh?" I murmured to him. I leaned my head down closer to his face, then pulled back. His eyes widened, and I did it again. And then he smiled and he had his father's dimples.

It was like a stab to the heart.

Brennan settled onto the sofa next to me. Wisely, he did not touch me. I looked up at Dahael, who was watching me from across the coffee table.

"Did you honestly think I was monster enough to hurt him?"

"Been through things, Mistress," she said apologetically. "Not the same."

I looked back down at the baby, who was still staring up at my glowing eyes. "No. I'm not the same. But I'll never be a monster, no matter how much it hurts."

"Molly--" Brennan began.

"Do not talk to me. Not right now," I said. "He's hungry, by the way," I told Brennan, and, after a moment, he got up and headed to the kitchen.

"We'll be okay, kid. You and me. I'm not gonna go all evil stepmother on you. I promise."

Sean gurgled, and smiled, and I shook my head.

Brennan came back with a bottle, and Ada and Stone came back from downstairs. I handed the baby to Brennan.

"Okay. I'll be right back," I said, standing up.

Brennan reached out, still holding the baby in his other arm. He grabbed my wrist gently. "Where are you going?"

"We have two team members being held captive. Time to get them out."

"I'm going with you," he said.

I shook my head. "I don't need you."

I felt anger from him. At himself, more than me. And a little pain. Maybe I'd wanted that.

Okay. There was no maybe about it. I wanted to hurt him. A lot.

I think he saw it in my eyes. He still didn't let go of me. "How? You can't just march in there and bust them out."

I pulled my wrist out of his grip. "Watch me."

And then I focused on the Wayne County Jail. I'd been there once, mostly because I was curious about what it was like, early on in my crime fighting career. I'd had so many thugs thrown in there. I wanted to know where they were going.

I closed my eyes, and the next thing I knew, I was

standing in the ladies' room on the first floor of the prison. There was a reception area, and this restroom was in that.

Shit, my head ached. The pain was back, tenfold. Okay. So using my powers was a whole different experience now that I was back.

I did my best to ignore it. *Nain,* I thought as loud as I could.

Molls. What the fuck are you doing here?

I smiled to myself. *Getting your ass out. What cell are you in? And where's Jones?*

I'm on 10. Last cell on the west block. He's in the cell to the right of mine.

Right. I'm getting him out first, then you. Are you alone?

Yeah.

I left the bathroom. There was a guard not too far away, and I made my way into his mind, trying to get a picture of the tenth level. I'd never tried it this way, but it was the best I could do, and I just had to hope I didn't screw it up completely. I rifled through the guard's thoughts, and, there it was: he knew the tenth floor well. I used the memories in his head, visualized where I wanted to go. I closed my eyes and focused, felt myself pulled elsewhere. When I opened my eyes, I was in the corridor on the tenth level. I walked toward the end of the block, keeping an eye out for guards. One came around the corner, and I broke into his mind, made him walk the other way, forgetting all about me.

Fuck, it *hurt.*

I could see their cells, feel both men's power signatures clearly. I looked through the small window in the door of the first cell. Jones was sitting on the cot, and after I had an idea of the room, I rematerialized inside.

Jones jumped up off the bed in surprise.

"Hey chief. Ready to go?"

"Hell yeah," he said, staring at me. "How?"

"Take my hand. Don't let go. This might be uncomfortable." And then I focused on the loft. When we

160

appeared in the dining room, I heard Ada gasp. Stone cursed in surprise and the coffee cup he'd been holding crashed to the floor. Brennan was standing nearby in the kitchen. I met his eyes once, then winked out again, back to the prison. This time I was right outside of Nain's cell, then I focused again and rematerialized inside.

My nose and ears were bleeding. I felt like my body was about to fall apart. My head pounded. I wanted to puke, and I felt like I was about to lose control of most of my bodily functions. I stumbled, and Nain leapt forward, caught me.

"Hey, baby," he said in his deep voice, cool hands on my upper arms. I shook my head, swiped at my nose. "Molls," he said, looking me over.

"I'm all right. One more time," I said. I put my hand in his and focused hard. I could hear chaos out in the corridors. They'd discovered that something was going on.

"You got enough in you to scramble their brains?" he asked, and I shook my head.

"Not if I want to get us out of here," I said. "Just a sec." I gritted my teeth. Someone shouted outside the door. I pictured the loft, held Nain's hand tighter. His ever-present rage was making itself useful again, feeding me. I focused harder, ignored the pain. And then I felt us fall apart just as the noise in the corridor started getting louder.

When we ended up in the loft, shouts of joy, applause greeted us. I let go of Nain and barely made it into the little powder room on the first floor before I lost everything in my gut. I puked, and blood streamed from my nose, my ears. My fingernails bled. It was torture, and it didn't seem to be ending. I stayed hunched over the toilet, unable to stop retching.

I felt a warm hand on my back, rubbing, soothing. Eventually, I stopped puking, and I started to stand. Brennan helped me, strong hands on my shoulders. I caught sight of myself in the bathroom mirror.

Blood leaked from the corners of my eyes. I shook my head. I could barely even move well enough to turn on the water. Brennan knew. His hands shook as he moistened a wash cloth and brought it to my face, started wiping gently at the blood leaking from my nose and eyes.

"Can you feel this?" I whispered. He gave a terse nod. His breathing was elevated. His body shook, the effects of my pain hitting him.

He worked anyway, holding me up with one arm while he used the other hand to wipe the wash cloth across my eyes, my mouth, my nose. Then he stood me against the wall so I leaned against it for support, and he rinsed the washcloth, then wrapped it around my still-bleeding hands.

I didn't want to cry. Hated the weakness inside. I bit my lip against the pain, both the physical and the emotional.

Brennan was taking shallow, uneven breaths. I felt regret, sadness, anger from him. He removed the washcloth from my hands. They'd started healing, the blood no longer collecting at the beds of my fingernails. Once he'd made sure I wasn't bleeding, he tossed the washcloth into the hamper and looked at me, his gaze meeting mine.

"I'm tired, Bren," I said, and it hurt to talk. I fought back tears again, and he pulled me into his arms. Then he picked me up and carried me up the stairs.

"Let me take care of you tonight. You can hate me tomorrow," he said as he carried me. We got into his room, and he kicked the door closed behind us. Then he laid me down on the bed and gently pulled off my shoes and socks, then my pants. I moved over so he could climb in beside me, and after stripping down to his boxers, he climbed in next to me and pulled me into his arms. I buried my face against his chest, put my arms around him. I fell asleep held tightly in his arms, just as I'd been dreaming about for what felt like an eternity, and I was too tired and in too much pain to care about anything else.

◆ ◆ ◆

When I woke up, bright morning sunlight was shining through the windows, and I could see the clear, blue autumn sky from my spot in bed. I could smell Brennan all around me, though I was in the bed alone. His scent was comforting and a punch to the gut all at the same time. I turned onto my side, buried my face in his pillow. I could feel him. I knew he still loved me, maybe more than he ever had. And I knew I loved him.

I didn't know what to think about anything else. Yeah, I was pissed that he'd been unfaithful. But is it really unfaithful if he'd started to give up hope of me ever coming back? And he had given up hope; I got that from him, very clearly.

Was I making excuses for him now?

Really, it's not like I had any room to judge. Brennan and I were together less than a year after Nain had died.

Except that I'd been sure my husband was dead. Brennan had known I was still alive.

I took deep breaths. I didn't have to make any decisions right away. I had too much to do. My body still ached from when I'd used my powers the night before, and my head still throbbed. If this was going to happen every damn time I used my powers, this was going to be a problem.

I was trying to figure out how to avoid pain (what a joke, right?) when the bedroom door opened. I knew it was Brennan before he stepped into the room. Our bond made it so I was constantly aware of his presence. I sat up as he walked in and closed the bedroom door behind him. He wore a gray Detroit Tigers t-shirt and jeans, and he had a cup in his hands.

I couldn't help it. I smiled.

Coffee.

He laughed a little and handed it to me, then he sat on the edge of the bed. I took my first sip of the perfect, bitter, creamy, hot perfection, and shivers went up my spine. Brennan was watching me, eyes on my face, and I met his gaze despite myself.

We didn't talk. I drank my coffee. It kind of reminded me of the weeks after Nain had died, the way he and I would just sit together in silence, comforted by each other's company.

"So, how old is Sean?" I asked. I set the now-empty coffee cup on the nightstand and folded my hands in my lap. He reached over and took one of my hands gently in his. He ran his thumb over my palm, and an involuntary shiver went up my spine again, and this time it had nothing to do with a caffeine fix. The thought of pulling away didn't even enter my mind. As angry as I was at him, I'd waited forever to be close to him again.

"He's a little over four months old," he said softly.

"He looks just like you."

He nodded. "That's what I keep hearing. You know what I wish?"

I didn't answer.

"I wish he looked like you. I wish he was yours. I wish I hadn't fucked up so bad. I can't regret him being here, because he's my son and other than you, I've never loved anyone so completely in my life."

"You shouldn't regret him being here," I said. "And I wish he was mine, too. But he's not, and I'm not sure what that means for us."

He sat in silence for a bit, thumb still tracing the long line that ran across my palm. "I hope it means that we can try again. I don't have any right to ask that of you. But I belong to you until the day I die, and that's not going to change."

"Did you have any feelings for her?"

"No." Not a single instant of hesitation. And I could feel that he was telling the truth. "If I hadn't have been weak and stupid, nothing ever would have happened. I knew it was wrong. I knew I should have gone home that night. I was pissed off and feeling sorry for myself, and I was starting to believe you'd never be back." He paused, shook his head. "I'm not making excuses for this. It doesn't matter what I was feeling or thinking. All that matters is that I screwed up, and I'm sorry. You're the best thing that ever happened to me, and if I lose you now--"

"Shut up," I said. His eyes had been on mine the entire time, my hand clasped in his. The guilt and sadness coming from him told me better than words how sorry he was. How afraid he was of losing me. "I love you. I am so angry and hurt right now. And I don't know if things will ever be the same between us. There's really no way they can be." In fact, the anger part of it was threatening to overtake everything else at that moment, rising up suddenly. It was venomous. Part of me wanted to hurt him, and not just physically. It was so out of character for me that it scared me. I forced it down, tried to stay in control, calm.

He nodded, and I sensed crushing sadness from him.

"We're going to take things slow. We're going to see how things are now. I love you, Brennan. Maybe I shouldn't. But I don't have a whole lot of room to judge you, considering how we got together. Maybe karma's a bigger bitch than I realized, and I had this coming."

"Molly..."

I shook my head, stopping him. "I think you should break your bond to me."

He went absolutely still, stared at me. "No."

"Not because of any of that," I said, waving it off. "For whatever reason, I'm in agony whenever I use my powers now. And I'm going to try not to use them until I figure out what the hell is going on, but there's no guarantee I won't have to. I don't want you in pain every time I use them."

He shook his head. "I'd rather know if you're in pain."

"You felt how bad it can be, last night," I said. "And

you're going to be holding your son at times, and I don't want to put you in agony and hurt him by mistake if you drop him or something. You, I'm kind of okay with hurting just now. But I'd feel terrible if it ended up affecting him."

"No," he said after a while. "I can feel the pain coming on. There's enough warning. I'm not breaking my bond to you."

I let out an exasperated breath and tried to pull my hand out of his, and he just held it tighter. Then he pulled me toward him. "Stop being a stubborn ass," I said as he leaned toward me. "And do not even think of kissing me."

"Too late," he said, and his lips claimed mine. Before long, his hands were tangled in my hair, and I wasn't sure if I was pushing him away or trying to pull him closer. I felt him open his mind to me as he kissed me, which was something he'd never done before.

I love you, he thought at me. *I will spend the rest of my life proving that to you, if you'll let me.*

I knew he loved me. And I knew I loved him. What I didn't know was how to deal with the sense of betrayal that had lodged its way into my heart, the anger that I felt every time I even thought about him.

When he pulled away, I let him.

We sat, watching each other. I could feel it from him, how much more he wanted. How hard it was for him to hold himself back, stop touching me when he did.

Maybe it was a good time to distract him. I wasn't ready for anything else just yet, and I had a few things I needed to tell him.

"I think there's a reason our connection never died, even though Nain's and mine did," I said.

"We love each that other more?" he said, raising his eyebrow at me, and I shook my head.

"That would be very fairy tale, wouldn't it? But that's not why. And your son is going to be insanely powerful, like you."

He just watched me.

"Which one of your parents could shift into any animal form?" I asked him.

"My mom."

"And her favorite was the huge black cat too, I bet?" I asked.

He nodded.

I watched him, wondering how he'd take what I told him next. His experiences with beings from the realm of the immortals hadn't exactly been pretty. "When I came to in the Nether after I resurrected there, I made my way to a cave to regain my strength. Once, when I woke up, there was a huge black cat guarding me. It brought me clothes and food. The first time I saw it, I thought it was you. Its power signature even felt similar." And then I told him about Artemis, and about his ancestry, and about how the first child of those gifted with Artemis' powers would have them as well. I told him about how excited Artemis was to meet him, about how excited she'd been at the prospect of actually getting to know the next generation of her family. And when I was done, he just sat, staring at me. "So I think that a lot of our bond's strength comes from the fact that we're both descended from the immortals," I said. "There's a little something extra there."

"So you're saying I'll live a long time," he said.

"Unless someone kills you, yeah. Your natural lifespan, and your son's, too, will be very long. Artemis said it's not uncommon for her heirs to live a thousand years or more. So there are a few of you around."

"That's crazy," he finally said.

"It explains why you're so much stronger than other shifters we know."

"It doesn't explain our bond, though," he said. "That has nothing to do whether we're descended from immortals or not."

"You don't think so?" I asked, and he took my hand again.

"Maybe it explains why it didn't die. I can buy that. But you and me have never been easy. There's always some reason we can't just be together and happy. We seem to have to fight for every peaceful, happy moment of our life together. And some of that is my fault, and not just what happened while you were gone, but some of the dumb things I did early on. Even with all that, I think we're worth fighting for. Don't you?"

I met his gaze, gave a small nod. "We are. I just need time."

"Well, apparently I have a lot of that. I'll give you whatever you need." And then he brought my hand to his lips, and he pressed a lingering kiss to the inside of my wrist, and I swore it sent fire through my veins. My entire body warmed at that simple touch, and when he pulled back and released my hand, his eyes had that mischievous sparkle that had always made my heart race. He knew everything he did to me, and I knew what I did to him.

I wanted to hit him. I wanted to pull him down onto the bed, rip his clothes off and ride him hard. I wanted to scream at him and I wanted to kiss him senseless. And part of me, something lodged deep inside, wanted to see him bleed, and that terrified me. Was I really like that? Cruel? My love for him and the anger that had risen toward him since I'd been back battled, each trying to assert dominance in my emotions.

And so, for maybe the first time in my life, I did the smart thing.

I did nothing.

He got up a few seconds later, and I watched him walk out of the bedroom and close the door behind him.

"Yeah. That's a mess I don't need right now," I said to the empty room. I rubbed my hands together. I'd naively thought that being back in my own world would help me forget the sensation of grime and blood coating my body. You'd really think I would know better by now. I got out of bed and rifled through Brennan's dresser. I didn't know how to feel about the fact that my clothes were still there, just the way I'd left them. I don't know why I expected different. Did I expect to find some other woman's bra on my side of the underwear drawer?

Maybe I did. Maybe I should have.

I didn't even know how I was supposed to feel, and I hate that. I hate ambiguity. Tell me what to punch, and I'll punch it. Point me toward the bad guy, and I'll destroy him. This emotional shit made me want to gouge my eyes out.

I stepped under the jet of scalding hot water, did my crazy scrubbing thing, knowing how nuts it was but still not able to stop doing it. By the time I was done, my skin was raw and red and I didn't feel any cleaner. I dressed (stepping into my favorite pair of jeans was another kind of homecoming, and this one made me grin), dried my hair, and even went as far as putting on some lip gloss and mascara.

Look at me, looking all human and shit.

I grabbed my empty coffee cup off of the nightstand and headed downstairs. Eunomia gave a loud shout and flew at me, practically knocking me on my ass as she wrapped her thin arms around me. I stumbled back against the wall under the force of her embrace.

"I am so happy to see you, my friend," she said as she hugged me. I hugged her back and laughed.

"Same here. Where were you last night?"

She pulled back and looked at me, grinning. "I felt the gateway, so I flew there. Your parents were still there, and they told me you'd departed. It was a relief to feel access to the Nether again. My power has been badly depleted since it closed," a shadow crossed her face, for just a fraction of a second, and then disappeared, and she grinned at me again.

I hadn't even thought of that. "I'm sorry," I said.

She shook her head, still smiling. "Are you kidding? You saved countless lives, and you suffered for it, from what Brennan went through while you were gone." And then her face fell as she realized what she'd said. "Oh. I..."

I gave a tiny shake of my head. "It's okay," I said quietly. "We'll work it out."

She smiled then. "Good. You should." And then I sensed something from her: guilt.

"And what do you have to feel guilty about, my friend?" I asked her softly. I was aware of Brennan and Nain standing in the kitchen, Stone, Levitt, and Ada in the living room. Eunomia's eyes met mine.

"I... that's to say... your ex-husband--" she said quietly, and I had to laugh at how flustered she was. I was surprised, but not in a bad way.

"You and the devil, huh?" I asked her, laughing, and she smacked my arm.

"It was really more of a physical thing."

"Well. He's very good, physically speaking," I said, trying to keep my voice serious, and she blushed bright red and shoved me gently, which only made me laugh harder. Soon we were both laughing, supporting each other as we wiped tears from our eyes. She gathered me into another fierce hug.

"You were missed, Mollis," she said softly, and I hugged her back.

"Thanks. And thank you for rescuing Brennan. I owe you."

"You owe me nothing. I am ashamed that my family forgot their purpose," she said, and shame radiated from her. I gave her another squeeze.

"You're amazing. Were you hurt?"

She shrugged, and we pulled away from each other. "Broken wing, a few cuts. I am healed."

I observed my friend. "You are." And she smiled at me again and we headed toward the kitchen. Brennan was standing at the counter, pouring a bottle for Sean, and I glanced at both of them as I headed for the coffee pot. I set my coffee cup down and held my hands out for the baby after watching Brennan fumble with the bottle for a few seconds. He handed Sean over with a murmured "thanks" and finished making the bottle. I handed the baby back, and Brennan took him, eyes on me. Then he leaned down and brushed his lips across mine. Avoiding his kiss didn't even cross my mind.

I was in the middle of my third cup of coffee when the buzzer sounded. Brennan pressed the intercom button to answer it.

"I'm looking for Mollis," a deep voice I immediately recognized said over the com. Hephaestus.

CHAPTER FOURTEEN

Brennan looked at me questioningly.

"Let him up," I said. He did, and a couple of minutes later, Hephaestus walked through the door. He barely acknowledged the other people in the loft, heading straight for me.

"Queenie. Hope this is okay," he said, and I nodded. "I just thought you might want to know what everyone is up to."

Ada, Stone, Levitt, Nain, and Brennan were all watching the new arrival with interest.

"I would, thanks."

"Okay. Your father, your mother, Persephone, and your aunt are working with Aphrodite and Artemis right now. Overnight, Zeus and I worked on fixing street lights. You know there were whole blocks in this city with no lights?"

"I know. The lighting system is outdated and they weren't able to get parts to fix them anymore."

"Yeah. So I made new parts. Fixed. People started coming out of their houses like they'd just experienced a fuckin' miracle or something," he said, shaking his head.

"Considering it's been years since some areas have had streetlights, it is a miracle," I said, smiling. "Thanks for doing that."

He waved it off. "So now Zeus and Hera went home. They said they did their part. The others decided to keep working. Hestia discovered a soup kitchen, and the line out the door made her mad. So, they went grocery shopping and right now they're handing out bags of food to anyone that wants them."

"Uh. That's great. How are they paying for the food, though?"

He smiled. "Aphrodite has credit cards. She always did get a kick out of shopping here."

"Oh. Good," I said, smiling. "So, no trouble?" I asked him.

He shook his head. "I don't trust Zeus and Hera. I'm going to be keeping an eye out for them. And though Apollo is Artemis' brother, I'm not sure his pride will allow him to accept what you did to him."

"I know."

My friends were all still watching us.

"One more thing," Heph said, and I nodded. "You mentioned the possibility of staying on here, maybe. I'd like to take you up on that."

"You want to live here?"

He nodded.

"What about Aphrodite?"

"What about her? We've been over this, yeah? She has her life, I have mine. And I think I could be of use here."

"It's not my decision to make. And I'm not sure," I paused, took a breath.

"You're not sure you can trust me. I know. I thought of that. If you want, take a piece of me again. Having one connection shouldn't be a problem, right?"

"I'm..." I was about to tell him about the trouble I was having, and decided against it. "Okay. If Nain decides to

173

let you stay, I'll do that. No offense."

He nodded. "None taken."

I turned my attention to my friends. "Guys, this is Hephaestus." Ada and Stone gaped at him. Eunomia grinned.

"How are you, you great lout?" she asked him, and he laughed.

"Happy to see you, for sure, Guardian," he said. "Glad you're well."

"Happy to see you are as well," Eunomia said.

I continued with the introductions, and soon they were all exchanging handshakes.

This guy okay, really, Molls? Nain asked in my mind.

He was a big help to me while I was trapped. Excellent weapon maker, crazy smart.

You trust him?

As far as I trust anyone, sure. It really is up to you.

I'll take him, then. Can't be a bad thing, having another immortal on our side.

I nodded, and then Nain and Heph went into Nain's office, talking on the way there. I was downing another cup of coffee when the buzzer sounded again, and Ada answered, remarking that the loft was like Grand Central all of a sudden. Soon, Chief Jones was walking through the door. His gaze found me, and a huge smile lit his face. He opened his arms and walked toward me.

Jones was a good-looking man, mid-forties, just a teeny bit of gray sprinkled through his black hair. Considering that the man was chief of the Detroit police, and also the leader of his shifter pack, he had a genuinely disarming smile. I was glad he was on our side.

"Molly," he said, and he folded me into a huge hug. "Thanks for getting me out, Angel."

"It was my pleasure. Are you all right?"

He nodded. "Sure am. I wanted to see you and thank you properly, then I'm going to head back home to my family."

"What about work?"

A shadow passed over his face. "The story they were telling was that I was off on family medical leave. I'm ready to go back. Stuff has probably gone to hell in my absence."

I nodded. "So they weren't making it a public thing that you were being held?"

"Hell no. They had no proof."

"What's the name of your underling? The one who's been investigating the supers?" I asked him.

"McGregor. Don McGregor."

"Okay. So McGregor has no proof of anything?"

"Definitely not. He's suspected for years, but we have always been able to throw him off. And then during the worst of the craziness, some supers started being more open about what they were. Nain and Brennan and I did a good job of mostly keeping that crap under wraps, but it was all McGregor needed to decide it was time to act. So he set a trap, because he'd always suspected me, and Nain was unlucky enough to get caught in it." As he spoke, Nain and Hephaestus came out of Nain's office, and they stood nearby, listening.

"You could have broken away from them," I said, watching Nain.

He nodded. "We both could have. But to do that, we would have had to become what they were accusing us of. We would have proved them right. It was either that, or kill them, and the Chief has this thing against killing if he can avoid it."

"Call me crazy," Jones said, rolling his eyes. "I know you all handle things the way you have to. The less I know about that, the better. But me: I'm sworn to protect and serve, even those who don't deserve it."

"So we sat in jail, thinking they'd just have to let us go eventually," Nain continued. "But then a couple of weeks passed, and the only one I ever heard from was McGregor, usually trying to piss me off enough to do something supernatural in his presence."

"Did he really think it would be that simple?" I asked, shaking my head.

"He's an idiot," Jones intoned.

"We can make him disappear," Nain said, crossing his arms over his chest.

"No. I'm his commanding officer. I have all kinds of ways of making his life hell," Jones said, and the smile on his face then was not the friendly one I was so fond of.

"Where can I find him?" I asked Jones as I set my coffee cup down on the counter.

Jones watched me. Studied me. "Why?"

I held my hands up. "I'm just going to have a little talk with him, that's all."

Hephaestus snorted. I glanced his way. "You have something to add?"

"I've seen you 'talk' to people, queenie."

"Yes, well. I'm just going to make sure he knows, in no uncertain terms, that there are no such things as supernaturals, and he's been a deluded asshole for believing otherwise."

Jones chuckled a little. "I can still make his life hell though, right?"

I nodded. "I think he has that coming to him."

"All right." Jones told me an address not too far from my house.

"Okay. I'm going to go take care of a few things," I said, stepping into my shoes and heading toward the door.

"I'm coming with you," Brennan said, and then I turned and met his eyes.

"No. You're not. I've got this, and I need some alone time right now," I told him. Then I headed out and down the elevator, imps trailing me, just like they always had.

Bash, Dahael, and I climbed into my Barracuda, and I turned the radio up, loud. It was on the classic rock station, just like I'd always had it, and Van Halen poured from the speakers. That would do. I had a whole bunch of rage on, and I needed someone to take it out on. I'd noticed, since being back, that not only did it hurt like hell to use my powers, but my emotions were all over the place. Part of that was the whole Brennan issue. But I'd stood there in the loft feeling like I wanted to hit something, for no reason in particular, and now I felt like I would destroy any unfortunate soul who happened to cross my path.

So I had issues. What else was new?

I went to the address Jones had given me. I sat in the car for a bit, pulling myself together, forcing control that I did not feel. I didn't want to kill him, just manipulate his mind. I'd gotten so accustomed to using my power at full-strength in the Nether. That, and using my power without constant pain.

When I felt as cold and steady as I could be, I got out of the car. My imps shadowed me, dashing behind shrubs and parked cars. I stalked up the front walk of a pretty brick colonial. The front lawn was a mosaic of orange, brown, and red leaves, and a blue and red Big Wheel sat near the porch. I lifted my hand and knocked. I'd worn my sunglasses, hiding my eyes from the Normals. Like so many things now that I was home, it felt weird to hide what I was.

A tall, thin man opened the door. He had the round, soft look of a man who had just about reached his retirement years, gray hair badly in need of a trim. "Captain McGregor?" I asked. He considered saying he was not, but I picked up right from his brain that he was the captain.

"There is some information I need to give you regarding your search for supernaturals," I said.

I felt anger, frustration roll off of him. Clearly, he'd heard that his prize captives had escaped. He didn't know how. One check, they were in their cells, the next, they were gone. Hazy description of a woman who'd been spotted in the corridors when it happened. Short woman, dark hair. Like this one.

"What do you want to tell me?" he asked, and his voice was sharp. Distrust, suspicion from him.

I gathered my power around me, gritting my teeth against the immediate pain. "You need to stop your ridiculous investigation into supernaturals. You will admit that you were on a wild goose chase, and it got the better of you. You will admit, when asked, by any colleagues you involved in this, that you abducted innocent men. You have found, through your research, that there are absolutely no such things as supernatural beings." My power built, and the air was practically snapping with energy around me. "It will be so."

I hadn't raised my voice above a whisper. I saw the look in his eyes when my power took hold; first, a confused, searching gaze, a shake of the head.

"I'm sorry. What were you saying?"

"I was asking if you've found any supernaturals? I'd love to interview you for this article I'm writing!" I said, playing to his vanity, trying to ensure everything had taken hold.

He glared at me. "Miss, everyone knows there's no such thing as supernaturals. What, do you write for one of those supermarket tabloids? Stop wasting my time!" And with that, the front door slammed in my face. I gave a nod.

He'd meant every word.

The imps and I got into the car, and we pulled away. I was aware of the officer watching me from the window of his home. He'd gotten a second chance. If he acted against us again, I wouldn't be quite so gentle next time.

Okay. Next.

"My demons. Where are they?" I asked my imps.

"Most are living in a house the demon bought, not too far from the loft," Dahael said.

"Nain bought a house for them?" I asked in dismay.

They nodded. Great. Now I owed him money, too.

Bash took a breath, stopped, opened his mouth again. "As long as it's not about Brennan, please feel free to speak," I said.

"Not all your demons there, Mistress," he said.

I glanced at him. "Meaning?"

"Some lost their way, once you were gone," Dahael said. "Causing trouble. Demon Levitt hunts them. A few still can't be found."

"Is Elsoloth still around?" I asked. They both nodded, and I asked them where the house was. As they gave me directions in their gravelly voices, I drove to a large old house not too far from midtown. Most of the homes around it had been renovated already, part of the revival of midtown and the surrounding areas. But this house had a few boarded up windows, peeling paint, and a porch that sagged so badly I was sure it wouldn't hold my weight, let alone some of the huge demons who had sworn themselves to me.

I got out of the car and the front door opened. Demons, wearing their human skins, flooded out of the front door upon recognizing me. When they reached the bottom of the steps, they dropped to a knees, saluted me, heads bowed. About half of those I'd brought with me from the Nether.

"Rise," I said, feeling distinctly uncomfortable, looking around to make sure no one had noticed the odd display. "My demons. I've heard you've done good work for the city, worked alongside Nain and his team."

Elsoloth nodded. "We have, my Lady. It has been a pleasure to do your work in your absence, but we are very happy to have you back among us."

"There have been losses in your ranks, Elsoloth."

He nodded, kept his eyes on me. "There have, my Lady. Many lost their way, with no light to guide them. We've been hunting the deserters, aided by the demon Levitt."

"The imps tell me you've executed all but a few." As I

stood there, even amid this whole new batch of problems, I had another moment of gratitude. The sun was bright, and the air smelled like autumn. How had I never noticed how good the sun felt on my face? I tried to focus my attention back on Elsoloth. Someday, I'd take a day off and enjoy being home again. Eventually.

"Yes. There are four demons who elude us, even though we have at least one group out searching for them at all times. From what we understand, they have come under the control of the goddess, known as Eris, though she calls herself 'Strife' now. She was trapped here with us when you closed the gateways. Apparently, she wasn't happy about that. And she's not too fond of you, my Lady."

Oh. Damn it. In all of the other insanity, I'd forgotten about her. One more thing to add to the list of shit I needed to take care of.

"Their names?" I asked, crossing my arms over my chest. The demons watched me, and I felt the same thing from them I always did: awe, adoration, respect. They'd seen me as their true leader, due to my blood and the fact that I'd bonded with a demon when I'd married Nain. The fact that we were no longer together hardly seemed to matter. All that mattered was that I did not write them off as worthless Netherspawn, the way the other gods did.

"They were Rafel, Azra, Szilek, and Daiv," Elsoloth said.

"Azra was female," I remembered, and he nodded. "Yes. One she-demon. The rest are males." He paused, looked uncomfortable. "I don't need to tell you that the things they're doing are not good. They are truly sickening individuals."

"I will find them. Thank you for everything. I'll be calling on you soon. In the meantime, please contact me if you need anything. The imps can always find me."

"Yes, Mistress," he said, saluting, bowing his head. The other demons followed suit. "It is a pleasure to have you back."

"Thanks," I said, trying not to sound as irritated as I felt. I said a few more words, then the imps and I got back into my car and we drove off.

"I need you guys to help me find them as soon as possible," I said to the imps.

"Have been. Slippery demons. Move a lot," Bash said.

"Try harder. This can't keep going on," I said, and they both nodded. I drove, listening to the stereo.

◆ ◆ ◆

I was on Jefferson. I was in the driver's seat. I had no idea why I was on Jefferson.

I shook my head, pulled over. I turned to the imps in the back seat. "What were we doing?"

They just looked at me, confusion rolling off of them.

"Why were we on Jefferson?"

They both watched me more. "Just came from Belle Isle, Mistress," Dahael said, staring at me.

"What did we do there?" I asked. My stomach twisted. What the fuck was happening now?

"Walked on the beach. Sat on a bench. Mistress doesn't remember?" Bash asked.

"Where were we going now?"

"Home."

"How long were we on Belle Isle?" I asked, not sure if I wanted to hear it.

"Almost an hour, Mistress. Mistress?"

"Was I acting funny?"

"No. Quiet."

I put my hands back on the steering wheel, stared out the windshield at nothing. I remembered none of it. The last thing I remembered was getting into the car after talking to my demons.

Oh, this was not good.

Was this the damage I'd caused by having the immortals all bound to me? Had I scrambled my brains so much that I'd blacked out for a while? Was it going to happen again?

No. That couldn't be it. I was tired. I was overwhelmed. I was an emotional wreck. So I'd zoned out. I shook my head. That was all.

"I'm not ready to go home yet. You have any leads for me?" I asked them. They told me about a husband and wife who were being held captive by a few warlocks. Levitt was supposed to deal with it. I'd take it instead.

It was unsatisfying.

I mean. I saved the couple. That goes without saying.

The imps and I pulled up to a nice-looking house in Eastpointe, and I marched up to the front door. Didn't bother knocking. I blasted it in with a push of energy. I should have thought before I did it. It hurt like a bitch.

Powers. Right.

I pulled off my sunglasses as I walked into the living room. I wanted them to know damn well what was coming for them.

There were four of them, and they had come running when the door had crashed in. Now they saw me, and fear rolled off of them, thick, heavy, and sweet. They put their hands above their heads, in the air, a posture of surrender.

"Where are they?" I snarled, and another warlock, a thin guy in his forties with greasy hair and a scruffy beard, came out of the other room, leading the woman and the man, who were cuffed together at the wrist, blindfolded, gagged. He, too, had his free hand above his head.

"Come here," I told the woman, and she did, bringing her husband with her and sobbing gratefully. She was in pain, and scared to death. I could easily see into her mind. They'd used her blood, over and over again, for different bullshit spells. Half-assed attempts. The whole point of it all was that they got off on causing pain, used their pathetic amount of ability to justify it. They were planning to kill both of them. They didn't like her. She was a woman two of them had worked with, and she'd fired both of them from their shitty janitorial jobs. I removed their gags, and the imps found the key for the cuffs. I removed their blindfolds, after I put my sunglasses back on.

"So. Bunch of big, tough men when you've got a couple of Normals at your mercy. What are you going to do now?" I said quietly. One of them pissed himself.

I wanted to kill them. They were pathetic. Useless. Sickening.

I craved their deaths. And it would be so easy.

One of them was crying.

I should kill them, I thought to myself, and I shook the thought away. They were weak. No significant power to speak of. There was no need to kill them, and I was a little freaked out that I wanted to do it so badly. I could visualize their lifeless bodies, their blood running across the floor, and it was tempting.

So tempting.

"Shit," I cursed, getting myself under control. I took a few deep breaths. I could feel the imps watching me.

"Kneel," I said to them, forcing the order into their minds. All five of them sunk to their knees instantly, so hard it was a wonder they didn't break their kneecaps. I reached into my pocket, found the zip ties I still carried out of habit. I handed them to the imps.

"Secure them, please," I said to them, and they went to work binding the warlocks' ankles and wrists. I turned to their victims, who were standing next to me. The man was in shock. They'd beaten him up pretty badly, and his eyes were swollen shut. The woman was trying not to freak out over the appearance of the imps, and she was wondering if I'd let her kick her captors a few times.

"Go for it," I told her, and she looked at me in surprise.

"It's okay. I don't really want to touch them at all," she said after a few seconds. She'd been tempted, though. "What are you?"

I gently made my way into her mind. I removed a lot of what she'd seen. Me controlling her abductors' minds. The imps. "You are going to call the police. You are going to tell them who you are. They've been looking for you. You will tell them to come to 14655 Lincoln. That's where you are. And when they ask how this happened, you will say the Angel rescued you, that she subdued your captors and tied them up. You will not be able to describe me, other than that I have dark hair. It will be done." I could have left that information out of it. But it was time for the troublemakers in my city to know I was back, and their days were numbered.

And my power took hold, and I wanted to scream from the pain. I could feel my nose bleeding again, that sensation of my body being shredded from the inside out. And then I left before I fell down in front of the woman I'd rescued. She'd had enough trauma for a while without that.

The imps and I drove away, and I had to pull over on the freeway when the nausea got too bad. I was sick at the side of the road as cars barreled past me at seventy miles per hour, and in my pain, for just a moment, I left my mind unshielded and I could hear the thoughts of the people in every single car that passed me. I whimpered against the onslaught and tried hard to pull it together.

Once there was nothing left to throw up, I crawled back into the car and rested my forehead against the steering wheel. I could feel the imps watching me, concern radiating from both of them.

I did my best at cleaning myself up with a few tissues, and, once I was sure I could drive without hurting anyone, I pulled back into traffic.

"Should rest, Mistress," Dahael said quietly.

184

"I will." I drove for a while in silence, taking I-94 back toward Midtown. "I should go to my house."

"Should be with the people you love. You were missed," Bash said.

"I feel out of place now. Maybe it's been too long. They've moved on, and I only feel like I left a few weeks ago."

"Haven't moved on. Most part, waited."

"For the most part," I grumbled, thinking of Brennan.

"He waited, too. Was weak," Dahael said.

I didn't want to talk about it. We drove the rest of the way in silence, and I pulled into the parking garage and headed up into the loft. Ada was in the living room, Sean in a little bouncy seat thing on the floor near where she sat. She was knitting something, soft blue and green yarn on her needles, and she looked up and smiled when I walked in.

"Hey, girl," she said. I kicked my shoes off and headed toward the living room.

"What's going on?" I asked her as I fell into Nain's chair.

"Brennan and Levitt are out on patrol. Stone is having lunch with Jones," she paused, grinned at me. "You hear Jones' troublemaker went back on his thoughts about supers?"

I smiled. "I wonder what made him change his mind."

"Yes, I do wonder," she said, laughing. She set her knitting down in her lap and leaned forward, put a warm hand on my arm. "It is so good to have you back, baby girl."

"It's good to be back, Ades," I said.

She studied me, her warm brown eyes seeming to take in more than she should. "You went through hell, and you came back changed. I can see it. Know that you are loved, Molly. Every one of us missed you. It felt like part of our hearts was missing, the whole time you were gone. Nain and Brennan were both a mess in their own ways. And

Stone and I just kept wishing you'd be back, because there was nothing else we could do. Nothing was right while you were gone."

"I feel so out of place," I said softly.

"That's normal. You're back from something none of us can understand. Normal life maybe isn't so normal for you anymore. Give it time, honey. Make your new normal. Just promise you'll let us be part of it." And then she smiled, and I couldn't help smiling back.

"Thanks, Ada."

She nodded and picked up her knitting again. "Nain is here. He's up on the roof deck. And your immortal friend? Hephaestus?" I nodded and she continued. "He moved in while you were gone. Shanti's old room."

Which reminded me that I needed to bind him to me again. If I even could. My powers were so screwy now that there was no telling what would work anymore.

I sat with Ada a while longer. I knew there was something I needed to do, but I kind of dreaded doing it. I excused myself, got up, and headed up the stairway that led to the roof.

CHAPTER FIFTEEN

I walked out onto the roof and was hit with a barrage of memories. Learning how to fight better. Learning how to shield my mind. Kissing Nain for the first time. Arguing with Nain, constantly. Mourning him.

And there he was, punching the bag I'd used so often when I'd been mourning him. Sweat darkened the back of the dark gray t-shirt he wore. He was facing away from me, and I watched for a few moments as he hit the bag, huge muscles bunching with each movement, then hard thumps as his punches connected. If it had been a person, the poor guy would have been dead after one punch.

I considered going back inside. There was no need to do this now. I had myself convinced of it, and was turning to head back in, when he stopped hitting the bag and stood still. He still faced away from me. "Are you leaving already?" he asked, and just the sound of his voice brought back hundreds of memories.

"I didn't want to bother you."

"Too late."

I let that go. Stood in silence as he wiped the sweat off of his face and guzzled most of a bottle of water. He turned and looked at me, and we stood in silence for several long, uncomfortable moments. "What do you want, Molls?" he finally asked.

I shrugged. Looked out at the city, because looking at my former husband still did all kinds of crazy shit to me. "I think I wanted to say I'm sorry," I said.

He snorted and sat on the wall, watched me. "Yeah? And what exactly are you sorry for?"

"I think I'm maybe getting a taste now of what I put you through."

He was silent. I could feel his eyes on me. He was pissed. Hurt. And underneath it all was the familiar undercurrent of desire. "Mr. Perfect isn't as perfect as he seemed, huh?"

I didn't answer.

"Tell me. I want to hear it. What exactly is it you thought you put me through?" he asked, and I started to regret starting this with him. But I owed him this, if nothing else.

"You died trying to keep me safe. I mean, yeah. You had your agenda, too. You wanted Astaroth dead, finally. But you wanted to keep me alive. Came back in the Nether, miracle of miracles. And you waited, and tried to find a way back to me. And then you did. And nothing was the same," I said. "And maybe thoughts of coming back to me kept you sane during the worst times. Maybe fantasies about the way it would be were all that kept you from giving up. And the reality is something else, and now you're not sure what was real and what wasn't," I finished, my voice barely above a whisper. I knew he could hear me, though.

We stayed in silence for a while. His emotions roared over me.

"I never expected you to wait for me. I didn't want you to be alone. If thoughts of you kept me going, well, whatever gets you through, right? Do I wish things were different? Did I fantasize about coming back and spending days with you trapped in our bed? Yeah. But I'm not going to hate you for living when you thought I was dead."

"Our bond is broken," I said, because I didn't know what else to say.

"Yeah. Your blood still runs through my veins, though. I can still feel it." He paused. "Why do you think it finally broke? It was alive when I saw you in the Nether."

I shrugged. "I died a few dozen times. I guess even the demon marriage bond has its limits."

I sat down on the wall beside him, and we didn't say anything for a while. "We're okay, Molls. We always will be," he said. "And if you and Brennan ever split, you know where to find me."

I shook my head, and he laughed. "Hey. Your bond makes it so he can feel you, right?"

I nodded.

He leaned over, closer to me. "We could make out. You know, for revenge's sake. I'd make the sacrifice for you."

I shoved him away, laughed. "No. I don't think so."

"All right. Well, the offer still stands, whenever you want to take me up on it."

I shook my head, looked over at him. He was watching me, sapphire eyes that had often rendered me breathless studying my face. "Ever thought about how things could have been if we'd been able to stay together?" he finally asked.

"Yeah. We would have ended up hating each other."

He nodded. "And we would have broken up, and I would have never had to see you again. Clean break."

"Maybe it would have been better that way," I said.

He shook his head. "No. It hurt when I realized what was going on between you and Brennan. That I'd been replaced. But the idea of not having you in my life isn't something that appeals to me in any way. Every other woman I've been with, I was more than happy to show to the door and forget about. What the hell did you do to me?"

"It's my sparkling personality," I said, elbowing him, and he shook his head. "We went through some shit. I'm glad you still want me in your life, because I know I still want you in mine. Even if you're a complete pain in the ass."

We sat in silence for a while. "After he fucked up, he came to me. Did he tell you that?"

I shook my head.

"When he told me what he did, I wanted to kick his ass. And I think he wanted me to kick his ass. But I know him well enough to know he'd never forgive himself. He's going to spend the rest of his life trying to make it up to you. But I know you, too. And you don't trust easy, and he broke it. Didn't he?"

I gave a small nod.

"And I'm even worse than him, because I lied to you about what would happen when you killed Astaroth. I made you hurt someone you loved. You can believe I heard about it from just about everyone once I was back, how I destroyed you, how you were never the same after that."

"Maybe I should just stay away from men. My track record kind of sucks," I said, crossing my arms over my chest.

"Maybe. Or maybe you should see how strong you are. You can overcome anything, and come back stronger. I know you're fucked up over whatever happened to you in the Nether, on top of everything else. You're going to get through this, with Brennan or without him, because it's what you do."

I didn't answer for a while. *Maybe there are some things you can't come back from*, I finally thought at him.

"What did they do to you, Molls?"

I met his eyes, shook my head. "I can't. But it did things to me. I blacked out for over an hour today. Drove all over the city, hung out on Belle Isle, according to the imps. And I don't remember any of it."

Nain was watching me, and I could feel worry from him.

"And I have these crazy violent urges. I want to hurt people. I want to see them bleed. Brennan, more than anyone else. And that scares the shit out of me. And do you know what the worst part is?"

"What?" he asked.

I looked at him again. "If I go bad, if I lose my mind, there's not a damn thing any of you can do to stop me. I can't be killed. I'm stronger than all of you. I've killed the unkillable. None of you stands a chance against me if I lose control."

"Are you afraid of that happening? Really?" he asked.

"I don't know. I keep thinking, you know... I'm tired and messed up and my emotional life is a mess. Maybe when things calm down, I'll feel more like myself again. But I've had these moments since I've been back, where I don't feel like myself anymore."

"You're strong, and you're good. You'll fight to protect the people you love, even from yourself, because that's just the way you are. And if it comes down to it, I swear I will do everything in my power to try to keep them all safe from you."

"Burying me or trapping me at the bottom of the river would work," I said softly, sick that I was telling him this. "I'll keep coming back, but I can't grow my power if I keep dying from suffocation. It's the best way to keep everyone safe, if you have to do it. I think that, eventually, I'd just give up and resurrect in a new body, but it would give you a break, anyway."

I felt complete and absolute horror from him. "And you know this shit, how?" he asked.

I met his eyes and he read it there. I opened my mind

and showed him just a little of what I'd lived through, and I felt white-hot rage course through him. He growled, stood up and ended up punching the bag to try to release some of his anger. Then he hit it again and it went flying, the chain that was holding it up failing under the onslaught.

"And I'm just supposed to bury you alive if this shit happens?" he growled at me.

"It's not something I'm letting become common knowledge. There are plenty who would love to have me out of the picture."

"I'm not telling any one any fucking thing about it," he growled. "You expect me to do this?"

"If it comes to it. Brennan would never be able to do it. I'm trusting you to kill me. Consider it a compliment, demon."

He was watching me. "Fix this shit before it comes to that."

"That's the plan," I said, standing up and heading for the door. "But I expect you to do what you need to if I fail."

"Molls," he said, and I turned back to him.

"Yeah?"

"That shit about being friends? Just so you know, you can come back to me any time. I think we have a few more good nights left in us."

I rolled my eyes. There was the Nain I knew. And he wasn't kidding. Not really. Emotions did not lie, and his were very, very clear just then.

"Yeah, I'll keep that in mind," I said, shaking my head and turning back toward the door.

"Good," he said quietly behind me. I walked back into the loft without another word, though his rage followed me through, stuck with me. My energy level was higher than it had been in a while. Damn demon, feeding me with his anger, just as he always had.

I made my way back into the loft. Brennan and Levitt

had returned from patrol, and Brennan was sitting in one of the chairs in the living room, Sean cradled in his arms. I glanced at him, and, as always, his eyes searched mine. I turned away, started talking to Ada. Stone walked in a few minutes later, started chatting with us in the kitchen. Almost immediately, it was clear that things between my friends weren't the same as they had been.

"Why do you have to butt in every time I'm talking to someone?" Ada asked, irritated. She turned to the sink, started filling a large pot with water for pasta.

"Oh, right. I'm generally not wanted lately. I keep forgetting," Stone grumbled.

"Try to remember it. Everywhere I go, there you are. Suffocating," Ada said, setting the pot on the stove while Stone stood there and glared at her. That in and of itself was weird. Stone always helped her with stuff like that, even if she didn't need it. It was just the way they were. And she'd always let him. There was an understanding between the two of them: Ada could totally take care of herself. But she didn't always have to, and Stone liked doing things for her. I watched them as they kept sniping at each other.

"Yeah. Maybe I'll just stay away. Then you won't have so much to bitch about."

"I wouldn't have so much to bitch about if you'd take a break every once in a while," she said back, then she shook her head. She took a deep breath, put her hand on Stone's arm. "I'm sorry, baby. I don't know what came over me."

He looked down at her, and now he wore the expression I expected to see when he looked at Ada: complete adoration. "Me too. Must be tired. Getting too old. I'm sorry, honey." And then he leaned down and kissed her cheek, gave me an embarrassed grin, and headed upstairs to the room he and Ada shared. I turned to Ada, looked at her questioningly.

She shrugged. "We've all been on each other's nerves worse than usual lately. Too much time together, too much stress, I suppose." Then she smiled a little. "I think I was hoping you being back would solve some of that. Stupid, huh?"

I crossed my arms. "Especially since I bring additional stress with me everywhere I go," I said, trying to lighten the mood.

She laughed a little. "Yeah, but we love you. Stop looking so worried. Me and Stone are getting old. Crankier. It's all right. And I think you have enough on your mind right now," she said, dropping her voice, glancing toward Brennan in the living room.

Then she gave my shoulder a pat and headed upstairs as well.

Which left me, Brennan, Sean, and Levitt in the loft.

Ugh. Go upstairs? Leave again? Because there was no way in hell I was going to sit with him just then. Not that I didn't want to. Not that every cell in my body didn't scream to be near him. But because I didn't know what to say to him, and part of me wanted to kill him.

Literally. Every time I looked at him, the urge to cause real, actual damage to him rose within me. And it was crazy, because as angry as I was, as angry as I'd ever been at him, I still loved him. And I protect the people I love. Even the idea of wanting to hurt one of them, no matter how mad I was, was so crazy it freaked me out.

Shit was too awkward. I glanced at the stove. Ada had left the water boiling, dinner forgotten.

She never did stuff like that.

I shook my head, grabbed two boxes of spaghetti, dumped them into the boiling water. I found two jars of spaghetti sauce in the cabinet. The pasta finished cooking, and I drained it, dumped it back in the empty pot. Then I dumped the two jars of pasta sauce over them, stirred it around.

There, dinner. Cooking is not my strong point.

"You cooked?" Levitt asked, humor radiating from him as he grabbed a plate.

"It probably won't kill you," I said, and he laughed. He piled a mountain of the pasta in a plate, dumped Parmesan cheese on top, then carried it into the dining room. I shook my head. Demons tend to have humongous appetites. It was scary how much they could pack away.

I was just getting ready to sit down and try to eat, thinking maybe it would help the headache a little (and give me something to do while I avoided Brennan, who was wisely staying away from me), when Shanti let herself into the loft. Her eyes scanned everyone, then she spotted me.

"You crazy bitch!" she whooped. And then she was beside me, moving in a blur. Vampire reflexes. I laughed and she threw her arms around me in a bone-crushing hug.

"You gotta stop doing shit like that," Shanti said as she hugged me. "You're killing me."

I hugged her harder. "Nah. You're all right. but I'll try to stop. Really."

She laughed, then released me, stepped back. She wiped her eyes. Blood-tinged vampire tears. "I'm not kidding, Molly. Damn, girl."

"I thought you had to work tonight. Brennan said he thought you had tomorrow night off," I said as Brennan walked into the kitchen carrying Sean and an empty bottle. He glanced at me, greeted Shanti quietly, started rinsing the bottle with hot water.

A look crossed her face. "I did, but the queen let me switch." Then she took my hand and pulled me toward the living room. "Come on, let's sit."

I let her drag me into the living room, and we both at on the couch. Brennan brought me a cup of coffee, offered Shanti something, and she declined, with a coldness in her voice that I'd never heard before. Brennan went back into the kitchen, then took Sean upstairs. Nain and Heph arrived, sat at the dining room table, talking in low voices.

"So. Enforcer for the queen, huh?" I asked Shanti, and she grinned.

"Yeah. I hunt down assholes."

"Perfect for you,' I said, taking a sip of coffee, and she nodded.

"I love it. I track down garbage like the vampire that turned me. There are so many out there. Some are just so new they have no control. Those, I take in and the queen has someone work with them. But the serial offenders? I get to end those."

"I hear you're good at your job," I said.

She nodded. "I am. I learned from the best."

"Brennan," I said, nodding.

She looked up sharply at me. "Fuck Brennan. I learned from you. How to stand up for those who need it. How to fight even when you're afraid. That's what I learned."

I stared at her. "Fuck Brennan, huh?"

"Yeah."

"Care to elaborate?"

She took an exasperated breath. "Did you not notice the baby who isn't yours?"

I tamped down my irritation. I was surprised at how I immediately wanted to defend Brennan, even as I wanted to slap him. "So you're seriously this pissed off at the guy who helped take you in, trained you, taught you, because he messed around on me?" I asked her quietly. "This isn't your fight."

She stared at me in disbelief. "Why aren't you more mad?"

"Oh, I'm mad. I'm so pissed I don't even know what to do with all the rage in me right now. And I'm hurt."

"Right. I mean... you were only gone for three years. It's not like he waited fifty years and you never came back or something. He couldn't keep it in his fucking pants after a couple of years?"

"When did you become such a potty-mouth?" I asked her. Didn't want to respond to what she'd said, because it was the same thing I'd asked myself hundreds of times since I'd been back, and then I reminded myself how (relatively) quickly Brennan and I had gotten together after Nain's death. And then I got confused and I hate being confused, so then I stopped thinking about it.

"Well somebody had to take the role once you were gone," she said, still irritated. I sensed for her. Aside from the irritation and anger, there was sadness.

"You're disappointed in him," I said softly, understanding.

She was quiet for a minute. "Yeah. I saw what you two had and thought, man, that's what I want someday. And then he comes home one day and says oh, hey, here's my son." She shook her head. "I expected better, I guess."

Her and me both. I'd never been the type of woman to believe in a knight in shining armor. Maybe I started to see Brennan that way, though. My white knight wasn't looking so pure anymore. I was supposed to be too old for fairy tales, either way.

We sat together in silence for a while.

"Do you want to go get something to eat? I'm starving," I finally said. Kind of a lie, but I mostly didn't want to sit around in the loft anymore, and chance facing Brennan.

She nodded, and we got up. "Slows?" she asked.

"It's still there, right?"

She nodded, and we left, took the elevator down to the parking garage. We got into my car and drove down Warren, then turned onto Fourteenth Street, heading toward the restaurant.

"So tell me about the queen," I said as I drove.

"I like her. She's tough, and she's fair. She doesn't take any crap, but she isn't unnecessarily cruel. You'd like her, Molly. I think you two have a lot in common."

"I'm going to have to meet her soon. I'm happy she's here, as long as she's keeping the vampires in control. If she starts stirring shit... "

"Then I'm out of there. My loyalties are to you and the team first, even if I'm spending most of my time there now. I needed to move out. I wanted to do things on my own, and I'm glad I have."

"You always were independent. You were a lot tougher at seventeen than I was," I told her.

"I find that hard to believe," she said, patting the top of the car door in time to the music. Eminem this time.

I shook my head. "I was a freaking mess at seventeen. Jumping at every shadow. Sleeping with the lights on." No need to mention that I still slept with the lights on. "You had your shit together at that age. You came to me because you knew you needed help."

"But you were finding lost girls when you were seventeen," Shanti said. She'd heard that story before, about how I'd started. Her, Brennan, and Nain were the only ones who knew it all. My mother kind of knew the abbreviated version. It wasn't the kind of story I liked sharing.

"I was. Doesn't mean I had my shit together." We reached the restaurant, and I cruised Michigan Avenue, looking for a parking spot. We ended up parking about a block down and got out of the car. I glanced around, and, sure as the sun rising in the east, two of my imps were crouched nearby. Best car alarm system on the planet. I nodded at them, and they thumped their chests in response.

I'd have to bring them some ribs.

We started walking toward the restaurant, and I was pushing my sunglasses up again in irritation, when I remembered that I knew how to enchant my appearance. I focused, trying to make my eyes look normal. As in, not glowing white like some freaky alien. When I felt something happen (it's hard to describe. Kind of a tingly, fuzzy feeling in the area you're trying to enchant.) I pulled the sunglasses down a little and nudged Shanti.

"Are they normal?"

She studied me. Then she grinned. "Yep. Cool trick, boss lady."

I snorted, shoved the sunglasses in my coat packet along with my car keys. We walked into the restaurant, snagged a small table for two near the front windows. I'd always liked the feel of Slows. Dark walls, lots of wood. Nice place.

But I liked their macaroni and cheese even more.

We ordered (and I remembered to order a half-slab of ribs to go for my car-watching imps. And then I added an order for Brennan because he loved them. And then I realized what an absolute sap I am.) Then we sat and talked. She filled me in on how things were when I'd first disappeared, the chaos and fighting in the city. Not having power for weeks in some areas. Constant patrolling to stop rioters and troublemakers. The way some supernaturals had taken advantage of the situation.

"Me and Levitt usually patrolled together, the way you wanted us to," she finished, and then I sensed some embarrassment from her.

I watched her, raised my eyebrow.

"I hate that you can sense when something's up," she muttered.

"I know. Sorry. Do you want to talk about it?"

She shrugged. "We were a thing for a little while. We started up about a year and a half after you disappeared. I was already crazy about him. You probably knew I had a crush on him, like, the second I laid eyes on him," she said.

I nodded. "Yeah. I sensed that."

She rolled her eyes. "So we got close, and then we started up. We didn't last long. A couple of months. Our personalities are too different, and he has a very possessive streak that pissed me off."

"I think it's a demon thing. I mean, plenty of people have one. But demons make it into an art form," I said, and she nodded.

"Seriously. So we called it quits, but we're still friends. Sort of." Then she laughed a little. "Do all demons have the 'damn, boy, you have spoiled me for all other lovers' thing going? Cuz I gotta say, that part was almost worth staying through the bullshit."

I laughed. "I don't know if it's all demons. But, yeah. That's been my experience." Our food came, and we both dug in. "Someone will live up to it eventually."

"I can have fun trying to find him out there, then," she said, and I laughed again. "I don't think I'm the relationship type. Is that bad?"

I shook my head. "There's no wrong way to be. As long as you're true to you. That's all that matters."

She reached across the table and put her hand over mine. "I'm so glad you're back, Molly. Not gonna lie: everything was shit while you were gone. And I felt lost. You're like my mother, my sister, my best friend, my mentor, all rolled into one badass bitch. I need you."

I shook my head. "You don't need me. But it makes me all warm and fuzzy that you think you do." She laughed and started eating again.

"You want to talk about what happened to you while you were gone?" she asked after a few minutes.

"Not really. But I'll tell you some of it if you really want to hear it."

"Spill."

So I talked and she listened, and we picked at our dinners. I left out a lot of the details, but she got the idea. When I'd finished, she sat in silence a while, shredding her napkin with her fingers. Anger rolled off of her, and I realized we were a lot more alike than I'd ever realized. She didn't feel sorry for me. She wanted to hurt someone on my behalf. I could respect that.

"So you don't believe they're gods?" she finally asked.

"Not really. I mean, it's not like I know either way, and ultimately it doesn't even matter. But I don't." It might have seemed like a weird thing for her to focus on, but I knew that Shanti was Christian, and still took her faith very seriously. The idea that there were gods around, and they weren't her god, had bothered her a lot. I knew she'd tried to work it out, figure out how to reconcile it with her faith. She still believed.

"You probably think it's stupid, the whole faith thing," she said after a while.

"No. I don't. I don't know any better than anyone else what the truth is. I mean, isn't that kind of the whole thing with faith? You believe, even when there's no proof. Otherwise, you wouldn't need faith."

"Do you believe?"

"No. But I never did to begin with," I said, shrugging. "But that doesn't matter. Your faith is yours, and my faith, or lack of it or whatever, is mine. The only thing I know for sure is that there's no fucking way I'm a god."

She laughed then, and before long, we were both laughing at the ridiculous concept of my godliness. We paid our bill and left, heading toward the car. I handed the imps their order of ribs, and they grinned and disappeared with their treasure.

We got into my car. "Want to patrol or something?" I asked Shanti as I pulled into traffic. "The imps had a lead on a lost girl in East English Village."

"You really know how to show a chick a good time," Shanti said.

"I don't feel like going back to the loft just now."

She nodded, reached over and gave my hand a small squeeze. "Let's go then."

We drove back toward the east side, left the car parked on a side street and got out to patrol on foot. All the imps had had was a general location, so I'd do some listening and we'd see what we came up with. It was kind of funny how easily I'd fallen back into certain parts of my life. Too bad not all of it was as easy.

"I'm going to listen," I told Shanti, and she nodded. I opened my mind, dropping the protective shields that kept other people's thoughts from driving me nuts. I was barraged immediately with random thoughts from within the homes around us. Worries, minutiae, life-changing decisions, thoughts about laundry. It all hit me. The hardest part was trying to pick individual voices out of the cacophony. After the initial assault on my psyche, I forced myself to focus. Most voices, I could let fall to a dull roar in the background. I was listening for particular thoughts: worries about being caught or general thoughts of supremacy were always like flashing red lights to me. Lustful thoughts, too, unfortunately.

We walked in silence for several blocks, and I listened. I finally turned to Shanti and shook my head in irritation.

"Want to try for a little longer? I have a couple of hours before dawn," Shanti said. I nodded, and we kept walking. Every once in a while I got a glimpse of one of my imps, on top of a house or in a tree. Sometimes, climbing out of a window. After a while, I started to feel a familiar presence, considered turning around and walking in the opposite direction. But that would have been immature.

"Nain is around here somewhere," I said.

"Probably looking for your lost girl, too. Didn't you say Levitt was on this one?"

I nodded. Soon, I saw Nain's big black pickup truck, Chief Jones' car. Shanti and I jogged the rest of the way. We were about to go through the front door, which was wide open, when Nain came out and took me by the shoulders, pushed me back gently.

"You don't want to go in there, Molls," he said. I tried to shrug his hands off, and he held firm. I stopped, looked up at him.

"I was too late," I said, hoping against hope that he'd disagree with me.

"We all were. Whoever took her is long gone, but they left her here," he said, his voice low, deep. I felt anger coming off of him, guilt.

"You never cared this much about this kind of thing," I said. He still had his hands on me, big cool palms resting on my bony shoulders. He looked down at me, met my eyes.

"I cared. Not enough to specifically go out of my way to help, not enough to completely focus on it, but it mattered. You have this tendency to make others care about the same things you do."

"He's been in on lost girl searches since he got back," Shanti verified.

"Was it just the one we were looking for? Or were there more?" I asked. I didn't want to think too much about how touched I was that my dedication for finding lost girls had made Nain make it one of his duties as well. I shrugged my shoulders again, and then he did remove his hands. He crossed his arms over his chest and watched me.

"It was just her. We have to find these assholes. Elsoloth didn't know anything, did he?"

I shook my head, then I looked up at him sharply. "Wait. You're telling me my rogue demons did this?"

He nodded. "They've left a few bodies around. All the same as this one."

"What do you mean?" I asked him.

He opened his mind to me and showed me, and I was sorry I asked.

"I will find the fuckers," I growled, feeling my power rise in response to my anger.

"I know you will," Nain said. Our eyes met for just a second, and I looked away. "Jones is here for cleanup. He'll inform her family. There have been so many murders the last few years, the media has figured out something's going on. Story now is that there's a serial killer out."

"Technically true," I said, rubbing my temples.

"Yeah."

I glanced over at Shanti who was watching Nain and I with more interest than I felt comfortable with. And my ex-husband was a whole separate issue. As angry as he was about the woman and my demons, he was very much distracted by something else just then.

Me.

He did a good job of hiding it. His face was calm, his posture relaxed. If I wasn't able to sense emotions, I would have had no idea what he was feeling just then. He wasn't like Brennan in that way. Brennan's emotions were easy to read, and, at least when it came to me, he wore them plainly.

I took a step away from Nain. "Okay." I glanced at Shanti again. "We should get going so you have enough time to get back."

"Uh huh," she said, glancing between Nain and I again.

"Come on," I said. I glanced back at Nain one more time. His face was impassive. Not at all like the emotions coming from him. I walked as quickly as my legs would carry me in the other direction.

When we were about a block away, Shanti laughed. "Well, that wasn't a whole bunch of sexual tension or anything. Damn."

"It wasn't," I said, irritated.

"Right."

I shook my head, kept walking, fast. Shanti of course had no problem catching up with me. She smartly changed the subject, and we talked about where to look for my demons. She said she'd ask around with the vampires and see if anyone had heard anything.

We drove back to the loft, and she got in her car in the below-ground garage. Sporty little red thing. Very Shanti. She hugged me before she left, telling me we'd get together again soon, and she'd call me to let me know if the vamps had heard anything.

I made my way up to the loft, hoping to avoid a Brennan confrontation, and, for once, I ended up lucky. He was up in his room. Ada and Stone were in their room. Levitt was on patrol, as was Nain. E had headed to the Nether again.

Alone. I was blissfully alone, and I needed it, just for a little while.

CHAPTER SIXTEEN

I kicked off my shoes and padded into the living room, where I fell into Nain's big leather chair. I'd gotten used to sitting there after he'd died, and it was, without a doubt, the most comfortable seat in the house.

I leaned my head back, closed my eyes.

Unfortunately, my thoughts went right where I didn't want them to, and I forced them away.

I could admit it to myself: seeing Nain again did all kinds of things to me. We hadn't been finished when he'd died. Not by a long shot. I didn't doubt that we would have broken up eventually. The good parts of our relationship had been amazing, and I could admit that it had apparently been three years since I'd been with a man, and Nain very obviously wanting me the way he did was tempting as hell.

Lust. That had never been a problem between Nain and I.

I took a deep breath, pulled my legs up to my chest. Lust was one thing. I would probably have pretty vivid memories of Nain and I together for the rest of my life, however long that was. But the man I loved was upstairs. Maybe I shouldn't have loved him anymore. But I did. Maybe that made me stupid, or pathetic, or blind.

Considering all the mistakes I'd made, who the hell was I to judge? Now, if he screwed around on me now that I was back, we'd have problems. He'd broken my trust, and I wasn't sure that part of our relationship would ever be the same again.

I got up and walked through the loft, turning off lights, checking the messages. Nain had an assistant who'd started coming to the loft a few times a week, and she took care of things like messages and mail, all the crap that had always fallen to Ada. From what I'd heard, she was a Normal. Which was weird. I'd have to check her out.

Once I was done, I went up the stairs toward the bedrooms. I let myself into Brennan's room, went over to the dresser and dug out a pair of my pajama pants and a t-shirt. I went into the bathroom, brushed my teeth, started scrubbing my hands, my face. By the time I was done, my hands were red and raw and I didn't feel any cleaner. I took my hair down and changed, then went back into the bedroom.

He was awake in bed, lying on his back, hands behind his head. His chest was bare, and he looked just as good as he always had. He sat up when I walked into the room, watched me. I climbed into bed next to him, snuggled under the comforter. He put his arms around me, and I put my hand on his waist. He trembled at my touch, and the emotions coming from him were overwhelming. Love, desire, relief, sadness, longing. We rested there in each other's arms for a while. He ran his fingers through my hair.

"I wasn't sure you were coming up. You didn't want to be around me today," he finally said.

"I wasn't sure I was either."

He moved his fingers from the ends of my hair to my scalp, started massaging it gently, the way he knew I liked.

I sighed in contentment, closed my eyes.

"I'm sorry, Molly," he said softly. "I want so bad to make it up to you, and I know I can't."

"I just need some time," I said. "I know you love me," I said. "I'm just not sure it's going to be enough."

"If you believed that, you wouldn't be here," he said, pulling me close again. "I will do whatever it takes to make things right between us. I swear."

I rolled over, facing away from him. My warring emotions were making me feel like I was about to lose it. Brennan slung an arm over my hips, and I found myself relaxing back into his warmth even as I kind of wanted to shove him away from me.

This shit was going to be complicated.

I laid there. I felt when he fell asleep. It was like a veil falling over our connection. It still existed, but it was muted. I laid there awake, thinking, listening to Brennan snoring softly beside me. Anger toward him washed over me in waves, and I tried to shove it back. It was actually a relief when Sean woke up crying for his six AM feeding, and Brennan got out of bed and went downstairs. It seemed like when he was around, I either wanted to kiss him or kill him.

I punched my pillow in irritation, rolled over and pulled the blankets over my head. I was back. Yay, me. But I was back and very little was the same, and I could admit that I was petty enough to be pissed off that the entire world hadn't waited for me, hadn't stayed the same so I wouldn't feel so lost once I finally made it back. Shanti, Nain, Ada and Stone, my rogue demons. Brennan and his son. Did I even belong there anymore?

I pushed my thoughts away from feeling sorry for myself, because that was stupid. I was back. I should be grateful for that, no matter how crazy everything seemed. I started thinking about where to look for my rogue demons. Both Elsoloth and Bash had said they'd been looking, but that the demons were proving impossible to find. Which made no sense, since they were apparently leaving a trail of dead bodies in their wake. They weren't exactly being subtle.

Not just a trail of dead bodies, I reminded myself. A trail of dead women. Almost as if they were taunting me. And I wasn't sure anymore whether I was being realistic or paranoid, believing that everything that happened was about me. But it sure the fuck felt like a taunt. "Oh, hey, look, more dead lost girls, Angel."

So what was their game? Draw me out? If they wanted that, they sure were doing a good job of running. And it wasn't like I was hiding.

And then I remembered what Athena and the Furies had told me about Strife, that she gains strength through chaos, which always causes more chaos, which makes her more powerful. A string of murders was a good way to cause fear and chaos, and get back at me at the same time.

I wasn't sure how far off I was. Probably just paranoid. Still it was something to think about, and I knew that, either way, Strife wasn't someone I could keep ignoring.

I gave up trying to fall asleep (which was for the best. I felt less in control when I relaxed anyway.) I took a too-hot shower, scrubbed my skin raw. I could feel that I was on the edge of a freakout. If I didn't get hold of myself I'd be a bawling mess on the bathroom floor again. I shook my head, finished shampooing my hair, tried fighting off the panic. Being back, having my powers all fucked up only made everything worse. Even the panic attacks, which I was sure couldn't get any more hellish. My power rose in response to my emotions, and I gritted my teeth against the agony coursing through me. I punched the shower wall in my anger and pain, ended up cracking the black tiles. Panic attacks were a bitch already. It hardly seemed fair that I had to be in actual physical pain because of my powers on top of it.

I breathed through it, stood under the rapidly cooling water. I heard the bathroom door open. Brennan. Shit.

"Molly? You okay? I thought you fell or something," he said.

"I'm fine. Go away, Bren," I said, and I could hear the growl in my voice.

I sensed irritation, worry from him. Then he pushed the shower door open and turned the water off, pulled me out of the shower and into his arms. I shoved him, but he held tight.

"I don't want to hurt you," I growled.

"Yes, you do." He reached over and grabbed one of the towels from the cabinet, wrapped it around me while still holding onto me tightly with one arm. "But you won't, because you're you and even if I absolutely deserve to have my ass kicked, you'd never do it."

"I'm not totally in control anymore," I said quietly. He ran his hands over my body, drying me.

"What happened to you?" he asked softly.

I shook my head. I knew that telling Brennan would be different from telling Shanti. Him, I'd tell everything. Every detail, every second of pain, every thought I had while dying. And I was still pissed off at him, and the idea of being that vulnerable with him... I wasn't quite there yet.

He leaned his forehead against mine, held the towel wrapped around me.

"I broke a bunch of tiles. I'll pay Nain to get it fixed. And I owe him money for buying that house for the demons."

"Molly. Who cares? He's got money to spare. He bought that house because he figured it wouldn't be a bad idea to have another house nearby and he wanted to keep an eye on your demons."

I took a deep breath. I could feel the pain and panic subsiding as we stood there. Brennan was doing what he does best: soothing and taking care of me. And that would have been great if I didn't have that stupid rage monster, that darkness inside of me that was triggered by him. I pulled back.

"I'm okay now," I said, and he let me go. His eyes searched mine, then he stepped away. He wanted to kiss me. Hold me. Do a lot more with me. I could feel it. But he stepped away anyway, left the room and went downstairs, because he knew I wasn't ready.

I closed my eyes, took a deep breath. I made it through drying off, getting dressed, and braiding my hair.

I went downstairs, stepped into my shoes, left without interacting with anyone. I knew I was acting like an asshole. I couldn't put on a happy, calm, everything-is-just-fine face. I got in my car, and Bash and Dahael joined me, climbing into the back seat. I found the classic rock station, turned the volume up, and roared out of the garage.

Find my demons. Find Strife. That was my focus.

I drove all over the city. Packard Plant, empty neighborhoods, places where I'd always had good luck tracking demons down before. They fed off of human fear and pain, so they liked being around crowds of people. But they always retreated to dark, quiet, solitary places.

Kind of like me. It's a Nether thing, I think. We don't do well around others. We need silence, darkness. We recharge in solitude, even as we kind of hate it, because we need others to be strong.

Basically, we creatures of the Nether are a bunch of emo assholes. Walking, talking, murderous, parasitic stereotypes.

After a few hours, I'd run through my list of rocks to look under for my demons. I finished up by checking out one of the sleazy motels on Eight Mile. No luck. But I wished brain bleach was a real thing by the time I left.

I got back into the car, slammed the door hard in frustration behind me.

"We'll find them," Dahael said from the back seat.

"Every second they're out there, they're causing more pain," I said. "This makes no fucking sense."

"Like you said, probably working with Strife," Bash

said, and I nodded. "So, easier to hide. Have help now."

"Meeting with shifter chief. Don't forget," Dahael said, and I sighed in irritation. I'd agreed to meet with Jones about the uptick in murders caused by my demons. This wasn't going to be fun.

When I got to the loft, Jones and Nain were already there. Brennan and Eunomia were out on patrol. Stone was sitting in the living room, holding Sean while he watched his talk shows. He got a kick out of the trashier ones, the ones where they were all about proving who the father was and who cheated on who. Everyone had to have a vice, right? Ada was out, having lunch with a couple of her witch friends. Levitt was still sleeping; he'd had the late patrol shift the night before.

"Chief," I said, and he shook my hand. The three of us went into Nain's office. It had been my office for a while, after Nain had died. He was clearly back. The top of the desk was back to its ordered, immaculate appearance. When I'd been using it, the place had been a mess. He was watching me as I looked around.

"You know it took me like a week to get it back the way it was supposed to be? How do you work like that?"

I couldn't help smiling. "Not everyone is as anal-retentive as you."

"I know. But, damn, woman. It was like a hurricane hit in here."

I laughed then. "You know we would have driven each other nuts if we'd stayed married? They could have made a shitty sitcom about us."

He laughed then, too. "Every episode would have been us bitching at each other over stupid shit. And then you'd kick my ass and the credits would roll."

I shook my head and sat down in one of the chairs.

"In her defense," Jones said, winking at me, "she barely had time to breathe when she was in charge. She changed a lot around here." He took the chair next to me as Nain settled himself into his big chair behind the desk.

"No shit. You know how weird it was to have people checking with me before they made decisions about things? Of course, for the first three months, all I heard was 'oh, uh, where's the Angel? I'd really rather talk to her.'"

Jones laughed. "They said that, but I've personally heard from people who swore they'd practically pissed themselves meeting with Molly." Then he turned to me. "You're scary. I like you."

I shook my head. "Apparently not scary enough," I said, bringing us back to the reason we'd decided to meet. "What can you tell me about the deaths my demons have caused?"

He ran through what he knew. Twenty-seven deaths. All women, all left in horrid states, which Nain had shown me in his mind the night before. There was no pattern to who they chose, other than that the victims were all women. Always found in empty houses or abandoned storefronts.

"The really irritating thing is that we've never run up against shit like this with demons before. You know they're not usually subtle. They enjoy flaunting what they do, the ones that do shit like this."

Time to share my part of the blame.

"I'm pretty sure they have help." I told them about Strife, and how I'd trapped her here, and her relationship with Enyo and Ares. "So I'm pretty sure she's doing this to get back at me," I finished. "Targeting women and leaving them like that. Taking my fucking demons. You're right. They wouldn't stay this well-hidden on their own."

Nain stayed silent, watching me. Jones looked completely deflated.

"This is your mess to clean up, Molls," Nain said finally.

"Yeah, no shit, Nain," I said, glaring at him. "I'm working on it." Then I turned to Jones. "For now, your guys should know that if they come across anything when they're working this case, they need to call for backup. Meaning you. Meaning you call me and I come and deal with it. All right?"

He nodded. Anger rolled off of him in waves. He liked me, but he was pretty sick of his city being in danger because of me. He was stressed out, so I was able to grab that right out of his mind. So was Nain, apparently.

"Just remember that she's saved a hell of a lot of people in your city when your department has dropped the ball before you get all judgmental, man," Nain said, with just enough threat in his voice to make Jones look up at him sharply.

"Relax. I know that." He stood up. "I'll relay your message to my guys." Then he shook Nain's hand, then mine, and took off. Nain and I exchanged a glance.

"We'll find them," he said to me.

"Same for you, Nain. If you come across them or Strife, don't take them on yourselves. It has to be me. Don't do anything stupid."

After a moment's hesitation, he gave me a terse nod and I walked out of his office. I grabbed a cup of coffee, and was gulping the hot heavenly liquid down when Eunomia came in from her patrol shift.

"Good day, devil girl," she said. I greeted her and grabbed my car keys off of the counter. "Going somewhere?"

"Hunting. Wanna come?"

She grinned, giving me one of her creepy little smiles. "Only if you leave that monstrous contraption behind. Let's fly."

"I hate heights."

"Get used to it. What good are wings if you refuse to fly?"

I tossed my car keys back onto the counter in case Brennan would need them, and we walked out together. We looked for my rogue demons, with zero luck, and we rescued two lost girls the imps alerted us to. We checked on the immortals, who were, for the most part, keeping themselves busy getting their hands dirty feeding and building and healing. I talked to my dad for a few minutes, as he took a break from preaching the word of Hades, which was basically "straighten the fuck up or I'm gonna hurt you" to a group of young men he was talking to. It seemed like they got the message. Apparently my mother and aunt were back in the Nether, doing their Fury thing. Zeus and Hera still hadn't returned from the Aether, and Apollo had joined them, along with Aphrodite.

"She was angry when she learned that Hephaestus had decided to live here full-time," Hades finished, and I rolled my eyes.

"As if she even cared, ever, what Heph was doing."

He shrugged. "She's the goddess of love. The idea of someone not being completely in love with her is hard to handle."

"Poor baby," I muttered.

"You'll want to watch your back with them, daughter," he said, his voice low and serious.

"I will. I know."

"And she has friends watching her back as well," E said, and I gave her a small smile.

"Have you visited the Nether yet, Guardian?" Hades asked Eunomia, and there was a note of worry from him. I watched his face.

"Yes," she said reluctantly.

"And did you notice anything amiss?"

"Why are you asking her that?" I asked, still watching my father.

"I need to hear if I'm imagining things or not."

I looked at Eunomia. "E?"

She glared at Hades. "Would you let her rest for a while? Um... my Lord," she added in a more neutral voice.

"What's going on?" I asked them.

"What did you feel, Guardian?" Hades pressed.

E looked at me, an apologetic look in her eyes.

"Something is wrong with it. It's weak. I didn't gain nearly as much of my strength as I'd hoped I would."

Oh, for fuck's sake, I thought to myself, and felt another instance of massive amounts of rage. It twisted my mind, made me want to hurt every living thing around me. I closed my eyes, took deep breaths, trying to fight it, whatever the hell it was, back. Too much stress. Too much craziness, I thought to myself. I sensed worry from E and my father, but I focused on getting my emotions under control again. Once I felt like I wouldn't destroy anything, I opened my eyes and looked at them. They were both watching me, concern in their eyes.

"It's fine. I'm just tired," I said. "So it's weak. What are we supposed to do about that? Did I do it, when I made the gateway?"

"Tisiphone and I think so. If that's the case, then it's not as though it can be un-done," my father said. Then he met my gaze. "But this loss of power puts the other Nether gods and I at a disadvantage, especially considering that those most likely to harm you are from the Aether."

"And the Aether hasn't experienced any loss of energy?"

Hades shook his head.

"Well, shit," I said, for lack of anything better. "I'll figure something out."

Hades took my arm. "No. You won't. Leave it, Mollis. It can't be fixed, and you're likely to kill yourself or us trying. Let it be. Live your life."

"I'm sorry," I said.

"Don't be. So we lost some power from the Nether. I'm gaining some power by being here, the power they give me by believing. It will balance out over time. I believe that."

I nodded, took a deep breath. Eunomia was glaring at Hades, and he was doing his best to ignore it.

Eunomia and I scanned the city some more after we left, trying to get even the tiniest sense of my demons or

Strife. We talked as we flew. She told me stories about things that had happened while I was gone, and I gave her the very abbreviated version of the Tale of Molly and the Immortals. After a while, we gave up, frustrated, and flew back to the loft. It was dark, and the night was cool. I could almost relax as we flew over the city. As we flew, I thought about how I really should move back into my own house. It was weird living in Nain's house, sleeping with Brennan. Living in the same house with Brennan and his son.

But part of me just wanted to be with all of them, no matter how awkward it felt sometimes. That was selfish. I'd figure it out.

E and I landed on the roof, and she took my hand and led me inside. Maybe she could sense how unsure I felt about everything. I followed her in. Ada, Stone, Nain, Heph, Brennan, Sean, and Levitt were all sitting at the huge dining room table, passing Chinese food containers back and forth. Brennan's eyes found mine immediately, and he set Sean down into the little bassinet that was near the dining room.

"Go on. I got him," Stone said, and Brennan nodded and grabbed one of the containers, then took my hand and pulled me toward his room.

I went.

It screwed me up, how much I wanted to be with him while wanting to hurt him. How I still craved the way he looked at me, the way his warm hands felt on my body, even as my heart shattered every time I let myself think about him and his one-night stand.

He pulled me into his room and closed the door behind us. He sat on the bedroom floor, and I sat down next to him.

"You like almond chicken, right?" he asked, and I nodded. He picked up some chicken with the chopsticks and held it toward me.

"I'm not a baby, Brennan," I said.

"I am well aware of that, Molly," he said, a low growl in his voice. "But I like watching you eat, and I want to feel useful, even if you don't need me."

I met his eyes, opened my mouth and accepted the food. I kept my eyes on his as I chewed. He fed me another bite when I was finished with the first, then took a bite for himself. We sat, eating in silence, and I couldn't stop looking at him.

"I didn't mean it, the other night," I said quietly. "When I said I didn't need you."

"I think maybe you don't need me. You don't need anyone, Molly. But I hope you still want me. I hope you still love me."

He put another morsel of food in my mouth. We finished off the rest of the container in silence, and he left and came back with two cups of coffee. He settled back onto the floor, sitting across from me. It felt like we should have been playing a board game or something, sitting on his bedroom floor like that. And then I had a thought, and I smiled in spite of myself.

"What are you thinking, with that little smile?" he asked softly.

"I was thinking it seems like we should be playing a board game. And then 'strip Scrabble' popped into my mind. It's something we would have done, I think."

He nodded, smiled a little. "Yeah. Maybe someday you'll want to actually do that."

"Maybe." I brought my knees up, hugged them to my chest. "Tell me about your day."

"Why?"

"Because I need to hear something other than the shit in my head."

So he did. He told me about his patrol. He told me about how a couple of shifters had stopped them, going on and on about the appearance of streetlights in their neighborhood, and I laughed. He told me about what a bad driver Hephaestus was, and he swore he'd never let the immortal drive my car. He talked about nothing, and it felt so normal. It was what I needed, and he knew it. He didn't talk about the Nether, or us, or his son. He stretched out on his back on the floor beside me, hands under his head, and he filled me with gossip and made me laugh over some of the crazier things he'd seen while I'd been gone. The room was lit only by the city outside, and neither of us bothered turning on a light. Sometimes, it's easier to find your way in the dark.

Eventually, he went silent, and we sat there, just keeping each other company. I knew, then, that I'd find a way to get past the pain I was feeling. He could have been begging. He could have been making excuses. He could have been telling me all the reasons we should make up and try to be happy. Instead, he fed me and talked himself hoarse trying to show me what normal life looked like.

He wasn't perfect. But I sure the hell wasn't either.

I yawned, and he got up and pulled me into bed with him. We both stayed in our clothes, too tired to change, and it didn't matter. I started to doze in Brennan's arms, his heart beating against my chest as I buried my face against him.

"I love you," he murmured after a while.

"I know. I love you too," I said softly. "We'll be okay."

He held me tighter, and I fell asleep with his fingers tracing up and down my spine, the curve of my lower back.

I was back in my grave again, blackness surrounding me, the weight of the soil heavy on my chest. Arms bound.

Helpless.

Suffocating.

I thrashed, whimpered, tried to scream despite the soil filling my throat.

"Molly!"

I woke up screaming, forced the weight off of me, the same way I'd forced the soil away as I'd emerged from the grave.

A loud crash, breaking glass.

I sat up, trying to catch my breath, ready to scream again. And I heard a groan.

I looked around wildly. It took a bit for me to remember where I was: home, in the loft, in the bed Brennan and I shared.

Brennan.

He was on the floor, across the room. He'd crashed into the wall, and the shelf full of photos and books was laying on the floor next to him. He was sitting up.

I stared in horror, then shook myself out of it, leapt out of bed and went to him.

"Oh god. Oh my god. I'm sorry," I said, kneeling next to him, running my hand over his neck, his back.

My fingers came away covered with blood.

"Oh---" I started getting up to get the first aid kit, and he reached up and grabbed my arm, held me still.

"Molly, it's okay," he said quietly.

"Hey! Everything okay up there?" Stone shouted from downstairs.

"Yeah. Dropped something," Brennan called back. He was still holding my arm.

"You're bleeding. Let me go."

He held on tighter. "Stop. I'm okay. It's a cut, and I've had worse."

"Brennan," I said helplessly, tears threatening. I'd hurt him. "I think I should move out," I whispered.

He pulled me down onto his lap, put his arms around me. Partially to comfort me, partially to keep me from taking off. "Yeah? Where would you go?"

"To my house," I said quietly.

"I would follow you."

"I hurt you. It could have been worse," I said, and he held me tighter. "You're going to hate me." That thing inside, the thing that wanted to hurt him, radiated satisfaction, and I wanted to scream.

"Sense for me, Molly. I there any sense, at all, that I hate you?"

I closed my eyes, felt his gaze on me. I sensed for him. Love. Warmth. Anger.

"You're angry," I said.

"Not at you, though," he said, resting his forehead against my hair. "Never that. I'm angry that things happened to you that I couldn't protect you from. I'm angry you have all of this fear in you now. I hate whatever happened to you to put that fear there. I'm angry you can't talk about it, yet Hephaestus seemed to know all about it."

"Only because he was there. Do you really want to know?" I asked him.

He picked me up, turned me around on his lap so I was facing him, legs on either side of his hips. He looked into my eyes, ran his fingers gently through my hair. "Yes. I have an idea, from what I felt on my end. But I have the feeling it was worse than I wanted to believe."

I took a deep breath, and I looked into his eyes. Then I rested my forehead against his, and I started talking.

By the time I'd gotten to the part where I'd been buried alive, the rage coming off of Brennan was worse than anything I'd ever felt from him.

I told him about coming to in my grave. About suffocating and dying, over and over again. About how the Nether saved me, made me more powerful, but demanded a price.

His arms were tight around my body. He sat in silence for a few long moments, and I knew he was trying to get himself calm enough to talk. He felt helpless. Enraged. His shoulders under my hands were tense.

"What was its price?" he finally asked.

"I'm tied to it," I said quietly. "It took all the power I had to break away from it. I don't think I was supposed to be able to leave the Nether. I was in pain when I went to the Aether. Being here is excruciating. Everything hurts, all the time. And when I use my powers, I kind of want to die."

"You've gotten a lot stronger."

"I have." I pulled back from him. "I need to show you something."

CHAPTER SEVENTEEN

"I've been dying to hear you say that," he said, running his hands firmly over my hips.

I laughed. "Besides that."

He grinned, and there was a glimmer of the way things used to be between us, me always too serious and him balancing me by lightening things up. "Show me."

"Don't freak out."

"Have you ever known me to freak out?" And he opened his mind to me again, showed me every thought he was having. His way of letting me know he meant what he said, and it meant the world to me just then.

I smiled, leaned forward and kissed him. "No. definitely not."

He smiled at me, and I took a deep breath, met his eyes. And then I let the enchantment fall, letting him see my wings for the first time.

He stared at me, his eyes taking in the black feathers.

His first thought was "holy shit."

His next was "I want to touch them."

I laughed. "Are you lusting after my wings?"

"If they're attached to you, I'm lusting after them," he said. Then he reached a hand out and ran his fingertips lightly over the edge of the wing on my left side. I shivered a little at the sensation.

"Does that bother you?" he asked quietly.

"Opposite of bother," I said, trembling as he ran his fingertips through the feathers.

"They're sensitive, huh?"

"I didn't realize how much. No one's ever touched them before."

He groaned, and then he thought that he really wanted to do a few things that involved a whole lot more than touching, and the next thing I knew, I was pulling his t-shirt up over his head, and he was unbuttoning my top, his lips on my throat, my collarbone. The thing inside me threatened to rise up, and I fought it down. It, whatever it was, could hate Brennan all it wanted, but I needed this.

Brennan's hands were all over my body, firmly squeezing my waist, my hips, running up and down my spine, then spanning my ribcage as he kissed me breathless. I ran my palms over his bare shoulders, his chest, traced that tattoo of my initial he had over his heart, leaned forward and kissed, then nipped the side of his neck, and he pulled my head back and kissed me again, hard, hungry. I pulled my bra off as he kissed me, and he pulled back and looked at me. His breathing was ragged, his body responding to me the way it always did.

"Are you sure?" he asked, and his voice was hoarse. Full of need.

"Yes. I'm sure," I said softly, and he picked me up and carried me back to the bed, and that was the last intelligible thing I said for the next few hours while Brennan made me remember what it felt like to be alive, what it felt like to be loved by someone who knew my soul completely.

By the time he finally rolled off of me, I was sweating, aching, exhausted. He'd taken me over the edge over and over again, gave me everything I wanted, worshiped my body with his the way only he could. I was filled to the brim, satisfied. That sensation of our power, our energy entwining as we'd thrashed and trembled against each other... damn, I'd missed that. He pulled me into his arms again, my front to his, pulled my thigh up over his waist, his arms around me. He was still trying to catch his breath, and his heart pounded against me. I was still trembling, coming down from the last waves of ecstasy.

"Holy shit that was amazing," I said, and he held me tighter, buried his face in my hair. "I love you."

"I love you, Molly," he said, his voice muffled. "I want this, forever. I'll do whatever it takes to earn it back."

"We're not keeping score," I murmured. "We're going to move forward, together."

I felt a wave of contentment, relief from him, and he kissed my shoulder and we fell asleep and I relaxed for the first time in an eternity.

Later, I woke up on my stomach, Brennan's lips and tongue working their way along my spine, right between my wings, his heavy body covering mine, bare skin to bare skin. I raised my body, and he claimed me again from behind before I was even fully awake.

"Sorry," he gasped when he rolled off of me a while later.

"Do you hear me complaining?"

"Well. I know you're not much of a morning person," he said, laying back and wiping his brow.

I sat up and straddled his bare body, then I leaned down over him. "Keep waking me up like that, and I think I could be," I whispered. Then I kissed him and got up to shower. To neither of our surprise, he followed me and did such a good job washing my body, I forgot all about trying to make myself feel clean again. He finished washing my hair, then ran his fingers down my arm, over the armband.

"This is... really cold," he said, looking down at my arm. "What is it?"

"Souls of my enemies," I said, looking up at him.

He met my eyes. "That is creepy as hell," he said, laughing. "Good. It does something for you, I'm guessing?"

"Gives my powers a little extra boost. Which would be awesome if I could use my powers without wanting to die. I'm pretty sure this is what made me strong enough to be able to pull away from the Nether."

He nodded. "And you can't take it off because this is probably one of those things that would be bad if it fell into the wrong hands," he guessed.

"To put it mildly," I said, soaping up his chest and stomach.

He held my hands still, and I looked up at him. "There's more you're not telling me," he finally said.

"I had a blackout the other day," I said. "I'm hoping it's just stress, that once I'm settled again, it won't happen anymore."

He just looked down at me. His emotions told me everything I needed to know. He loved me. He was angry I'd been through so much. He wanted to fix it, but couldn't, and he hated that.

And I hadn't even told him the worst of it. That there was something in me that wanted him bleeding, dead, broken. And that every second we were together, the thing raged harder. I was having a hard time keeping its rage from overtaking me. I didn't want him to know that. He'd think it was me, being mad at him (rightfully, but still) over his one-nighter. But I was starting to realize that this was something different, something separate from me.

Frankly, it scared the hell out of me.

A few minutes, a few kisses later, Brennan stepped out of the shower and I finished up by myself.

Once I'd dressed and braided my hair, I headed downstairs in search of one thing:

Coffee.

When I got downstairs, Brennan was sitting in the living room giving Sean a bottle. Ada was standing in the kitchen with Stone, him putting away dishes from the dishwasher while she looked over some papers in her hand. Nain was sitting at the dining room table, reading something.

Oh. He was really, really pissed off about something.

He looked up and glanced at me as I walked past.

"Morning," I said, watching him. He just grunted. I got my coffee and headed toward the living room.

"Have a good night?" he said under his breath.

I stopped short and looked at him, raised an eyebrow.

You want to do this now? Really?

Why the fuck not? The gang's all here, right?

"That was fast," he said, loudly enough now for Brennan to hear. "Didn't even make him beg, did you?"

"And this is your business how, exactly?" I said, and I knew there was a threat in my voice.

"He shows he's perfectly willing to betray you, and you go crawling back," Nain said, disgust in his voice. And it hurt me more than it should have.

"Betray? Like lie to someone so they do the one thing they couldn't live with? Like that kind of betrayal?" My power rose in response to my anger, and I felt the building tremble slightly.

"Or betray like start fucking your husband's best friend months after he died? Like that?" Nain growled, and his eyes were glowing red. He stood, came toward me, and I stood my ground.

"Don't even, demon. This isn't a fight you want. Believe me," I said, glaring up into his face. *What the hell is wrong with you? We were fine.*

"Guys. Hey!" Ada shouted from the kitchen, and Stone put a hand on Nain's arm, tried to pull him away from me. Brennan had put Sean down in his bouncer and raced to my side. He was shouting at Nain, rage pouring off of him.

"You think I'm afraid of you, little girl?" Nain snarled.

"If you were smart, you would be. I never betrayed you, you asshole," I said, forcing myself to calm down. I wasn't doing this. Brennan took my shoulders and put me behind him, glared at Nain.

"Yeah. Protect her," Nain growled. "You think she won't toss you aside when the time is right, Bren? She'll take what she wants and move on. Watch her."

Rage rose inside me, overshadowed everything else. Any rational thought I might have had, any sense at all, was obliterated in that moment by the desire to show the demon what happened when he tried to threaten his betters.

I darted out from behind Brennan. I sensed Hephaestus coming down from his room. I reached Nain, punched him hard in the stomach, and when he bent over in pain, I kneed his face and he dropped to the floor.

"You want to say anything else to me, demon?" I growled as I bent over him, grabbed his hair and pulled. Power, rage, coursed through my body, and I felt the darkness inside me rising. My flamesword appeared in my hand, and I heard Ada gasp. The loft was silent around us.

"What the hell?" Nain said, and the snarl was gone from his voice. I felt confusion from him, fear. I fought back the rage, the images of me removing his head from his body in one quick swipe of the sword. I let him go, stepped back, made my flamesword disappear. Nain stood up, stared at me. "What the hell just happened? Why did you kick my ass, Molls?"

"You weren't yourself," I said shakily, meeting his eyes. What the hell had I nearly done? *Do you remember what you said?*

He shook his head.

"What's going on?" Brennan asked. His fists were still clenched at his side. He was ready to shift, ready to rip Nain's throat out. I put my hand on his arm.

"You were going off about how I'd betrayed you, about how Brennan proved he was capable of betraying me because he slept with that wi..." I trailed off, then looked toward the living room, at Sean.

All of the arguing. Ada and Stone at each other's throats. Nain being a bigger asshole than usual, when we'd just decided we were fine. Eunomia's unexplainable moment of anger at Hephaestus a few days prior. None of it was normal. None of it made sense. Unless...

Fucking Strife.

I remembered the things my mother and Athena had told me, back in the Nether, about the spirit daemon I'd trapped in my realm.

"Ada, you scanned the baby, right?" I asked, hoping I was wrong.

"Molly, what are you talking about?" Brennan asked. "He has nothing to do with this. Nain's an asshole, that's all."

"Ades?" I asked again, ignoring Brennan.

Embarrassment flooded from her. "No. I didn't. Didn't even think about it. Brennan brought him home and we were just all so busy loving on him."

"Molly?" Brennan asked, worried now.

"Check him, Ada," I said. I met Nain's eyes, then turned to Brennan.

"How did you meet his mother again?"

"I rescued her from two of your demons, some of the ones that went rogue? I killed the demons, then offered to take her home. And it turned into a drink and then something else," he trailed off, anger and shame flooding from him. "Why?"

I didn't answer. Turned to watch Ada as she picked up Brennan's son. She brought him into the dining room, then laid him on the table. He looked up at her calmly, giant blue eyes taking in every detail. I could feel him. He was not afraid. He trusted and loved Ada.

Ada focused on the baby, made a low humming sound every now and then as she moved her hands over him. She placed stones on his head, his chest, and then closed her eyes and focused some more.

"Oh, hell," she muttered a few minutes later.

"What?" Brennan asked, going over to the table. He picked up his son, looked him over.

Ada's eyes found mine.

"Brennan, kiddo. I think you were set up," Ada said gently.

"He's mine," Brennan said softly.

She nodded. "He's yours. He's also hosting a spirit miasma," Ada said.

"What the hell does that mean?" Brennan asked, looking down at his son.

"His mother imbued him with the spirit of discord. It picks up on negative emotions: anger, hatred, jealousy. And it temporarily infects those feeling it, amplifies the feelings. There are witches who are talented at these kinds of spells. The main point is usually to cause chaos and strife. Those witches usually are followers of Eris." Then she looked at me. "This explains a hell of a lot."

"But what does that have to do with anything?" Brennan asked.

Ada took his arm, gently. "It was no coincidence that you rescued that particular witch, from those particular demons," she said. "Or that you ended up with her that night. If I was able to guess, I'd bet you were spelled. You're not stupid enough to cheat on Molly, and I've always thought so, but I wrote it off to desperation and depression." Her gaze shifted to me. "And you have too many enemies, girl."

"Tell me something I don't know," I muttered. "Strife. Eris. I trapped her here when I destroyed the gateway."

"And fuckin' Strife found your demons," Hephaestus intoned. I nodded.

"And put them to work going after those I try to protect and using bullshit tactics like this to hurt those I care about," I said.

"It's not just that," Ada said. "The worst part is that a possessed being is often a kind of conduit between the one who spelled them and their current station. So chances are good that we've been being watched for the last few months, and we haven't realized it."

"Fuck," Nain growled.

Brennan had been quiet, looking down at his son during our exchange. Then he looked up at me. "She didn't put a spell on me. I mean, maybe she would have if I hadn't been willing. But it never got to that point." He glanced at Ada, who was shaking her head sadly. "I know you were trying to give me an out, Ada, and I love you for it." Then he met my eyes. "But I'm not going to lie. I messed up, but I'm the one that did it, and I'm going to take responsibility for it."

I nodded. "Okay. So where does that leave us?" I asked Ada.

"I'm so sorry. I should have thought of it," Ada said, looking at me helplessly.

"It's okay. Can you do anything about it now?"

Brennan looked at me like he didn't know me, held his son tighter.

"Brennan," Ada said sharply, and he turned his gaze back to her. "I think I can remove the miasma. Maybe. It won't hurt him, but it will make him very tired. Do you understand?"

"He'll be okay, though?" Brennan asked, and I could feel the fear for his son rolling off of him.

"I promise. I'm not sure I can remove it, but I'll try. But you need to give me the baby, and you need to trust me. I need a quiet place with no external interference. Just me and him. Okay?"

He stared at her.

"Would I ever, *ever* hurt that baby, Brennan Michael Riley?" Ada asked sternly, and he shook his head. He handed the baby over, and she took him.

"This will take a while. Do not come into my room. I need to be able to focus," Ada said, carrying the baby upstairs.

We all watched her go. Brennan went and sat at the foot of the stairs, stared at his feet. Stone went back to the kitchen, and Hephaestus went in the living room and started tinkering with some contraption he was building. Nain and I exchanged a look.

"Strife uses emotions that are already there," I said quietly. "Is there something you want to say to me?"

Nain shook his head. "We already had this out, Molls. You knew I was jealous. You know I want you. And I'm an asshole, but not that much of an asshole. I said we were okay the other day, and I meant it."

I nodded. "I think it's time for me to move out," I said. "It's for the best."

"Time for *us* to move out," Brennan said from the stairway. "I'm coming with you."

I took a deep breath, felt the certainty of what I had to do settle over me. Remembered what Athena had said to me, during our training: what we want doesn't matter. I thought of all the things I'd wanted, all the dreams I'd had for Brennan and me.

His infant son had been spelled to try to get at those who cared for me.

Brennan himself had been the target of the shifter plague. He'd been taken and tortured by Hermes' minions, a bargaining chip to use against me.

And so, I thought of all the things I wanted, and I let them go. I made my face expressionless, my voice mild, no matter how I felt my heart shredding.

"Brennan, I don't think I'm the best person to raise a baby around. Your son was targeted because of me."

"So, what? We're done? Bullshit, Molly. I already know you have crazy enemies. I'm not going anywhere."

I took a deep breath. "We'll see each other around. You continue to be used against me, and I can't let that go on. It's for the best."

"And you get to make every decision for us now?"

Us. The word threatened to make me lose it. The "us" I could never have, because I'd pissed off way too many powerful beings. The "us" I had to walk away from to keep the love of my life safe. The "us" I'd never have, not the way I'd dreamed of.

"No. I get to make the decisions that need to be made, the ones that you're too emotionally involved to make."

He shook his head. "Forever. That's what we said. Yeah?" He met my eyes, and I nodded. "Okay, then. Forever means forever, no matter what bullshit gets thrown at us."

"Not for us, it doesn't," I said quietly.

"You're putting extra pressure on her," Nain said to Brennan. "You really think she needs that now?"

"She needs to be surrounded by people who love her," Brennan said.

"She," I said loudly, "is standing right the fuck here, and she tends to get pissed off when people try to make decisions for her." I looked back at Brennan. "This is how it has to be. You have a support network here. This is the safest place for your son. And no matter how much you love me, you owe him a safe place to grow up. You owe him time with his father. We'll see each other around, and I will always love you. But I'm not going to put you and Sean in danger because I want you by my side. That's it." I felt anger, frustration roll off of him, and I headed up the opposite stairway, to his room. As I walked up the stairs, I heard Nain tell Brennan that I was right, and Brennan tell him to shut the hell up.

I packed a duffel bag with the few items of clothing I had in Brennan's room. Before that, they'd been in Nain's room, sharing his dresser drawers.

I was really, really good at making mistakes. Screwing up people's lives. I shook my head.

I sat down on the edge of the bed, t-shirt in my hands. Trying to keep it together. The darkness inside me, smugly satisfied. The emptiness I felt, even though I knew it was for the best. It would have been so easy to lose control, to let whatever it was inside me take over. Maybe I'd feel less.

Of course, then everyone I loved would end up dead.

There was a knock at the door. Eunomia. I told her to come in, and she did, closing the door behind her.

"Stop it, devil girl," she said softly as she sat down next to me.

"Stop what?"

"Second-guessing everything you do. You love who you love. You make the decisions you make for a reason."

"That's the thing, E," I said, shaking my head. "I have no goddamn idea what I'm doing. I'm lost, and I'm going to make all of you lost with me."

"Well, for what it's worth, if I was going to be lost with anyone, I'd want it to be you, my friend," she said. Then she leaned into me, and we rested the sides of our heads together. "You're too hard on yourself. You always have been."

"I'm not hard enough on myself. And I make stupidass decisions."

She sighed. "I don't think you have to leave. You have to understand on some level that the safest place for all of us is wherever you are. Even if your enemies come right at you, you're the only one here who's able to really fight them off. If Strife comes for any of us, you're the only one who stands a chance."

"If Strife comes around, it will be for me. I don't want you guys in the crossfire."

"If Strife comes around, she'll likely try to hurt those you love. Look what she's done already."

"Exactly. I need to find that witch. I need to find Strife. I need to find the rogue demons." And that was just for starters. While I would have liked to believe that my rage and blackouts could be blamed on the miasma in Brennan's son, I knew better. Most of my episodes had occurred when I was nowhere near the baby. And I had a bad feeling about what it could be. If it was what I was starting to suspect, then that was all the more reason the best place for everyone was as far away from me as possible.

"And when do you get to live your life, Mollis?" Eunomia asked gently.

I looked at her. "Maybe I don't get one. Maybe this is what I'm here for. Maybe I need to clean up the messes I made, and then focus on doing what I can to keep everyone safe. Could be I'm not meant to have a family, or anyone else close to me."

"Too late," she whispered, smiling a little. "You've got us, and we all love you. And we just got you back and I have the feeling every one of us would chase you to the end of the Earth, to the Aether, the Nether, and back if you decided to leave us again. You are loved. You're needed."

"Why?" I asked, and felt the tears threatening. "All I bring is chaos. You know it."

She shrugged. "So?"

I stared at her, and she wrapped a thin arm around my shoulders, hugged me. Then Eunomia got up and walked out, closing the door behind herself.

They loved me. All the more reason I was determined to keep them safe.

Okay. Brennan needed me right that moment, because his son was going through something scary. Once I knew Sean was all right, that was it, I told myself. I couldn't just desert him when he was worried over what was happening with his son.

I dropped my bag on Brennan's bed and walked out of the room. He was still sitting on the step, looking at the floor. He knew I was there; he could feel me just as easily as I could feel him. And he was worried, and confused, and angry. I walked over to him and nudged him a little, and he moved over so I could sit on the step next to him.

I sat, my thigh and hip pressed against his. He reached over and took my hand. I rested my head on his shoulder. We sat like that, silent, until we heard Ada's bedroom door open, then we both sprang up and watched her carry Sean down the stairs. The baby was sleeping. He looked healthy and whole, but when I sensed for Ada, all I felt was sadness. Disappointment. Frustration. Her hair had escaped its braid, and her face, which normally looked so young and vibrant, was showing its age; she looked haggard, and the wrinkles around her mouth and eyes were more pronounced. She noticed me watching her.

"I'm sorry. Miasmas are not fun to deal with, and this one is..." she shook her head, tears glistening in her eyes. "I couldn't get rid of it. All I could do was layer another spell over it, one that would keep whoever cast it from watching us. But it's still there, and it'll still affect us," she said, and I hugged her. Then Stone came rushing over, and he ushered Ada back to their room and closed the door.

Brennan was looking down at Sean, then he looked up at me. "Now what?"

I took a deep breath. Time to contact someone more powerful. No matter how much I disliked the idea of indebting myself to her. I sent a thought to my imps to find my father and give him a message.

"We wait. I have more help on the way." We went in the living room and sat side-by-side on the couch, Sean still sleeping in Brennan's arms.

A few minutes later, I heard a distinctive "crack" and I looked up to see my father and Persephone standing in the center of the loft.

"Daughter," Hades said in greeting. "Your imps say you have need of us."

I nodded. "You remember Brennan," I said to Hades. "Brennan, this is my stepmother, Persephone."

Persephone was studying Brennan and his son with a knowing look on her face.

"So. The shifter you moved Earth and the heavens to save. And he holds a child that is his and very much not yours," Hades said, glaring at Brennan.

I stood up, walked over to my father. I shook my head a little. "That's my problem, not yours." Then I turned to Persephone. "His son was infested with a spirit miasma. Strong one. Our witch friend tried to remove it and couldn't. We need someone more powerful."

"Wait. You mean you didn't need me?" Hades asked me.

"No. I only needed you to bring her." Then I looked at Persephone again. "Will you help him? Please?"

She nodded, eyes on me. I walked back to Brennan and held my arms out for the baby. He settled Sean into my arms without any hesitation. "He'll be okay," I said softly.

"I trust you."

Sweet words; a knife to the heart. I turned away, carried the baby over to Persephone.

"You will come with me," she said to me. "We need a quiet place." Then she turned to Hades and Brennan. "We'll leave you to discuss whatever it is philanderers discuss."

I rolled my eyes (though I couldn't help admiring her bitchiness when it wasn't directed at me) and headed up toward Brennan's room, and she followed me. Mostly, I focused on not dropping Sean, who was still sleeping. I am totally not a baby person.

We walked into Brennan's room. The bed sheets were still twisted and rumpled. I tried not to think about it. Another thing I was turning my back on: the best sex I could ever hope to have.

I am an idiot.

Persephone was looking around. She closed the door behind us, then she stood and watched me. I set Sean on the bed.

"Well. Go ahead. You've earned a cheap shot or ten," I told my stepmother.

She raised one of her perfect eyebrows, her model-gorgeous face unreadable. "I am above cheap shots, abomination."

I looked away.

"You've forgiven him. This room reeks of sexual energy."

"Oh, Christ," I muttered. "I haven't totally forgiven him, but..." I shrugged.

"You love him."

I looked down at Sean. "It doesn't matter. I can't stay."

We stood in awkward silence for a few seconds. "The witch, the kid's mother, cursed him before she turned him over to Brennan. I'm pretty sure she's a follower of--"

"Eris," Persephone finished, nodding. "Yes. The feel of the curse is very familiar. Not the first I've dealt with." She walked over to the bed, sat down beside where Sean was still sleeping. "You are very good at making the wrong beings mad at you."

"I know."

"You don't expect me to do this for you and get nothing in return, do you?" she asked me.

"I figured that was too much to hope. What do you want?"

"Nothing just now. Just remember that you owe me a favor someday."

"I have the right to turn you down, though, just as you could have with this."

"Fine."

She started running her hands just above Sean's sleeping form. "Yes, this is a strong miasma," she murmured. "She set the curse when he was in the womb, and it finalized at birth. That is very, very potent magic."

"Can you remove it?" I asked her, sitting on the other side of Sean.

She gave me a withering look. "Please. There isn't a mortal witch alive who can place a curse I can't remove. Now be silent. You're mainly here so I can draw off of your obnoxious amount of power if I need to."

I crossed my arms, watched my stepmother as she worked. She ran her hands gently over the baby, closed her eyes as she focused. Her hands seemed to hover for quite a while over Sean's head, then again over his chest. I could feel the power she was drawing, the hairs on the back of my neck rising in response to the energy flowing through the room. She was breathing harder, her brow creased in concentration.

After a while, the energy level decreased, then fell completely. Persephone opened her eyes and looked at me, then at Sean. She pulled her hands back and folded them in her lap.

"He is rid of the curse," she said. "He's very strong. Because of the way she planted the miasma, it was very much part of him. He was kind of fighting me there for a while."

"Thank you, Persephone," I said softly, picking Sean up. She nodded. I was ready to carry Sean out of the room when she put her hand on my arm, held me back gently.

"The only advice I have for you is to remember that whatever he did has nothing to do with you. It's him. His weakness, his moments of idiocy. Don't let it affect the way you see yourself."

I met her eyes, nodded. Then I grinned. "Did we just have a moment?"

She glared at me. "I will deny that to my dying day, abomination." Then she headed out of the room and I followed her down the stairs to where Brennan and Hades were waiting in the dining room. They were sitting at the same end of the table, and Hades was talking in low tones to Brennan when Persephone and I started down the stairs. As soon as they saw us, they both stood up and

Brennan raced to my side. I handed Sean to him, and he held him closely, looked him over.

"He is fine. I've removed the curse completely," Persephone told him.

"Thank you so much," Brennan said, bowing to her.

"It was deeply embedded in him. He will sleep for quite a while. When he wakes, he will likely be quite disoriented. He will need plenty of comforting, shifter. It may take a while for him to get used to life without the miasma."

Brennan nodded, thanked Persephone again. I showed my father and his wife out, and Hades gave me a small hug as he walked out. "Call me if you need me, daughter. You are not alone," he murmured, and I nodded. I closed the door behind them and headed back into the living room. Brennan was sitting on the couch, holding Sean. I went and sat next to him, dreading what came next.

"Thank you so much for calling her. I know you're not crazy about each other."

"I'm just happy she was able to help. Poor kid," I said.

We sat in silence for a few minutes, things getting more uncomfortable as more time passed. I knew what I had to do, couldn't make myself stand up and do it.

"I have to leave for patrol in a bit," he said, looking down at Sean.

"No you don't. I'll take it tonight," Nain said, walking out of his room.

"Thanks, man. I'll take one of yours to pay you back."

"Damn right you will," Nain said, heading for the door.

When he was gone, Brennan and I sat for a while in silence. "So, you're really going to do this? You're leaving me," he said.

My stomach twisted. Sadness rolled off of him. "Yes."

"And I can't talk you out of it, because you're stubborn and infuriating that way," he said.

"That's me," I said, trying to keep my voice steady.

"And I'm just supposed to do this now? Live without you? See you around the city and act like you're not the other half of me?"

I didn't trust my voice to answer.

He set Sean down on the sofa next to him, covered him up with a blue afghan. And then he turned back to me, and his gaze bored into mine. "I love you, Molly. You are my heart. You're everything to me. By your side is the only place I ever want to be. If I beg, and rage, and threaten, would you let me be there? If I try to convince you that the danger of being with you is worth it, would you listen?" I shook my head, tears already spilling over.

"My enemies won't stop trying to get to me. They'll use whatever they can, and there are too many of them now. You know that, better than anyone else. One of these times, they'd kill you. And I can't allow that. The best place for you is away from me." I paused. Time to tell him the whole story, so he'd see how lucky he was to be rid of me. "And there's more. Whatever happened to me in the Nether... I'm not myself. And for whatever reason, you trigger this thing inside me. I can't trust myself around you anymore. It wants to hurt you. It wants you dead. And one of these times, I'm not gonna be able to hold it back."

"God damn it, Molly," he said, a plea in his voice, and I shook my head.

"You know I'm right. Don't make me have to live with your death."

He didn't answer. He was angry. He was hurting the same way I was, and feeling it only made it all the harder for me to breathe. And then he took my face gently in his hands, and he kissed me, softly, gently, and this time, it really was good-bye. He pulled away slowly, his lips lingering on mine as if he couldn't make himself break the contact between us. "I miss you already," he whispered against my lips. "Don't do this. Don't make me live without you again." I didn't answer, and he kissed me again, and I made myself savor it, made myself memorize the sensation of his lips on mine, his warm, strong hands cupping my face. "I don't know how I'm going to do this."

"Me too," I whispered. Then I removed his hands from my face, set them into his lap. I went up to his room and grabbed the bag I'd packed, stepped into my shoes. I walked back down the stairs and out of the loft, and I didn't turn back to look at him, because if I did, I wouldn't have had the strength to walk out the door.

I managed not to cry until I was in my car. And then I rested my forehead on the steering wheel and bawled, barely able to breathe around the emptiness inside me.

I heard the passenger door open, and glanced up. Bash and Dahael climbed in and closed the door behind them. Bash climbed into the back seat, and Dahael stayed in the passenger seat.

"Sorry, Mistress," she said, sadness in her eyes. "So sorry. Mistress should be able to be happy. He belongs to you."

"I know he does," I said, my voice hoarse from crying. "Sometimes, it's just not enough. And what we want is not the most important thing. Not right now, anyway."

CHAPTER EIGHTEEN

When I was able to drive, I pulled out of the garage and drove through the streets to the east side, finally pulling up into my driveway. It was a little after midnight. I got out of the car and unlocked the back door. I'd ask Stone to bring my dogs the next day. I'd spent a little time with them in their yard near the loft, but they needed to be home now. Time to make a clean break.

I went through the house, plugging in appliances, turning on lamps. Nain or Brennan or whoever had done a good job of making sure the power and everything stayed on, so the house was ready when I got back. It needed an airing out, a good dusting, and to be vacuumed, but it was livable.

I wandered up to my old office. All those photos of lost girls, found girls, on the walls, starting to yellow and curl with age and the effects of a few years of humid Detroit summers. I stood and stared at my desk. This had been my life. This had been everything. Simple. I did good, and I kept to myself. I'd been smarter than I'd given myself credit for.

Then I walked to my bedroom, clicked on the overhead light. My bed, the plant stand, the plants long-since dead now. Even succulents can't live forever without someone around to care for them. I looked at the bed. I'd shared it with Nain, not nearly as often as either of us would have liked. We'd made our marriage bond there, promised each other forever.

Well. Nothing lasts forever, right? Except for me.

I went to work, changed the sheets. The imps stayed out of my way. All of them were there with me now; not just Bash and Dahael, but my entire imp army, which numbered a few dozen, give or take. Some of them were always out on patrol, scouting the city for my lost girls or other problems, while the rest guarded me, alerted me to danger.

I went to the front door, called a small group over to me. "You guys are in charge of watching the loft. Any sign of danger, you let me know immediately."

"Yes Mistress," they said in low voices, then they bowed and thumped their fists to their chests. I watched them head out into the night, then I headed back in and locked the door. Bash and Dahael were still inside. They both looked up at me.

"Find that witch, and my rogue demons," I said. "That's your focus now, okay?"

They both saluted me, grabbed a few more imps, then headed out into the night, through the window. I closed it behind them, leaving it open a crack so they could get back in when they returned.

I climbed into bed in my clothes. And I cried myself to sleep, like some ridiculous cliché, and instead of dreams, I saw blood and death. I killed Brennan over and over again, and when he begged for mercy, I laughed. And I heard a voice, chilling, cold, tell me that this was what was coming.

I dreamed that I murdered everyone who'd ever hurt me, and, worse, everyone who'd ever loved me, that I bathed in their blood and was reborn. And even though I cried, I could feel something inside me exalting in the violence, and that thing, whatever it was, was in control just then. It showed me Brennan dead, broken, and I couldn't even scream.

"Mistress," someone said near my ear. Then louder; "Mistress!"

I jumped up. My forehead was soaked with sweat, and I felt like I could barely breathe. "Huh? What?" I asked hoarsely. Bash and Dahael stood next to my bed.

"Found your demons." Dahael said. I glanced at the clock on the nightstand. It was a little after three-thirty. I'd lost a couple of hours again, and didn't feel rested. It hadn't been sleep as much as me and that thing inside me battling for control. And I'd lost. I knew that for a fact, and it was just lucky that the imps had stirred me when they had.

I wiped my face. "Anything else?"

"Got four women, two men captive. In rough shape, all. Probably getting ready to move again. Hurry." Bash said.

"Okay. Where?"

They told me, and I went into my backyard, figuring I'd fly there. Artemis was there, just outside of the gateway. My heart felt like it was bleeding in my chest. Was everything going to remind me of him now?

"How are you, dear girl?" she asked. "Surprised to see you here."

I forced my face into a mask of emotionless distance. "You have another descendant. Brennan has a son."

She stared at me.

"And I can't be with him anymore. It's not safe. You love them? You care for your descendants so much? Watch over them. Keep them safe."

She watched me a moment, then she reached forward and pulled me into a hug, and I forced down the sob that rose to my chest, bit my lip hard to keep from crying.

When she pulled away, I took a deep breath, determined to pull myself back together again.

"I will keep them safe. I promise you that, Fury," she said. She studied me. "I would have loved to have had you in my family, my dear."

I nodded, because I couldn't trust my voice. And then Artemis shifted before me, turning into a big black cat. I ignored the stab to my heart, gestured to an imp. "Show Artemis where the loft is, please," I said to him, and he nodded, thumped his chest.

I took a few breaths, tried to make myself focus. I had people to save, asses to kick. I took another deep breath and kicked into the air, flying into the night. I headed east. There were a bunch of duplexes on Kelly Road, straddling the border between Detroit and Harper Woods. The imps told me they were in one of them, at least for the moment. I flew over the area, getting an idea of the layout. At least four demons. Maybe the witch, if I was lucky. There was definitely a mist over the area, the same kind Ada used when she was trying to shield us from the eyes of Normals. Demons couldn't do that.

I hoped they'd put up a fight. I had all kinds of rage to work off.

I found the duplex they were hiding in. It was boarded up in front, but I could see from my flyover that the back door was open. It was brick, two story, like two little colonials side-by-side. My rogue demons were in the right-hand side of the duplex.

I landed in the back yard, sensed the area. Yeah. Four demons, a few Normals. I wasn't picking up the witch, but she could have been shielding herself. Some of the stronger ones knew how to do that, and if she was working with Strife, there was a decent chance she could do it. If she wasn't there, one of them would spill their guts about her. I'd make sure of that.

No powers, I reminded myself. The pain would distract me, and if I was facing four demons, I couldn't weaken myself for the quick hit. I remembered the things Athena had taught me, reminded myself to thank her for all those times she kicked my ass, shouted at me to use my head once in a while.

I held my hand out and my flamesword appeared at my side.

I could feel them inside. They knew I was there, and a mixture of fear and rage roared over me, from them.

I walked up the crumbling concrete steps and into what used to be a kitchen. The counters and cabinets were still intact, and aging yellow paint adorned the walls.

"Don't you want to play, my demons?" I asked the empty room. "All this running, you'd think you were a bunch of cowards."

They were in the next room. I smiled, my adrenaline pumping, my bloodlust full on. I walked through the doorway, and they charged me, as I figured they would. I swung out with the sword and caught the first unfortunate (and stupid) demon, slashing through his throat as if it was made of tissue paper. His blood washed over me, and I remembered my dreams.

They'd pay.

The remaining three demons circled me. One had a knife, and one had two cruel-looking daggers. The final one, the female, pointed a gun at my head.

"Oh, please, bitch," I muttered. "I've been taking out thugs with guns since I was seventeen. You aren't shit." And I brought my sword arm up and knocked her arm aside, just as she pulled the trigger. Then I brought the blade down again, and her hand, still holding the gun, hit the floor. I kicked the gun back into the kitchen as I dodged the demon with the daggers. He lunged for me, but I can move a hell of a lot faster than any demon. All that muscle tends to slow them down. That, and the fact that they rarely ever have to actually fight, since they usually rely on cheap tricks to surprise their prey.

But me? I learned how to fight on the streets when I had nothing but the conviction that I was needed. I was taught by the most hardass demon I'd ever known, then by one of the best pure fighters I've ever met.

I've sparred with Athena. I've fought my way back from death. Demons? Please.

While the female demon tried to pull herself up and together, I fought the remaining two, the one with the knife and the one with the daggers. I parried, slashed out at them when they tried to stab at me. Soon, they were both bleeding, angry. And it started to be accompanied by just a little bit of fear, and it fed me. I grinned and slashed out at Daggers, taking his left arm off at the elbow, and he howled, and I ended the noise with a quick slash to his throat.

The floor was slick with blood. Their pain and fear fed me, that inner part of me that is of the Nether, my demon. If we're talking demons, I'm the most demonic bitch in this realm or any other. Born of the Lord of the Dead Himself. I drew on that, let myself forget everything else, just for a while, and felt the joy of battle, the screams and agony of my enemies.

The demon with the knife kept coming at me. He managed to stab me in the shoulder when I tripped over Daggers' body, and I growled in pain. The female demon was trying to rise, and I jabbed behind me with the sword, heard her flesh sizzle as the blade entered her stomach. She gave a final gurgle and fell over. She wouldn't be getting up again.

Knives charged me again, and I ducked him, placed a hard kick to the side of his knee, and he screamed and crumpled to the ground. He tried to grab me on his way down, and I brought my knee up and broke his nose.

After that, he just tried to get away from me.

"Where are you going?" I growled. He whimpered, still trying to put distance between the two of us. I kicked him, hard, and he fell over. I kicked him onto his back, put the point of my sword at his throat. He looked up at me, fear rolling off of him. He put his hands up; a gesture of defeat. I knew better. I'd been lied to too often to take anything at face value.

"Where's the witch?" I asked him, and the power filling me hurt. I was full, and there was no way in hell I'd be able to release it now. Not if I wanted to stay conscious and in control.

He shook his head wildly, and I kicked him in the stomach. He grunted. "Where is the witch?" I repeated, my voice starting to turn into a snarl as my power thundered through me.

"Don't know. Haven't seen her. She stays with Strife. They only find us when they want us. Please. It was Strife."

He was lying. Not about Strife, though.

"Do not make excuses," I roared. "You betrayed me. Me. It's not a mistake you'll live to repeat."

I broke into his mind, then. I'd have to risk using my powers. I had to find out where she was. It was absolute agony. He squirmed, and panicked, and I tried to focus on sifting through his thoughts.

Ah. There.

She was supposed to meet them at our current location at four. Make Strife's mark (each body had had a weird little design cut into it; now I knew what it was) and then mist everything again so they could go into hiding. I smirked.

Something else would be greeting her instead.

I bored the rest of the way into his mind, took his will to live away from him. I watched the light in his eyes fade; the last of my rogue demons. As he died, crows flooded into the house, started claiming the souls of the demons. I'd forgotten. These were the Guardians' replacements, and now that the gateway was back, they could do their work, bringing the souls to my family to face their eternal judgment. There was no chanting, no ceremony. The crows came in, claimed their treasures, and left.

Once they were gone, I went into the back bedroom, found the humans the demons had been keeping captive. I could see what the demons had done to them, both the men and the women, and I wished I could kill each of the demons a few more times.

I pulled my phone out of my pocket and dialed Chief Jones. I told him what was going on, where to find the captives. And then I went to work trying to comfort them. I'd have to use my powers on them, after Jones and his shifters got here. They'd heard and seen too much, and it would only traumatize them if they were able to remember it all.

I untied each of them, offered them bottles of water I'd found on the kitchen counter. A couple of the women drank gratefully, but the rest sat there. In shock. They were all afraid of me, but grateful at the same time.

"You're one of them. You're not human," one of the women said.

"I'm not human. But I sure the hell am not one of them," I told her.

"You saved us. We didn't think anyone was coming... no one knew we were gone, all this time," another of the women said.

"Why not?"

"None of us have anybody. While we've been stuck here, we've been talking. Realized nobody was ever going to bother looking for us."

One of the men nodded. "We were pretty sure we were dead, as soon as they got tired of us. And no one would know or care, either way."

I looked them over. Four women, two men. Varying ages, shapes, some black, some white. One of the women was Middle Eastern. Lost.

"Well. I care," I said. "I'm sorry I didn't get to you sooner. They did a good job of staying on the run."

"Thank you," one of the women said, and she was crying. She buried her face in her hands, and one of the other women comforted her.

I heard a couple of car doors slam outside, and the humans all tensed. I held my hands out, letting them know to stay calm. "I'm pretty sure that's my police officer friend," I said, soothing them. They relaxed, a little.

Within a few seconds, Jones walked in the house. "In here," I called, and he made his way into the bedroom where we were all standing. He'd seen the carnage in the living room, and now he looked over the humans who had been captive.

"Chief," I said quietly.

"Angel," he said, holding his hand out.

"It *is* you!" one of the women said. "I prayed to you. You answered." And then she started bawling, and two of the other women put their arms around her.

I turned to the chief, met his eyes. "I'm going to have to use some of my powers on them. They saw way too much," I said in a low voice.

He nodded. "You're going to let them remember you, though. I think they need that, after this."

I gave a short nod. "I need you guys to all clear out ASAP. I'm expecting the witch that was working with them."

"Not a problem. It's good to have you back, Angel. We'll be back after sunrise to handle clean-up."

I turned to the humans. "Guys," I said softly, and they all looked at me. I felt my power rising, let it lace my voice. "You were held captive by four sick individuals. They were humans, but they were deranged, and they hurt you. You were rescued by the Angel and the Detroit Police, who were forced to kill your captors when they wouldn't surrender. You won't remember much about tonight, but you will remember me." Oh, damn. Everything hurt. I could feel blood dripping from my nose, and I brought my hand up to staunch the bleeding. "Remember me. I care about you. Someone cares." I gritted my teeth against the pain. "It will be so."

My power snapped, took hold in the humans, who had the tell-tale glazed look in their eyes. I turned away, not wanting them to see my glowing eyes or the blood all over my body, both mine and the demons'.

"Thank you, Angel," Chief Jones said softly. Then he looked at me. "Hey. You okay?"

"I'll survive," I said. And then I walked out into the backyard, putting a little distance between them and me while the chief and his men got the humans out. I went to a far corner of the backyard, stumbling, in agony after using my powers again. I could barely breathe around it, and I tried to pull myself together. I breathed, thought un-painful thoughts, threw up a couple of times. I listened to car doors slamming, low voices as Jones got the humans away from the house.

I should have kept one of the demons alive, I thought to myself. I could have used a little pain and anger to feed my power while I waited for the witch.

I wiped my sleeve across my mouth, trying to clean myself up a little. Then I walked back through the yard, up the back stairs, and into the yellow kitchen. I went into the living room (cleared now of demon bodies; the chief and his crew didn't leave anything to chance) and leaned up against one of the walls. I closed my eyes, waited for my body to return to more manageable levels of pain.

I was really going to have to figure something out regarding my powers. Either I needed to stop using them, or I needed to figure out how to make this crap stop happening every time I tried to use them. I could only guess that this was some way of the Nether punishing me for breaking away, somehow. The Nether had taught me plenty of ways to punish my enemies; undoubtedly, it had a few tricks it hadn't shared with me. Such as how to completely screw with someone who broke an oath to it.

I was just starting to think that maybe the darkness in me, the urge to seriously hurt, even kill, Brennan, had to be related to that. I mean, he was the main thing I thought of in my grave. He was the one thing I couldn't wait to get back to. I'd have to ask Persephone. Maybe it was nothing more than a curse of some kind, and I'd have my life back.

Well, sorta. My life with my mate who had a kid that wasn't mine. Right.

Almost as if on cue, I felt a presence nearby. Witch.

Time to meet the murdering, lying, evil-ass baby mama.

CHAPTER NINETEEN

I stayed still in the living room, though I did draw my flamesword. I knew already that she was a powerful witch; the miasma she'd placed on Brennan's son hadn't been the work of an amateur. Which held with what my mom and Athena had told me about Strife. She was more likely to pick the strongest witches, because they could cause the most chaos.

I listened as the back door opened, soft footsteps treading on the linoleum kitchen floor.

"Are you worthless shitheads sleeping again?" I heard a voice call. It was a husky voice. The woman who walked into the room was not entirely what I'd expected. She was tall, willowy. A shock of purple hair was cut into a severe bob, and the second her eyes found me, she lifted her hands, readying a spell.

"Stop," I ordered, trying to force the thought into her mind. She laughed at me.

"Oh, please." And she lifted her hands again, and I charged her before she could get her spell off. I knocked her back into the wall, and she let out a grunt of pain.

I felt the air kind of tingle around me, and within

seconds it felt like my skin was being pricked by millions of needles. It was like being attacked by a swarm of hornets, and it distracted me just enough, and she danced out of my grasp.

The attack, whatever she'd done, kept going, and I forced myself to try to ignore it. After all the things I've been though, it shouldn't have messed with me as much as it did. She was readying another spell, and I shot fire at her, igniting the black leather jacket she wore. She let out a scream and started thrashing around, trying to put the flames out. The hornet-thing stopped, and I tackled her again, knocked her to the ground.

Her jacket was still on fire. I let it burn, and she panicked.

Oh. It was good. Exactly what I needed. Fear. It strengthened me, and I felt my body repairing itself from the trauma of using my powers against her. I put my hand on her throat and squeezed, hard. She still thrashed, trying to put the flames out. I sent a strong blast of power at them, and they stopped burning.

I kind of regretted doing that. But, I was currently holding her down, and it's not like I especially wanted to catch fire. It had done what I wanted it to do: distracted her.

I looked down at her, and felt complete hatred course through me. This time, it had nothing to do with the thing living inside me. It had everything to do with the fact that she'd participated in the deaths of twenty-seven innocent people. She'd worked with the demons. Helped them.

She started laughing at me, even as I still grasped her throat.

"He was good. But you already know that, don't you?" she taunted.

Christ. She thought I was mad about Brennan. Shallow, delusional bitch.

I punched her, hard, in the face. She stopped laughing then.

My skin prickled as she started preparing another spell, and I punched her again. To my surprise, she raised her knee and caught me in the gut, and it was just enough to distract me enough so that she was able to roll out of my grip on her throat.

I charged her again before she could get the spell off, and she met me with a kick to my knee. She missed, but caught my thigh, which threw me off-balance. Then she did manage to get a quick spell off, and I found myself totally unable to move.

"Yes!" she shouted when she realized I was immobile. "Oh, hell yes!"

I rolled my eyes, trying to show her that I was clearly unimpressed. Fucking newbies.

"You can't even talk, can you?" she taunted, laughing. Then she clapped her hands in her glee. She wiped at her nose, which was still bleeding. "Oh, she is going to be so happy with me," she said, watching me.

I just watched her. She grinned at me, totally relaxed now that she apparently had me subdued. "He was good. I actually meant that. I wouldn't have minded keeping him around a while, but Strife insisted I let him go back to his life. I had no idea how simple it was to ensure I got pregnant," she shook her head, still smiling. "She really is a genius."

I tried getting into her mind. She had a decent shield, actually, but she was so busy taunting me that she wasn't paying attention. She should have been able to feel me in her mind, trying to break in. I rolled my eyes again, and she took it as irritation over Brennan.

Lovely. Keep thinking that, I thought.

I worked at her mind a little more. I didn't give a shit about anything but Strife just then. She had to know something, obviously.

"You know, I really wasn't sure what to believe about how you looked. I mean, you hear things. Some people are all 'oh, she's gorgeous,' and others say you don't look like much of anything at all. Gotta say, Angel," she sneered, "I have to agree with the second group."

I kept working at her, made my way in as she prattled on. She was a prideful idiot. Her mind was filled with thoughts of how powerful she was, how amazing she was, how she was absolutely Strife's favorite. Sweet words whispered straight to her ego by Strife herself, about how glory lay ahead for someone as talented as her.

I searched her thoughts regarding her son. Nothing but pride over the miasma she'd managed to infect him with. He'd been a tool, a means to an end, a way to get more of Strife's approval. Nothing more. She was ambitious. I had to give her that much.

She was still fucking talking, which was actually starting to annoy me a little. "I mean, really. It's not all that surprising he was so easy to seduce, considering what he'd been sleeping with," she said, laughing.

There it was. Her thoughts about Strife herself were actually kind of hazy, confused. The only thing I really got from her head was that she was definitely responsible for working with the demons with all of those murders. Her main task had been to make sure the demons did their job, help them remain undetected, and to carve Strife's symbol (kind of a little weird squiggle; we'd noticed it on several bodies, but didn't know what it was) onto the flesh of each of the bodies. Kind of a prayer of thanks to her favorite goddess.

Yeah. The murders were meant to taunt me. At least I knew I wasn't being paranoid about that now.

"I don't even know what to do with you now," she was saying. "You killed all my demons. And Strife isn't supposed to even call me until Thursday." She stood, watching me, a bit of a pout on her lips. "I guess I can just keep you like that until then. Not like you're going anywhere." And then she laughed again, clearly pleased with herself.

There is only so much self-congratulatory crap I can be expected to stand.

I focused, hard. I could have used mental knives on her. Kind of wanted to, really. Could have set the bitch on fire again. That would have been fun. Unfortunately, I didn't have a whole lot of power left to work with, and I was already in agony from working my way into her mind.

In the end, I used one of the more useless powers I'd stolen back in my earlier days. It made the victim vomit uncontrollably. So I sent that at her, and she bent over, puking loudly.

Her spell broke, and I was free.

I stood, watching her vomit and whimper.

The imps came into the room, and Dahael watched her for a moment, then glanced at me, humor rolling off of her.

"Good one, Mistress," she said.

"It's not all about chopping heads off all the time," I said wisely, echoing Athena's words to me, and Dahael gave a small bark of a laugh. I sent some of the imps out to find my mother.

"Find Strife now?" Dahael asked.

I shook my head. "She didn't know where Strife is. I doubt Strife would have shared that with her; she's not going to advertise her whereabouts. She knows I'm stronger than she is."

"Bleeding, Mistress," Bash said, walking over to us.

"I know." My nose was gushing blood again, punishment for using my powers. I was trying to ignore the pain. I'd just have to toughen up a little until we figured out how to make it all stop. It had taken a lot of power to get into her mind, and I didn't have a hell of a lot left to work with to subdue her. Luckily, I hadn't had to do much; useless powers like making someone puke uncontrollably don't take a whole lot of power to pull off.

"Gonna make her stop now?" Dahael asked, glancing over at the still-puking witch.

"When my mom gets here."

"Not gonna kill her then?" Bash asked, and I shook my head.

"No. She's worthless. And my mom and aunt can spend some time finding out if there's anything else she knows." I felt fear from the witch, in addition to the pain she was in.

I enjoyed that. So I'm a little on the petty side.

A few seconds later, I felt my mother and aunt nearby, and then they walked through the back door and into the living room. My mother glanced at the witch, then raised her eyebrow at me questioningly.

"You didn't kill her?" she asked.

I let out a huffy breath in exasperation. "Why does everyone assume I was going to kill her?"

My aunt grinned. "Can you make her stop vomiting so I may escort her to her punishment, niece?"

I focused for a second, and the retching sounds stopped.

"That is disgusting," Megaera said.

"I know."

My mother shook her head.

"This witch was responsible for working with the demons who cause all of those murders. Twenty-seven deaths in all, and she was an accomplice. It was Strife's idea, but she was responsible for hiding the demons who did it and carving Strife's symbol into the bodies."

My mother nodded. "That's a common tactic Eris uses. Leave the symbol, cause panic because no one understand what it means other than that it keeps appearing."

"Right. So, she has a lot of punishment coming her way. If it had been left up to me, I would have killed her painfully, and then we would have learned nothing." *I can't poke at her mind too much more. Her shield is strong and my powers are still not working right*, I thought at my mother. *Please do that for me.*

Tisiphone met my eyes, nodded. *You wanted to kill her.*

Badly. She feels no remorse for the things she's done. This was all I could do just now, and it satisfied my own juvenile need to see her brought low.

My mother smiled a little. *We will handle it. We will strip her of her powers, her memories, when we are finished with her.*

I nodded. *Tell me what you learn.*

She hugged me, and she and my aunt dragged the witch from the room.

Well. One witch down, anyway. Hopefully she knew more about Strife than I'd been able to get from her. The imps filed out of the room, and I was left, trying to get my aching, bleeding body to stop.

Eventually, the pain receded enough that I could fly the rest of the way home. It still felt like my insides were being shredded as I walked into the duplex's back yard and rose into the air again. All I wanted to do was fall into bed. Instead I headed in the opposite direction, toward the bright lights downtown. I circled around, then flew to the top of one of the buildings on Wayne State's campus. I could see the loft from there, city shimmering beyond. The windows at the loft glowed, lit from the inside. Every once in a while, a shadow would cross one of the windows. I stood on the roof, my city below me, the home of the only people I'd ever loved nearby. And I wasn't part of it anymore, any of it, but it was mine. I'd protect it. I'd give them something to believe in, the reassurance that someone was watching over them.

I stood there a long time, the cool night breeze drying the blood on my clothing. The lights of the city, the freeways beyond lit the night sky. I felt my body healing itself from the damage caused by using my powers. My heart was still shredded. It would stay that way, probably. I couldn't deal with that anymore. I had enemies to find, people to save. I was here, for better or worse. I'd do what I do best: fight.

Even if it meant fighting the darkness within myself.

EPILOGUE

I landed in my front yard. It would be morning soon. Time to stop flying around where everyone could see me. I needed a shower and a warm bed.

Granted, it would be an empty bed, but whatever.

Instead of an empty yard, though, I was greeted with four beings standing on my front porch.

Eunomia, Levitt, Shanti, and Hephaestus stood there, and, once they saw me, they all put a fist to their chest.

"What the hell are you guys doing here?" I asked as I walked toward the porch.

"We go where you go," Shanti said.

I shook my head. "They need you."

"So do you," Eunomia said. "You have too many enemies, devil girl. We're not going to stand aside while you have all the fun."

"Agreed. We want in on the fight," Levitt said.

"You have a team, queenie," Hephaestus said. "Put us to work, already."

I stared at them, turned to Shanti. "What about your other duties?"

"I'll still be working for queen Rayna. But when she doesn't need me, I'm here."

"Uh. So, where do you plan to live?" I asked them. Eunomia grinned and picked up a large duffel bag, and Levitt followed suit.

"You have a few extra rooms," Eunomia said. "Any chance you're up for house guests?"

The imps had gathered around now, and they watched me and the group on the porch.

"You all are freaking suicidal. This is the dumbest place you could possibly want to be," I told them.

"I'll take my chances here, just the same," Eunomia said. I hesitated, stood staring at them, trying to find a way to talk them out of this stupidity.

"Look at us, Molly," Shanti said, desperation in her voice. "We were all lost in our own ways. And then you came along and showed us what we could be. You gave us a place when there was nowhere else to go. I'd rather die fighting by your side than live, leaving you to face this shit alone. You made me the kind of person who doesn't give up. I'm not freaking giving up now."

I felt it from all of them: certainty. Stubbornness. Devotion, to me. Warmth.

I could run from Brennan. I could run from Nain and his team. There was no way I could run from the people who'd had ended up living this crazy life because of me. I owed them more than that.

I shook my head and walked up the porch steps, and they parted, giving me a path to the front door. I unlocked it and pushed it open.

"Fine," I said, and my friends, my team (insane as they were), filed into the house.

"Tomorrow's another day, Scarlett," Shanti said as she

walked past me. "That's from another crappy book you made me read, by the way." I rolled my eyes and closed the door behind us.

"Welcome home, team."

THE END

Keep reading for a sneak peek of

HIDDEN BOOK FOUR: STRIFE

KNOW YOUR ENEMY: CHAPTER ONE

My name is Molly Brooks.
Vigilante.
Godslayer.
Oathbreaker.
Daughter of the Lord of the Dead.

The Angel.

What a joke.

I now lead a team of supernaturals who chose me when I'd split from my old team. The people of my city consider me a legend, a god. A hero.

You want to know what I am?

I'm someone who's afraid to go to sleep at night. I'm someone who scrubs my hands so often I make them bleed. I'm someone who re-lives every single one of my deaths, over and over and over again.

I'm a powerful being who can't use my powers without ending up in agony.

I'm afraid of myself. The darkness inside me grows, and I am losing hope that I'm strong enough to contain it. If I lose control, if I unleash whatever this is that is inside me, everyone I've ever loved will suffer for it.

One, in particular, more than others.

And the easy solution would be to get rid of the problem: me. Except that, unfortunately, I can't die.

As in, plenty have tried to make that happen. But I just keep fucking coming back.

Lucky me.

◆ ◆ ◆

I drove the route I'd driven dozens of times, from my house to the loft where Nain and his team lived. Every block that closed the distance between me and the people who lived there made my stomach clench more.

My hands gripped the steering wheel, hard enough to snap it if I'd unleash my powers just a little. As it was, the stress was stirring my powers, heightening them, and it was starting to hurt. Eunomia reached over and put her cool hand over mine on the steering wheel.

"Relax, my friend," she said softly.

"Better to be on edge than relaxed, considering. Don't you think?" I asked her. I glanced over at her, then into the rear-view mirror. The rest of my friends, my team, sat in the back seat. Levitt, Hephaestus, and Shanti. The imps had gone ahead; they'd meet us there. My team knew about the problems I was having. They knew that the moment I relaxed, the darkness inside me threatened to take over. They knew how close I was to giving in to it, to becoming the thing I feared most. They fought beside me. They watched out for me. And, maybe most importantly, they watched me, always prepared for that moment when whatever was inside me took over for good. And they knew that, when that moment came, their job was to put me down.

Yes. I trust my best friends to try to destroy me. Doesn't everyone?

We'd gotten to know each other better than I could have imagined over the past few weeks. We lived together, worked together, fought together. My house, which had seemed so big during all the years I'd lived there alone, felt cozy now. Granted, it was a crazy combination of gods, demons, vampires, and imps, but it was mine.

They knew my weaknesses. My problems. The promises I made to myself. We were more than a team. We were a family, and I trusted them with my life, as they trusted me with theirs. Considering how many powerful beings I had gunning for me, I thought their trust was misplaced. They ignored me when I said stuff like that.

They knew, better than anyone, that I was not as tough as most of the world believed. They knew I still tried to scrub unseen blood and gore off of my body. They knew I had nightmares, when I managed to let myself sleep. They knew that, in my weakest moments, I cursed my life for the things I couldn't have.

"This is exactly why ya should have talked to the fuckin' shifter on the phone all those times he called. Now yer goin' in with all this pent-up shit. Not healthy, queenie," Hephaestus said from the back seat.

"Well, that's why you guys are here, right?" I said, glancing at him in the rear-view mirror. "Keep an eye on me. Make an excuse to leave if it seems like I'm going to lose it. But I can't keep putting Nain off about this meeting, considering we're all trying to hunt Strife down and she's here because of me."

Strife.

I'd trapped her here in my realm back when I'd initially destroyed the gateway between here and the Nether, cutting off this world from the world of the immortals. She was not my biggest fan. I'd killed one of her closest friends, Enyo, the Goddess of War. And I'd trapped her other pal, Ares, the God of War, in a talisman that added to my power. She'd been doing her best to cause chaos, even going as far as using Brennan's infant son (another thing I tried not to think about too often) to harm those I cared about.

And we'd all been hunting her, but she was wily. We hadn't even gotten close.

So I'd finally given in, and agreed to meet with Nain and his team.

I hadn't seen Brennan since the night we'd decided to stop seeing each other. So I'm a coward. But it hurt too much, and I had enough on my mind. I knew it was for the best. It didn't make it any easier. Not when I loved him more than anything in this world or any other, and I knew he felt the same way about me.

Sometimes, love doesn't conquer all. That's a bunch of bullshit.

I pulled into the parking garage, and we all got out of the car. My team, for better or worse, had adopted my uniform as their own: black cargo pants, black shirts. The imps were there already, waiting for me as they'd said they would. And it wasn't just them. My parents, Hades and Tisiphone, stood by the elevator. Hades leaned against the wall, arms folded over his chest. My father never looked worried about anything. Though, I guess if you were the Lord of the Dead and ruler of the afterlife, you wouldn't be worried about much, either. Tisiphone, as always, looked like she was on guard, ready to kick ass.

"What are you two doing here?" I asked them as my team and I walked toward the elevator. "Not that I'm not happy to see you," I added. My mother gave me a small hug, murmuring a hello, and my father studied me.

"There's a reason you've been avoiding this. We're here

in case we're needed." I hadn't been thrilled about telling my parents about the issues I was having, but E had insisted, and I had to admit it was smart. If I lost my mind, they were two of the few beings who had any decent chance of getting me under control.

I nodded. My parents, as always, were also dressed in black. "Go team death," I muttered under my breath as I pulled the gate up and we all got onto the elevator.

"We need a secret handshake," Shanti said. Then she hit the button to take us up to the loft. I took a deep breath. My stomach was turning. It wasn't seeing Nain and the team. I was fine with that. I'd had lunch with Ada and Stone the previous week, seen Nain around town. It was Brennan. I loved him. I missed him. And when I had my blackouts, I had visions of murdering him, brutally, in ways that made me sick. And even though I'm hurt, I know I'd never do any of those things to him. It was this... thing, whatever it was that was inside me. It was even more bloodthirsty than I was, and it wanted to hurt everyone I cared about. Especially him, because that would break me. It hated him. I knew that without knowing how, and that alone scared the shit out of me.

I'd tried to talk Nain out of this dozens of times. But my ex-husband was not the most accommodating man. And he'd finally just growled that I needed to get over it, that I was being weak.

And he knows me well enough to know which buttons to push. The weakness button is almost guaranteed to make me move my ass.

So there we were. I just wanted to get through the meeting without crying. Or, you know... killing anybody. Either or.

"I'm going to say as little as possible. Maybe this will be quick and painless," I said to them as the elevator creaked up to the main living area.

We poured out of the elevator, and I lifted my hand to knock on the heavy mahogany door that led into the loft. When I'd lived here, I'd just walked in. But this wasn't my home anymore, and I wasn't going to let myself fall into my old habits now.

Any of my old habits.

The door opened, and Ada stood on the other side. She smiled when she saw me, pulled me into a huge hug, and I hugged her back. "Good to see you again, baby girl," she said softly, and I gave her another squeeze. She greeted the rest of my team, and they greeted her politely, Shanti and Levitt hugging her when they stepped into the loft.

I could feel him. Our connection was still alive, and I could practically feel every breath he took. I could feel his eyes on me, desperate need flowing from him like lava. It was torture. I took a deep breath, tried to calm myself down. My heart was racing in response to his presence, and I knew for sure he would be able to sense that. We followed Ada into the dining room, my team trailing behind me. Nain, Brennan, Stone, and Chief Jones were all sitting at the dining room table. Brennan's son, Sean, played quietly in a playpen nearby.

Nain stood, eyes on me. Then he glanced at my team.

"Didn't know you traveled with an entourage now, Molls," he said, deep voice practically making the floor vibrate.

"Yeah, well. You know me. There's nothing I like more than feeling important. Hence: entourage."

He studied me for a minute, and I kept my eyes on him. He knew at least a little bit of what was happening with me. I'd confessed it to him before I'd moved out, warned him he might have to try to put me down. Told him how to do it.

"You look good," he said, and I felt the usual from him: anger, desire. Mixed together. It was our signature blend. Always had been.

Then Chief Jones stood and shook my hand, said a few words in greeting, and Stone wrapped me up in a huge bear hug.

Brennan stayed where he was. He seemed unable to stop looking at me, and I did my best to avoid looking at him. But I failed, as usual, and when I looked at him, our eyes met.

"Hey," he said quietly.

I nodded at him, then looked away, unable to trust my voice. Jesus, I just wanted to make it through this so I could go home and bury my face in my pillow and scream. I sat down, and my team arrayed themselves behind me. They stood, Levitt and Shanti at attention, hands folded behind their backs. My parents and Hephaestus stood with their arms crossed, watching everything. Especially me. And Eunomia took the seat beside me. My right hand. She was able to read me better than most, and I needed her now because I couldn't trust myself.

It was maddening. He was sitting right the hell there. Not even six feet away from me, and everything sane in me screamed in desperation, needing to be closer to him.

I tamped it down. I'd made my decision for a reason, and I'd stick to it no matter how good he smelled or how much I'd missed his touch.

"Okay," I said. "I'm here. Let's get this over with."

READ MORE IN
HIDDEN BOOK FOUR: STRIFE
AVAILABLE NOW

Visit http://www.colleenvanderlinden.com/hidden for news, updates, and more

ABOUT THE AUTHOR

Colleen Vanderlinden is the author and publisher of the *Hidden* series, which currently includes *Lost Girl, Broken, Home, Forever Night, and Strife*. She lives in the Detroit area with her husband, children, and two lazy cats. She enjoys reading, obsessing over comic book characters, gardening, and playing World of Warcraft.

Website: http://www.colleenvanderlinden.com
Facebook: facebook.com/colleenvanderlinden
Twitter: @C_Vanderlinden

The Hidden Series

Book One: Lost Girl
Book Two: Broken
Book Three: Home
Book 3.5: Forever Night
Book Four: Strife
Book Five: Nether - Available Fall 2014